The Inspector and Mrs. Jeffries: When a [...] own office, Mrs. Jeffries must scour the premises to find the prescription for murder.

Mrs. Jeffries Dusts for Clues: One case is solved and another is opened when the inspector finds a missing brooch—pinned to a dead woman's gown.

The Ghost and Mrs. Jeffries: When the murder of Mrs. Hodges is foreseen at a spooky séance, Mrs. Jeffries must look into the past for clues.

Mrs. Jeffries Takes Stock: A businessman has been murdered—and the smart money's on Mrs. Jeffries to catch the killer.

Mrs. Jeffries on the Ball: A festive Jubilee celebration turns into a fatal affair—and Mrs. Jeffries must find the guilty party.

Mrs. Jeffries on the Trail: Mrs. Jeffries must sniff out a flower peddler's killer.

Mrs. Jeffries Plays the Cook: Mrs. Jeffries finds herself doing double duty: cooking for the inspector's household and trying to cook a killer's goose.

Mrs. Jeffries and the Missing Alibi: When Inspector Witherspoon is the main suspect in a murder, only Mrs. Jeffries can save him.

Mrs. Jeffries Stands Corrected: When a local publican is murdered and Inspector Witherspoon botches the investigation, trouble starts to brew for Mrs. Jeffries.

Mrs. Jeffries Takes the Stage: After a theater critic is murdered, Mrs. Jeffries uncovers the victim's secret shocking past.

Mrs. Jeffries Questions the Answer: To find the disagreeable Hannah Cameron's killer, Mrs. Jeffries must tread lightly—or it could be a matter of life and death.

Mrs. Jeffries Reveals Her Art: A missing model and a killer have Mrs. Jeffries working double time before someone else becomes the next subject.

Mrs. Jeffries Takes the Cake: A dead body, two dessert plates, and a gun. Mrs. Jeffries will have to do some serious snooping around to dish up more clues.

Mrs. Jeffries Rocks the Boat: A murdered woman had recently traveled by boat from Australia. Now Mrs. Jeffries must solve the case—and it's sink or swim.

Mrs. Jeffries Weeds the Plot: Three attempts have been made on Annabeth Gentry's life. Is it because her bloodhound dug up the body of a murdered thief?

Mrs. Jeffries Pinches the Post: Mrs. Jeffries and her staff must root through the sins of a ruthless man's past to catch his killer.

Mrs. Jeffries Pleads Her Case: The inspector is determined to prove a suicide was murder, and with Mrs. Jeffries on his side, he may well succeed.

Mrs. Jeffries Sweeps the Chimney: A vicar has been found murdered and Inspector Witherspoon's only prayer is to seek the divinations of Mrs. Jeffries.

Mrs. Jeffries Stalks the Hunter: When love turns deadly, who better to get to the heart of the matter than Inspector Witherspoon's indomitable companion, Mrs. Jeffries?

Mrs. Jeffries and the Silent Knight: The yuletide murder of an elderly man is complicated by several suspects—none of whom were in the Christmas spirit.

Mrs. Jeffries Appeals the Verdict: Mrs. Jeffries and her belowstairs cohorts have their work cut out for them if they want to save an innocent man from the gallows.

Mrs. Jeffries and the Best Laid Plans: Everyone banker Lawrence Boyd met became his enemy. It will take Mrs. Jeffries' shrewd eye to find who killed him.

Mrs. Jeffries and the Feast of St. Stephen: 'Tis the season for sleuthing when a wealthy man is murdered and Mrs. Jeffries must solve the case in time for Christmas.

Mrs. Jeffries Holds the Trump: A medical magnate is found floating down the river. Now Mrs. Jeffries will have to dive into the mystery.

Mrs. Jeffries in the Nick of Time: Mrs. Jeffries lends her downstairs common sense to this upstairs murder mystery.

Mrs. Jeffries and the Yuletide Weddings: Wedding bells will make this season all the more jolly. Until one humbug sings a carol of murder.

Mrs. Jeffries Speaks Her Mind: Everyone doubts an eccentric old woman who suspects she's going to be murdered—until the prediction comes true.

Mrs. Jeffries Forges Ahead: A free-spirited bride is poisoned, and it's up to Mrs. Jeffries to discover who wanted to make the modern young woman into a postmortem.

Mrs. Jeffries and the Mistletoe Mix-Up: There's murder going on under the mistletoe as Mrs. Jeffries and Inspector Witherspoon hurry to solve the case.

Mrs. Jeffries Defends Her Own: When an unwelcome visitor from her past needs help, Mrs. Jeffries steps into the fray to stop a terrible miscarriage of justice.

Mrs. Jeffries Turns the Tide: When Mrs. Jeffries doubts a suspect's guilt, she must turn the tide of the investigation to save an innocent man.

Mrs. Jeffries and the Merry Gentlemen: When a successful stockbroker is murdered just days before Christmas, Mrs. Jeffries won't rest until justice is served for the holidays.

Mrs. Jeffries and the One Who Got Away: When a woman is found strangled clutching an old newspaper clipping, only Mrs. Jeffries can get to the bottom of the story.

Mrs. Jeffries Wins the Prize: Inspector Witherspoon and Mrs. Jeffries weed out a killer after a body is found in a gentlewoman's conservatory.

Mrs. Jeffries Rights a Wrong: Mrs. Jeffries and Inspector Witherspoon must determine who had the motive to put a duplicitous businessman in the red.

Mrs. Jeffries and the Three Wise Women: As Christmas approaches, Luty, Ruth, and Mrs. Goodge turn up the heat on a murderer to stop the crime from becoming a cold case.

Mrs. Jeffries Delivers the Goods: When poison fells an arrogant businessman at a ball, Mrs. Jeffries and Inspector Witherspoon must catch the culprit before the misanthrope murders again.

Mrs. Jeffries and the Alms of the Angel: When a wealthy widow is murdered right before Christmas, Mrs. Jeffries investigates what happens when money can't buy your life.

MRS. JEFFRIES
DEMANDS JUSTICE

Emily Brightwell

BERKLEY PRIME CRIME

NEW YORK

BERKLEY PRIME CRIME
Published by Berkley
An imprint of Penguin Random House LLC
penguinrandomhouse.com

Library of Congress Cataloging-in-Publication Data

Names: Brightwell, Emily, author.
Title: Mrs. Jeffries demands justice / Emily Brightwell.
Description: First edition. | New York: Berkley Prime Crime, 2021. |
Series: A Victorian mystery; 39
Identifiers: LCCN 2020037106 (print) | LCCN 2020037107 (ebook) |
ISBN 9780593101063 (trade paperback) | ISBN 9780593101070 (ebook)
Subjects: LCSH: Jeffries, Mrs. (Fictitious character)—Fiction. |
Women detectives—England—Fiction. |
Housekeepers—England—Fiction. | Murder—Investigation—Fiction. |
Police—England—Fiction. | GSAFD: Mystery fiction.
Classification: LCC PS3552.R46443 M6486 2021 (print) |
LCC PS3552.R46443 (ebook) | DDC 813/.54—dc23
LC record available at https://lccn.loc.gov/2020037106
LC ebook record available at https://lccn.loc.gov/2020037107

First Edition: January 2021

Printed in the United States of America
1 3 5 7 9 10 8 6 4 2

Cover art by Mark Fredrickson

MRS. JEFFRIES
DEMANDS JUSTICE

CHAPTER 1

Bert Santorini hoped this wouldn't take long. He didn't have all night and despite it being almost springtime, it was still bloomin' cold. Princess, the old pony, swished her tail and gave a soft whinny. He climbed down from the seat of his ice cart and straightened the bouquet he'd saved to give to a certain lady who was annoyed with him at the moment. He put his hand on Princess' back, hoping to soothe her. "Don't fret, my lovey—we'll be home soon. Just got to take care of this bit of business."

He glared down the dark mews and tried to keep a lid on his temper. It was past time for the meeting and he was tired; Mondays were always a tough day. He told himself he should just leave, that he wasn't going to be dancing to a fancy toff's tune, but there was too much at stake. This was business, and there was more than a little money to be made, maybe a lot more if he kept his head and held his tongue.

Wind gusted down the mews, and Princess snorted faintly, as if telling him they should be moving on. "It's alright, love—it'll not be much longer." He glanced at the far end of the mews, squinting in the dim light. He and Princess were only a few feet off the Commercial Road; but the radiance from the streetlamps didn't reach this far, and the only illumination was from the two kerosene lights on his cart. It was enough to see by, but just barely.

He glanced up at the four-story brown brick office building on his left before turning and examining the two-story warehouse on the right. Both places were dark and closed for the night. Good—the last thing he needed was prying eyes. Satisfied, he turned toward the Commercial Road. Traffic was heavy at this time of evening, but nothing turned into the mews. Where was the blighter? Money or not, he wasn't going to wait much longer.

He whirled around as he heard footsteps coming from the opposite end of the mews. He had a story ready if it was a copper on patrol, but it wasn't a copper, it was the one he expected. Dragging in a deep breath, he readied himself for what might turn into a nasty row. As he exhaled, he realized there was something funny going on here. His eyes narrowed as the figure came closer. It was him, of course, and he'd not seen him since before the trial, but from the way his overcoat hung, he'd put on a good half stone or more of weight. "Guess 'e can afford to stuff his face anytime he wants," he muttered. Princess snorted.

"It's about time you got 'ere." Bert tried and failed to hold his tongue. But his visitor said nothing; he simply shoved his right hand into his coat pocket and kept moving.

"What's wrong with ya? Cat got yer tongue?"

Again, the advancing figure said nothing.

Princess whinnied again and tossed her head, jangling her harness. Bert was suddenly uneasy; something was wrong, but he couldn't put his finger on it. He told himself there was nothing to worry about—he'd taken precautions. What they'd done had been much more dangerous for the toff than for him. He'd made bloomin' sure the toff knew better than to try to squirm out of their deal. He'd taken a big risk for this one, and he'd made it crystal clear that if anything happened to him, there was a friend who'd point the police his way.

"Come on, come on, pick up your feet and get your arse over 'ere. It's cold and you're late. I want to get Princess home. I've got plans for tonight."

But instead of moving faster, the blighter stuck his left hand inside his overcoat. Bert's eyes widened in surprise as he saw a pillow appear.

"Have you gone mad? Why are you carryin' around a pillow?"

But instead of answering, he suddenly increased his speed while shoving his hand into his other coat pocket.

Alarmed, Bert stumbled backward. He'd survived the crime-ridden streets of the East End by trusting his instincts, and right now they were screaming at him to run.

But it was too late.

The figure raced toward Bert, pulling a gun out of his coat pocket as he narrowed the distance between the two of them. Bert turned and ran toward the end of the mews. His only chance was to make it to the Commercial Road. But the cobblestones were damp, and before he could go more than a few feet, he slipped and fell hard onto the ground. He landed next to Princess, scaring her enough so that she danced away from him. He grabbed at her harness, his fingers closing around the soft leather straps as he tried to get up. But the animal tore away from his grasp, confused, and bolted toward the busy road.

The killer stood above him with the gun pointed straight at his forehead. Bert's eyes widened as he saw who held the weapon. "You. What in the name of all that's holy are you doin' 'ere?"

"My God, you always did ask stupid questions." In one quick movement, the murderer shoved the pillow into Bert's face, rammed the gun against the fabric, and pulled the trigger. The sound of the shot was muffled by the traffic noise.

Bert slumped to the ground. It took only a moment to make sure he was dead. The assailant saw that the pony, frightened even more by the unfamiliar noises, had now reached the end of the mews and, with the cart lurching drunkenly behind it, ran out onto the busy street. That was good—part of the plan, actually. At this time of day, the street would be crowded with both pedestrian and road traffic. By now, someone would have spotted the animal and realized where it had come from and, more important, that something might be wrong. No one let a valuable horse and cart go running off on its own, not in this part of the city. Within minutes, someone would be here to see what happened and that was just fine.

The faster the police arrived, the better.

The killer carefully placed the gun next to the body, turned around, and walked calmly back the way they'd come.

Constable Poole spotted the pony and cart rushing into the heavy traffic of the Commercial Road. He raced toward it, dodging coopers' vans, hansoms, four-wheelers, and two omnibuses before he managed to grasp the animal's bridle. He'd been raised in the country, so he knew better than to try to stop the runaway. He ran alongside the pony, gradually slowing it down.

Poole petted the pony's head and spoke in a low, soothing voice as they slackened their pace and moved toward the edge of the pavement. Both of them were panting and out of breath as they finally came to a stop. "Not to worry, my pretty one, you're safe now. But where's your owner? Where'd you come from?"

By this time quite a crowd had gathered. "He come out of the end of Felix Mews." A flat-capped young lad pointed. "He come out like he was bein' chased by the devil hisself."

"Can someone hold on to him?" Poole called. He wanted to have a look in the mews. The owner should be close by; perhaps he'd been making deliveries or had stopped to give the beast a rest. But if that was the case, where was he? Whatever the reason, Poole needed to find out what was happening.

"I'll hold him," a middle-aged man volunteered.

Poole nodded and hurried to the mews. He stepped inside and realized how little light came from the street. For a brief moment, he wished he had his hand lantern, but he'd been on fixed-point duty and all he had was a truncheon and a whistle. He moved farther inside the mews and then came to a full stop. Even in the darkness, there was enough light for him to see a body splayed out on the cobblestones. Poole hurried over to where the man lay, knelt down, and shoved his fingers against the man's neck, feeling for a pulse. He prayed he was doing it right. But after several minutes of Poole prodding the poor fellow's neck and wrist, he was fairly certain the man was dead. The bullet hole in his forehead was a clue, but he'd been on the force long enough to know that people could survive all sorts of wounds, including bullets to their head. He took a deep breath to steady his nerves and leaned back on his heels. That was when he spotted the gun lying next to the body.

Poole stood up and charged out of the mews, blowing his police whistle as he ran. Several members of the crowd surged forward, but he held out his arms. "No one goes inside here," he yelled.

"You"—he nodded toward a street lad who was petting the pony—"run to the Leman Street Police Station and tell them we need help here. Hurry." The lad raced off.

"What happened? Why can't we go in the mews?" an elderly woman asked. Several others echoed her questions. They were a pushy bunch here in the East End. But Constable Poole ignored them and blew his whistle again and again.

Relief flooded through him as he saw two constables coming around the corner. For once, Constable Poole was glad that White-chapel was such a high crime area that there were always constables on patrol.

"We're lucky that pony bolted," Inspector Vincent Havers muttered as he stared down at the body. "Otherwise he might have lain here all night." The inspector was a tall, burly man with curly black hair sprinkled with gray at the temples and an elegantly shaped mustache. "Does anyone know who he is?"

"Bert Santorini, sir. He's an iceman who mainly works in the West End, but he supplies some of the nicer pubs around 'ere with ice," Constable Farrow, one of the men holding a lamp, replied. He'd been born and raised in Whitechapel and knew all the locals.

"Does anyone know where he lives?" Havers asked.

"He lodges at Frida Sorensen's," another constable said.

"We'll start there then," Havers muttered. "Hold the lamps higher," he ordered as he knelt down, looking for the weapon Poole had said was next to the body. It was lying next to Santorini's head. Havers moved the weapon carefully, making sure it wasn't pointing at anyone before picking it up. "No doubt, this is the murder weapon." He raised the barrel to his nose and took a whiff. "I can smell the powder; it's been fired."

"You mean the killer left it here?" Constable Farrow said. "That doesn't make much sense, does it, sir? Guns are expensive."

Havers frowned slightly as he held the firearm closer to the lamp. "Indeed, it doesn't, especially when the weapon in question looks to be quite valuable." He drew back. "This is a dueling pistol. It's got fancy carvings on the handle, and it looks as if this filigree is made of gold. Good gracious, the inlay looks like mother-of-pearl."

"May I have a look, sir?" Poole asked. "It might be one that we saw at the station recently."

Havers looked up sharply. "At the station? Good Lord, man, if it belonged to a prisoner and was used in a crime, why didn't you confiscate it and take it into evidence?" He handed the weapon, handle first, to the constable.

Poole took the firearm. He said nothing for a few moments as he stared at the gun in his hand. He'd paid no attention to the details when he'd seen it lying next to the body, but now he knew he'd seen it before, and very recently at that. "Well, sir, we didn't confiscate it because it didn't belong to a prisoner."

"Who does it belong to?" Havers demanded.

"Inspector Nigel Nivens, sir. He brought it into the station because he was getting one of the guns repaired. You're right, sir, it is a dueling pistol. It's part of a set that Inspector Nivens said had been in his family for generations. According to Inspector Nivens, it's very old, something called a single-shot flintlock, which only fires one bullet and then has to be reloaded."

Havers said nothing for a moment. Poole shifted nervously. He wasn't sure what to do now. He knew that Inspector Havers had no great liking or admiration for Inspector Nivens, but he also knew that when it came right down to it, those at the top always stuck together. "Are you certain of this, Constable Poole?"

But despite his trepidation, Poole was an honest man, raised in the best traditions of his late mother's Presbyterian church; he'd not lie just because the truth might cause him a bit of trouble. Besides, he wasn't the only constable who'd seen Nivens' guns. "I'm very certain of it, sir." He handed the weapon back to Havers. "Inspector Nivens brought the guns into the station last Thursday, sir. He laid the gun box on the sergeant's desk and opened the lid. The two guns were inside. Several of us saw them, sir. Inspector Nivens held one up and told us the filigree design on the handles was an intricate working of his mother's maiden initials, so he had to be careful who he let repair the one that wasn't working. Apparently, there aren't many gunsmiths in London who Inspector Nivens trusted with his family heirloom. He didn't want the gold filigree or mother-of-pearl destroyed."

In truth, Inspector Nivens had used the opportunity to brag about his mother's family wealth, claiming the guns had been a gift to her grandfather by a maharajah of India. No one knew whether what he said was true or not; for that matter, no one cared. Every constable that had the misfortune of working under Nivens hated him.

"And you're absolutely certain this gun was part of Nivens' set?" Havers loathed Nivens as well, but before he questioned the fellow, he had to be absolutely sure of his facts. Nivens had been sent to the East End because he'd been accused of deliberately withholding evidence in a murder investigation, conduct that would normally have gotten a detective sacked. But Nivens' family had intervened, so instead of the man getting chucked out, the Leman Street Station was stuck with him. Furthermore, Nivens had recently solved a series of burglaries and sent the Irish brothers who'd committed the crimes off to prison, so his star was on the rise.

Havers was no fool: Nivens' family was powerful, and it wouldn't do to start hurling accusations based on very few facts.

Poole stared at the weapon for a few moments and then met his inspector's gaze. "It looks the same to me, sir, and when the inspector was talking about the pistols, he claimed they were the only ones ever made with a gold filigree handle and mother-of-pearl inlays. But Constable Farrow and Constable Blackstone were standing there when Inspector Nivens showed us the pistols. You might want to double-check with one of them, sir."

"It's the same weapon, sir," Constable Farrow said quickly.

"Did Inspector Nivens leave the pistols lying on the sergeant's desk?" Havers asked.

"No, sir. He took them into the duty inspector's office, and later that day I saw him carrying the case when he left."

"Did he say anything as he left with the case?" Havers asked.

"Not that I can recall, sir," Poole replied.

"I overheard him say he was stopping at the pub, sir," Farrow added.

"Do you know which one?"

"He didn't say, sir, but he generally goes to the Crying Crows."

Havers nodded. "Let's not jump to any conclusions. I'm sure there's a reasonable explanation as to why a weapon that resembles the ones Inspector Nivens brought into the station would be here. We'll see what he has to say about the matter. In the meantime, keep constables posted at each end of the mews and when daybreak comes, make certain the entire area is thoroughly searched."

"There's already crowds at each end of the mews." Constable Farrow jerked his chin to his left, then to his right. "Should we try and send them off, sir?"

"No, leave them be. Trying to disperse them will just cause a fuss," Havers ordered. He knew they had far too few constables present to be effective in clearing the area. East Enders didn't like getting pushed about by the police, and he'd just as soon not have a scuffle on his hands that ended up in tomorrow's newspapers. "Pubs are open now, so most of them will move along on their own."

"The police surgeon is here, sir," one of the constables guarding the entrance to the mews called.

Inspector Havers handed the pistol to Constable Poole. "Right, then, take this into evidence, and we'll see what the doctor has to say about this."

Charlie Bowman sighed in relief as the heavy door of the *Sentinel* actually opened. He hurried inside and then skidded to a halt as he faced several rows of huge machines, several of which had grumpy-looking men standing behind them. "What ya want, lad?" the man nearest him called out.

"I've got a note for one of your reporters," he yelled. "There's been a murder in Whitechapel."

"So, there's always a murder down that way. But if you're lookin' for a reporter, go up to the second floor—the stairs are over there." He jerked his thumb to his right.

Charlie nodded his thanks and dashed off. He climbed the stairs and came out into a big room filled with desks, typewriters, and cabinets. But not many people.

"Bloody 'ell," he muttered. "This place is empty."

"What do ya need, lad?" A man wearing spectacles wandered out of an open office door at the far end of the room.

"There's been a murder in Whitechapel," Charlie cried as he hurried toward what he hoped was a reporter. "Bert Santorini—

he's the iceman—he's been shot. 'Ere." He thrust the note into the man's hand. "Someone give me this to bring to ya. They give me a whole shillin' to get 'ere before you closed up shop."

"We're a newspaper, we never close," the man muttered as he opened the folded sheet of paper and read the three lines that were written.

> *The police are already trying to cover up a crime by one*
> *of their own.*
> *The gun used to murder Bert Santorini belongs to*
> *Inspector Nigel Nivens.*
> *Don't let them get away with killing someone.*

The man fixed Charlie with a hard glare. "Where'd ya get this?"

"Outside the Felix Mews."

"Who gave it to you?"

"I don't know—there was a big crowd of us watching the coppers, and all of a sudden someone shoved this note into my hand and give me a shillin'. I just told ya that." Charlie wanted to get going. It was a long way home, and his mam didn't like him staying out too late. Mind you, she'd be a bit nicer about it when he gave her the money.

"Was it a man or a woman?"

"Don't know—it coulda been either. It was pitch-dark and bloomin' cold—everyone was bundled up so I couldn't see nuthin'. Someone shoved the note in me hand, give me the coin, and told me to get 'ere quick."

"Don't be daft, lad. What did the voice sound like? A man or a woman?"

"They had a low voice, but it coulda been either. Mrs. Cayley at the butcher's has a voice like that, and she's a woman. That's all I know, and I've got to go. Me mam don't like me bein' out late."

The man watched the lad leave. By this time another man, a reporter named Jerome Corey stood in the open doorway. "Should I go have a look?"

"Someone spent a shilling to send the lad here, and in that part of London, that's a lot of coin. It might not be a hoax." He handed Corey the note. "If this is true, it'll make a good headline for tomorrow's edition. But you'll need to get there and back here with a story by nine o'clock. That's the latest we can hold off in time for tomorrow's edition."

At Scotland Yard the next morning, Chief Superintendent Barrows entered his third-floor office, stopped by the door, and hung up his gray overcoat on the coat tree. He yawned as he went to his desk and took his chair. The chief superintendent was a tall, balding man with tortoiseshell spectacles and a luxurious mustache.

There was a short knock on the door and then Constable Dingle stepped inside. He carried a stack of mail in one hand and a file box in the other. "These are for you, sir. It's the daily reports as well as the post."

"Of course. Put them on the desk," Barrows instructed. "What time did you come on duty?"

"Midnight, sir." He put the post on top of the box and laid the stack on the side of the desk within the chief's reach.

"Was it quiet last night?" Barrows asked.

"For the most part, sir. There was a murder in Whitechapel," he began, only to be interrupted.

"Whitechapel? Ye gods, it wasn't a woman, was it?" Barrows asked quickly.

"No, sir." Dingle tried not to smile. Everyone at Scotland Yard knew that Chief Superintendent Barrows was one of the officers who'd investigated the Ripper killings and, even though that had been years earlier, he was still very nervous about killings in the East End. The Ripper murders had never been solved, and a number of the older officers at Scotland Yard were very skittish whenever there was a murder in that part of London. "It was a man, sir. An ice seller."

"You read the report?"

Dingle shook his head. "No, sir. Constable Blackstone told me when he came on duty this morning. His brother works at the Leman Street Station. Said a bloke named Santorini was found shot in Felix Mews."

"Shot? With a gun?"

"That's what he told me, sir."

"Ye gods, how do these criminals get their hands on so many firearms? I tell you, it's a disgrace, an absolute disgrace. Most unfair—we don't carry guns, yet half the blackguards and knaves in London seem to be armed to the teeth."

"Yes, sir." Dingle edged toward the door. The chief superintendent's views on guns were widely known at the Yard, and he didn't want to get stuck listening to him go on about it now. His shift was almost over; he was tired, bored, and wanted to go home and have a nice cup of tea. "Uh, that's really all I know. If that's all, sir, I'll be off."

"Yes, yes." Barrows waved him away. "I'm sure all the grisly details will be in the reports." He reached for the stack, put the post aside to open later, and flipped open the file box containing the daily reports. The reports were divided into districts, with one central station in the district reporting the arrests, incidents, accidents, and civilian inquiries made each day.

Barrows went through the pages diligently, noting it was the usual litany of stolen goods, lost purses, petty thefts, burglaries, two accidental traffic deaths, a drowning off the East India Dock, and a raid on a house of prostitution in Bethnal Green. But when he got to the report from the Leman Street Station, he was so stunned he read it again. Barrows sat back in his chair and stared at the door. He shook his head in disbelief. Ye gods, why on earth was a police inspector's gun found at a murder scene, and why did it have to be the one police inspector who had done nothing but cause them trouble?

Across town in the kitchen of Inspector Gerald Witherspoon's home on Upper Edmonton Gardens, Mrs. Jeffries, the housekeeper, came down the back stairs, her brown bombazine dress rustling as she entered the kitchen. She dumped the huge green book on the table and sat down. "I've put this off as long as possible, but if I don't get the housekeeping ledger caught up, we'll have no idea what we've spent or where we've spent it." She was a plump woman of late middle age with dark auburn hair streaked with gray, light colored freckles over her nose, brown eyes, and a ready smile.

Mrs. Goodge, a portly woman with snow-white hair under her floppy cook's cap and wire-framed spectacles said, "I'm glad you're in charge of that and not me. I've always found numbers confusing."

They heard the back door open and a few moments later, Phyllis, the housemaid, rushed into the kitchen. She unfastened her coat as she headed for the coat tree. She was a pretty lass with dark blonde hair, sapphire-colored eyes, and a porcelain complexion that now had very red cheeks from being outside in the wind. "You'll never guess who died."

"Who?" The cook, who'd just bent down to pull her big brown bowl out from beneath her worktable, straightened up and turned to look at the maid.

Phyllis hung her coat on the peg. "Mr. Soames, that's who." She hurried to the table, her attention on Mrs. Jeffries. "But before I forget, Mrs. Jeffries, Mrs. Morgenstern told me to thank you for the tea you sent over last week. She said it really soothed her throat and that it broke her fever. She was ever so grateful for the batch you sent today."

"Is she finally getting better?" Mrs. Jeffries asked.

"She was up and well enough to wave me down from the kitchen door. She stood there chatting for five minutes with the door wide-open. Honestly, it's so cold out, I was afraid she was going to catch a chill. From the way she was going on, you'd think that ginger tea of yours was a magic potion."

"Compared to that awful stuff you get from the chemists, it probably is." The cook put her hands on her hips. "Now come on—we're all glad Mrs. Morgenstern is on the mend, but don't keep us in suspense. Tell us about Mr. Soames."

Phyllis pulled out a chair and sat down. "As I was leaving the Morgenstern home, Hannah Sebold, the housemaid for the Soameses came outside. When she spotted me, she came running over. You know how Hannah is—she loves to talk. She told me that Mr. Soames got out of bed in the middle of the night and plummeted down the back stairs. He bounced and banged around so much he woke up the whole place. By the time anyone got to him, he was unconscious but still breathing. They sent for the doctor right away, but apparently the fall must have caused a concussion or some sort of brain injury because he died early this morning."

"Was he alone when he tumbled down the stairs?" Mrs. Jeffries asked. It wasn't an idle question. Mrs. Jeffries and the household of Upper Edmonton Gardens knew more about foul play than the average domestic servants. They worked for Inspector Gerald Witherspoon, and they'd helped their dear inspector solve more murders than anyone in the history of the Metropolitan Police. Not that he had any idea that they assisted him, and they were determined to keep it that way.

"He was and he wasn't. Mrs. Perrin—she's the Soameses' housekeeper—saw the whole thing. According to Hannah, Mrs. Perrin said that Mr. Soames made such a racket when he left his room that she heard him. Her quarters are at the back of the house on the third floor. She got up because she thought someone was trying to break into the house, and she spotted him just as he reached the back stairs," Phyllis explained. Like everyone else in the Witherspoon household, she understood the importance of details, and she'd questioned Hannah quite thoroughly.

"Why on earth was the master of the house using the back stairs?" the cook exclaimed. "Especially an old snob like Soames?"

"Hannah said she overheard Mrs. Perrin tell their cook that Mr. Soames was drunk, that she'd seen him take a bottle of whisky up to his room."

"He does drink a fair bit," Mrs. Jeffries commented. "He was so drunk at Christmas that he wandered out into the communal garden and thought Mrs. Enright's bulldog was a pig. He tried to catch the poor animal for his Christmas dinner. The Enrights were not amused by the incident."

"I shouldn't laugh, either." Phyllis giggled. "But it was funny, especially when Mrs. Enright started smacking him with a tree branch. Anyway, Mrs. Perrin went after him to see if there was something wrong and then saw him trip over his own feet and go flying down the back stairs."

"At least now that he's dead, poor Mrs. Soames will have a moment's peace." The cook leaned down again and grabbed the bread bowl.

Mrs. Jeffries looked at the cook, her expression shocked. "Mrs. Goodge, what a thing to say."

"Now don't get on your high horse, Hepzibah," the cook said, using the housekeeper's Christian name, which she generally only said when the two of them were alone or when she wanted to make a point. "You couldn't stand him, either. I'm just being honest. He was a dreadful man. I'm amazed that his wife hadn't pushed him down the ruddy stairs ages ago." She reached for her tin of flour and pried open the lid. "Besides, he threw rocks at Samson and would have kicked poor Fred's head in if Wiggins hadn't stopped him." Samson was the cook's bad-tempered tomcat, and Fred was the household dog. Upon hearing his name, Fred looked up from his rug by the cooker and thumped his tail.

"Mrs. Goodge is right," Phyllis said. "He's a horrid tyrant, Hannah said he constantly criticized poor Mrs. Soames, was always late paying their quarterly wages, disinherited his own daughter because she married a man he didn't like, and worst of all, turfed out that young housemaid last year just because she chipped his teacup."

"That may all be true—he was a nasty human being," Mrs. Jeffries admitted. "But still, a death is never to be celebrated."

"If I was Mrs. Soames, I'd be celebrating." Wiggins knelt down as Fred leapt up and trotted over to him. He'd just come inside after helping the laundry boy carry the big wicker basket of linens out to the wagon. He was a tall, brown-haired young man in his twenties with fair skin and a handsome face. Though technically a footman, Wiggins did everything and anything that needed to be done in the household. "And I think everyone at the Soames home will be breathin' a bit easier now that the old man is gone," he continued. "Fred wasn't doin' anything except tryin' to find a spot to do his business. He was only walkin' past when Mr. Soames started kickin' at him, and he'd have killed him if I'd not heard the poor dog screamin'. Anyone who kicks a dog just for the fun of it is downright evil." He gave the animal one last, loving stroke and stood up. Fred went back to his rug, curled up, and went back to sleep.

Mrs. Jeffries knew when she was beaten. "I've no doubt you're right. Still, it seems wrong to make light of the man's death."

"God works in mysterious ways," the cook murmured. "Perhaps the Almighty got tired of watching that wretched man bullying and browbeating everyone. Strange, isn't it, that death means freedom for some, while for most others, it's a heartbreaking moment."

"It means things will change in the Soames household." Phyllis got up and went to the cupboard next to the pine sideboard. Opening the bottom cabinet, she pulled out her feather duster and a bundle of clean rags. "Now Mrs. Soames can help her daughter; she's goin' to have a child."

"Death always means change," Mrs. Jeffries murmured. "If it wasn't for a death, none of us would be here."

"What do you mean?" Phyllis tucked the duster under her arm.

"Well, if the inspector's Aunt Euphemia hadn't died when Smythe returned from Australia, none of us would be here, and we certainly wouldn't be helping him solve murders."

"I never thought of it like that," Wiggins mused. "But you're right. None of us would be here if it hadn't been for Miss Witherspoon's death. She took me in when I was just a lad, and she was a nice mistress. She didn't put on airs, and she treated us decently. It was right awful what 'appened. When Smythe come in and took over, I was ever so happy. He did everything he could to save 'er, but the poor lady died anyway."

"What happened?" Phyllis looked at the footman curiously. Compared to the others, she was relatively new to the household. She'd heard of Euphemia Witherspoon, and she knew some, but not *all* of the details of how they'd all come together.

"She got ill with bronchitis and sent me for the doctor," Wiggins explained. "Mind you, I don't think he was much good at doctoring—he just said for her to put a smelly poultice on her chest and keep to her bed. But she got worse and worse. She was so ill, she couldn't get out of bed. That's when the other servants started pinchin' her stuff."

"They started stealing?" Phyllis exclaimed. "That's terrible, especially as she treated them well."

"That doesn't matter to some people." Wiggins shrugged. "But all of a sudden, some of her jewels went missing from her room, and some of the nice things from the house started to disappear. When I complained and said they oughtn't to do it, the butler cuffed me so hard on the 'ead I saw stars. I remember goin' back upstairs and tryin' to take care of her, but I was just a young lad, and I didn't know what to do."

"Couldn't you go to the neighbors?" Phyllis sat back down and put the feather duster and the rags on the chair next to her.

He shook his head. "No, for some reason they didn't seem to like the mistress—not that she minded, she had lots of other friends. I'd decided I was goin' to go and find Mr. Brooker—he was her special friend and very wealthy. Trouble was, I didn't know where he lived. But then that mornin', she roused enough to tell me where to find 'im. I was puttin' on my coat to go get 'im, but then I saw the housekeeper and the butler huddled together in the front hall, you know, like they was plottin' somethin' bad. I wasn't scared of them, but I wasn't goin' to leave her on her own." His handsome young face clouded as he remembered those awful days. "By this time, all the other servants were doin' whatever they liked. Eatin' everythin' in sight, drinkin' her liquor, and that awful housekeeper, Mrs. Gowdy, was even wearin' her pearls. I didn't know what to do.

"Then Smythe turned up. It was like a miracle. He used to work for the mistress; he'd been her coachman before he'd gone to Australia, and when he'd come back to England, he stopped in to pay his respects. Well, he took one look at what was goin' on and took matters in hand, he did." Wiggins smiled at the memory. "He sent me for a proper doctor and turfed out the rest of 'em. Mr. Cuccinelli—he was the butler—tried to bluff 'im out, but Smythe just twisted his arm around his back and showed him the door. That whole bunch got out of here right quick, I tell ya." His expression darkened. "But it was too late for the mistress. She died two days later."

Mrs. Jeffries patted his arm. "Wiggins, I'm sure that you helped make Miss Witherspoon's last days bearable. If you hadn't been there for her, she'd have had no one to take care of her."

"Ta, Mrs. Jeffries." He smiled gratefully. "She were a nice mistress, and she'd have approved of what we've been doin'. You know, 'elpin' our inspector with 'is murder cases."

"She sounds like a really good person," Phyllis said.

"She was," he continued. "I was there when she made Smythe promise to stay on here and make certain our inspector wasn't taken advantage of by anyone. Smythe might 'ave been just a coachman, but he made sure that you"—he looked at the housekeeper, then at the cook—"Mrs. Goodge, and even Betsy were decent people before he let you in the 'ouse."

"He told the inspector who he could and couldn't hire?" Mrs. Goodge laughed as she dumped a cup of flour into her bowl. "Gracious, I didn't know that."

"Not directly, but by the time our inspector moved in, he relied on Smythe and me to 'elp 'im out a bit. He'd never lived in a big, fancy house like this before. He and his mum hadn't had servants. He became a policeman because he needed to earn a living to take care of the both of them. When he inherited his aunt's fortune, it made it hard for him, and our inspector saw that Smythe knew what 'e was doin'. He's a good judge of character, is our Smythe."

"The inspector's mother had died by the time he inherited all this?" Phyllis waved a hand around the huge, well-equipped kitchen.

"She died a few months before Miss Witherspoon."

"It must have been a sad time for our inspector." The cook dusted the flour off her hands. "Losing his mother and his aunt. He barely knew Miss Witherspoon, but it's never nice to be alone in the world. Mind you, some good came of the situation. It brought all of us together. If I'd not got this position, I don't know what I'd have done."

"Surely you'd have found another position, Mrs. Goodge," Phyllis said. "You're a wonderful cook."

"Ta, Phyllis. That's nice of you to say. But most households wouldn't have wanted to hire someone my age. The only reason the clerk at the domestic employment agency sent me here was because no other qualified cooks wanted to work for a policeman and, to be perfectly honest, I didn't either."

Phyllis gasped in shock. She couldn't believe what she'd just heard. The cook had never struck her as someone who placed any importance on the status of her employer.

Mrs. Goodge looked at her. "Don't be so surprised. You've been in service long enough to know there's as much snobbery below-stairs as there is above. I was no better than most other servants of my generation. Our position, the way we were treated by our family and the neighborhood, was determined by the standing of the master of the household where we worked. Even if the wages were awful, most people would rather have worked for a stingy baronet than a generous butcher. I'd worked for lords and ladies, country gentry, and members of Parliament; it was quite a comedown to take a position with a mere policeman, no matter how wealthy he might be."

"It's true," Mrs. Jeffries said. "When she first arrived, she did look down her nose at us a bit."

The cook chuckled. "But that didn't last long. Before I knew it, Mrs. Jeffries had everyone out asking questions about those horrible Kensington High Street murders, and, despite myself, I realized I wanted to help. What's more, being here has given me a real purpose in life. Our investigations are the most important thing I've ever done."

Wiggins nodded in agreement. "They're the most important thing any of us has ever done."

"I know I don't contribute as much as the rest of you do." Mrs. Goodge stepped away from her worktable, pulled out a chair, and sat down. "But I'm happy to do what little I can."

"You do your share, Mrs. Goodge," Phyllis protested.

"Of course you do," the housekeeper echoed. "Why would you think you do less than the rest of us?"

"Because I don't leave the kitchen. The rest of you get out and about, talking to people and gatherin' clues, but all I do is stay in my kitchen and listen to gossip."

"Gossip that often turns out to be very important," Mrs. Jeffries insisted. "There are a number of cases we'd never have solved if it hadn't been for information you have passed along."

"Cor blimey, Mrs. Goodge, you've worked in some of the finest houses all over the country, and you stay in touch with all your old friends. The sort of gossip and information you've found out is right important. You've done as much as any of us."

"That's nice of you to say." The cook smiled as she glanced at their faces. "I just wish I could do more. Fighting for justice is so important."

"As you and Wiggins have said, it's the most important thing any of us have done and you do your fair share," Mrs. Jeffries declared. "We all do. Each and every one of us."

"I wish we had another one to work on," Phyllis muttered, then she realized what she'd said. "Oh dear, I don't mean that the way it sounded. Murder is never right, even when the victim is a dreadful human being. But let's be honest here—life is so much more exciting when we're on the hunt."

Mrs. Jeffries ducked her head to hide a smile. When Phyllis had first arrived at the Witherspoon household, she'd been a shy, frightened girl so terrified of losing her position she wouldn't even consider helping them with the inspector's cases. But now she was a vibrant, confident young woman who was saving her money to open her own detective agency! Life was simply full of surprises.

"She's right, Mrs. Jeffries." Wiggins gave the maid a broad smile. "None of us like to admit it, but life is excitin' when we're out and about and doin' our best to make sure innocent people don't face the 'angman's noose. But it's done somethin' else for me—it's made me realize that one of these days, I can be more than what I am now. Don't get me wrong, I love livin' 'ere and bein' with all of you, but one of these days, I'm goin' to take what I've learned and start my own business."

"What kind of business?" Mrs. Goodge asked.

"A private inquiry agency."

"You're going to open a detective agency?" Phyllis yelped. "But you know that's what I was planning to do."

"I can do it, too," he countered. "Cor blimey, if anyone should do it, it's me. I've been at this longer than you."

"But that's not fair," she argued. "I had the idea first."

"So what difference does that make? Besides, I might go abroad and open mine. I've always wanted to go to Canada or America. They need detectives there as well."

"Now you two quit squabbling," the cook interjected. "There's room for more than one detective agency in this world." She cocked her head, her expression speculative as she looked at the maid. "Are you absolutely sure that Mrs. Perrin didn't give Mr. Soames a shove down those kitchen stairs?"

CHAPTER 2

Inspector Nigel Nivens yanked open the door of the Leman Street Police Station and strolled inside. But despite being ten minutes late for his shift, he wasn't in a rush. Nivens was a middle-aged man with a shape that had once been muscular but was now running to fat. He boasted a walrus mustache and a full head of once-dark blond hair that was now almost completely gray. He whipped off his bowler as he nodded curtly to the duty officer behind the counter.

"Inspector Havers wants to see you, sir," Constable Rhodes said.

"What's he still doing here?" Nivens came to a halt. "Surely, he didn't take it upon himself to stay simply because I'm a few minutes late."

Rhodes, an old veteran of a copper who'd seen more than one like Nivens, wasn't impressed with Nivens' haughty manner. "I've no idea, sir"—he shrugged as he spoke—"but he's waiting for you in the duty inspector's office."

Nivens' mouth flattened in displeasure as he turned into the short corridor toward the duty inspector's office. He stopped in front of the closed door and lifted his hand to knock. But then he hesitated. What could this be about? It was unusual for the night inspector to stay this late on a quiet day unless something important had happened. Had there been a murder in the night? But if that was the situation, Inspector Havers would have caught the case himself. What's more, there were always murders in this dreadful district.

So why did Havers want to see him? They weren't working any cases together. Then he understood. Oh. He smiled as he realized what it meant. Thank God, he told himself, thank God and my own clever initiative that it's finally happened. It had taken these fools long enough. That burglary trial had been over for weeks, and he'd almost given up hope.

But now it was here—his ticket to freedom, his way out of the most miserable district in all of the Metropolitan Police Force. He hadn't expected to receive the news from Havers. By rights, he should have been called to Scotland Yard and given his transfer or his promotion by Chief Superintendent Barrows himself. It was a slight, and he was sure a deliberate one, but once he was out of here and back in a decent district, he'd make certain Barrows paid for this as well as all the other affronts.

Nivens lifted his chin and rapped on the door.

"Enter."

He stepped inside and came to an abrupt halt when he saw that Havers wasn't alone. Chief Inspector Boney, the most senior officer in the district, was sitting behind the desk. Havers sat in a chair next to him.

"Come in and take a seat." Boney, a tall, gaunt man with coarse white hair and vivid, deep-set blue eyes, gestured at a chair placed in front of the desk.

"Good morning, sir. I do apologize for being late, but I stopped to break up a ruckus between a cockle seller and a customer on my way here." Nivens was lying, but he was certain they couldn't prove it one way or the other. He smiled slightly as he sat down and unbuttoned his overcoat. He put his bowler on his lap.

"I'm not concerned with your tardiness," Boney said coldly.

Nivens began to realize something was very wrong and that perhaps the chief inspector wasn't here to announce he'd been promoted or transferred. What's more, Havers was staring at him with the same expression he reserved for criminals. "Nonetheless, I do apologize."

Boney said nothing for several moments. Finally, when the silence was almost too much for Nivens to stand, Boney said, "Recently, you arrested the O'Dwyer brothers for housebreaking. Is that correct?"

"That's right, sir. We've already gone to trial, and all three of the O'Dwyers were found guilty. They're now at Pentonville."

"I'm well aware of that, Inspector," Boney snapped. "However, I do want you to confirm several things about the trial."

"Of course, sir."

"The main witness linking the O'Dwyers to the burglaries was a man named Humberto Santorini. Is that right?"

"Yes, sir." Nivens could feel sweat breaking out along his hairline, and his heart began to thump so loudly he was sure the other two men could hear it.

"Santorini was an iceman with his own cart and pony. Is that correct?"

Nivens nodded.

"In your opinion, is it fair to say that without Santorini's testimony, the O'Dwyers wouldn't have been found guilty?" Boney asked.

"I'm not sure that's true, sir," Nivens said quickly. "It wasn't just Santorini's testimony that condemned the brothers. There were several witnesses from the neighborhood that testified the O'Dwyers were thieves."

"Yes, but they were on trial for the specific burglary of Sir Jonathan Freemantle's Mayfair house, and one of the charges against the brothers was that there was grievous bodily harm done to the butler. The poor man was knocked unconscious. Correct?"

"That's true, sir, but it wasn't just witness testimony. There was other evidence against them. Stolen items were found in their home, including a silver cup identified as being part of a set from the Freemantle home."

"But none of those items was from the recent burglaries done in the West End, and the only item you found from the Freemantle break-in was the silver cup," Havers said. "When you and the constables searched the O'Dwyer home, the only objects taken into evidence were a few pieces from a badly damaged silver tea service and two sets of brass andirons, all of which Mrs. O'Dwyer claimed belonged to her family. Additionally, Mrs. O'Dwyer claimed the silver cup had been planted in the house by the police."

"That's absurd, sir. You know as well as I do that the people around here are always claiming the police have planted evidence. Mrs. O'Dwyer couldn't prove the items were hers. The O'Dwyers had a very sophisticated system of fencing the goods they stole. They didn't keep anything more than a few hours."

"That's what Santorini testified to during the trial. As a matter of fact, he was the only witness to make that specific assertion,"

Boney said softly. "But he never explained how he, a simple ice-man, knew this alleged fact."

"But it was precisely because he was an iceman that he knew these things, sir," Nivens insisted. "He serviced a number of pubs in the East End, sir."

"I thought most of his business was in the West End," Havers interrupted.

"He had clients here as well," Nivens argued. "And during the course of his work, he got to know a number of . . . shall we say, less than honest members of the public. He heard things, and not wanting to risk life and limb, kept most of what he heard to himself. But recently, he's had a change of heart about his life and is determined to do the right thing. Which he did when he testified against the O'Dwyers. What is this about, sir? I think I have a right to know."

Boney stared at him stonily.

"Where were you last night?" Havers asked.

"Where was I? Why on earth are you asking me such a question?" Nivens protested. He sat up straighter in the chair and took a deep breath. He'd had enough of being treated like a newly sworn-in constable who didn't know what was what. He might have mucked up his last case, that dreadful one that landed him in this horrid district, but he wasn't without power and, by all that was holy, he'd use it again if he had to. "What is this about? I demand to know."

"Answer the question," Boney snapped.

Nivens gaped at him in surprise. "After my shift ended, I went to Baxter's Restaurant for dinner, then I went to my mother's home and spent the night."

"Why didn't you stay at your own home?" Havers asked.

"Because my mother's out of town and her butler, who was supposed to stay at her residence, was called away as his brother is ill. Lady Merton—that's my mother—didn't want the house empty, so she asked me to stay there until Lord Merton's valet arrives from the Merton country estate."

"How long have you been there?" Havers asked.

"Since Sunday night. The valet is arriving today, so I'm going back to my own home. Look, what's this all about? Why are you asking all these questions?"

Boney suddenly opened the top drawer, drew out a pistol, and laid it on the desk. "Do you recognize this?"

Nivens' eyes widened in shock. "My God, where did you get that?"

"Is it yours?"

"It certainly looks like mine." He shook his head in disbelief. "But mine should be at home in my study. It's a dueling pistol that was part of a set left to me when my grandfather died. It's been in my family for generations. What's it doing here?"

"When was the last time you saw it?" Havers asked.

"When I picked it up from the gunsmiths, Settler and Sons, and took it home. That was last Thursday. Good Lord, what's this about? Why have you got my gun?"

"What was wrong with the gun?" Boney asked.

"The spur below the finger guard was broken."

"So even with a broken piece to it, the weapon was still in working order?" Havers asked.

"Yes, yes, of course, it worked perfectly. Nonetheless, the set is so valuable, I had the spur repaired. The set may be old, but the original workmanship was of the highest quality."

"That's very interesting, Inspector Nivens."

"What is?" Nivens was now so confused he wanted to scream, but he wisely kept himself in check.

"The fact that you've admitted it worked perfectly." Havers smiled. "You see, this gun, a weapon you freely admit was in your possession, was used to murder Bert Santorini last night."

Inspector Gerald Witherspoon closed the open file box on the duty inspector's desk and put it to one side. He was a middle-aged man of medium height with thinning dark hair, spectacles on his deep-set hazel eyes, and a slight thickening around the waist of his slender frame. He glanced at the clock on the top of the wooden file cabinet and noted that Constable Barnes was late. That was highly unusual, as the constable was one of those people who hated tardiness in others and held himself to even higher standards.

Witherspoon looked toward the open office door as he heard footsteps in the hall. He spotted Constable Griffiths going past. "Have you any idea where Constable Barnes has got to? He was supposed to go over the witness statements in the Joffrey case with me."

Griffiths, a tall, lanky man with red hair and a very pale complexion, stopped in the doorway. He had a newspaper tucked under his arm. "He's in the lockup, sir. One-legged Billy insisted he needed to see him and discuss something. Shall I get him for you, sir?"

Witherspoon shook his head. "No, the witness statements can wait. If Billy Gaspain wants to speak to the constable, I'm sure he's something important to tell him." The inspector thought it rather mean to refer to someone's physical disfigurement instead of their proper name, but he'd not chastise Constable Griffiths. Most constables tended to use the street names of prisoners and informants.

"Gaspain's not one for makin' up tales, sir," Griffiths agreed. He pulled the newspaper out, unrolled it, and held it up. "Have you seen this, sir? It's a wonder they managed to get it in the morning paper. But luckily, it's only in the *Sentinel* and not the decent newspapers."

"No, what is it?" Witherspoon squinted as the constable came toward him. Then his eyes widened when he read the headline on the lead article: *Policeman's Gun Used for Murder in Whitechapel.*

"Good gracious!" Witherspoon exclaimed.

"You'll never guess whose gun it was, either." Griffiths paused for a moment. "Inspector Nigel Nivens', sir. It was one of his family's dueling pistols that was used."

"Who was murdered?"

"One of Nivens' informants, the one that testified for him in the O'Dwyer trial. Fellow named Bert Santorini."

"He was killed last night?"

"Early in the evening, just after dark. That's the only way the paper was able to get the story in time to print it. But it's odd that none of the other newspapers have it. The article didn't come right out and say it, but the paper is hinting that the police are tryin' to cover everything up to protect one of their own just because the gun belonged to Inspector Nivens." He snorted. "Mind you, they wouldn't be thinkin' like that if they knew how much most of us dislike Inspector Nivens. Still, it doesn't make us look very good, does it." He handed the paper to Witherspoon, who was so surprised by the information he didn't admonish the young constable for making truthful but rather insubordinate remarks about one of his superiors.

The article was short, so Witherspoon read it twice and then frowned as he put the newspaper down on the edge of the desk.

"I'm surprised they named Inspector Nivens as the owner of the weapon. How on earth did they get that information?"

"I don't know, sir, but they weren't shy about bandyin' Inspector Nivens' name about."

"This most definitely paints the force in a very bad light. Why does the gutter press always assume every police officer will lie to protect another police officer? It simply isn't true."

Griffiths said nothing. The truth was, there were lots of times when coppers lied to protect one another—he'd done it himself a time or two to shield a fellow officer who'd done nothing really wrong.

"Of course it isn't true, sir." Constable Barnes stepped into the office. "But some people think that it is, and articles like that one"—he pointed at the paper—"don't help us much." Barnes was an older officer with wavy iron-gray hair, a slightly ruddy complexion, and a ramrod straight spine.

"I'll be off, then." Griffiths picked up his newspaper, nodded respectfully, and left.

"I'm sorry to be late, sir, but One-legged Billy wanted to have a word with me before he went in front of the magistrate this morning." Barnes sat down in the chair across from Witherspoon. "And what he told me wasn't good news."

"What do you mean?"

"That article you and Griffiths were talking about—there might be something to what it said. Billy said there's lots of talk goin' around that Santorini had something he was holding over Inspector Nigel Nivens. Mind you, he wasn't specific, just said there was talk and that Santorini had been flashin' a bit of money about these days. Unfortunately, he didn't say enough for us to take it to Chief Superintendent Barrows."

"Perhaps that's just as well," Witherspoon replied. "I've a feeling this Santorini murder might get very nasty. Thank goodness it happened in Whitechapel. It's the Leman Street Station's problem, not ours."

At Scotland Yard, Chief Superintendent Barrows was having a very bad morning. His tortoiseshell spectacles had slipped down his nose, and his normally pale face was flushed with anger.

He slammed his fist against the newspaper on his desk. "I don't understand how this could have happened? How on earth did the *Sentinel* get this story so quickly? According to the morning report, Santorini was only killed last night."

Harry Wadsworth, the white-haired, clean-shaven head of the Criminal Investigation Division, said, "It was apparently early enough in the evening to get a reporter to the scene to start asking questions. Their offices are in Fleet Street, and the only way that could have happened is if someone tipped them off."

"We can only hope the decent papers don't pick up the story," Sergeant Pickering, the third man in the office, added. "If it's only the gutter press that runs articles like that one"—he nodded at the paper—"it should be fine, and the Santorini murder can be investigated just like any other."

"Don't count on it." Wadsworth snorted. "Even the so-called decent papers aren't above reminding the public that Jack the Ripper was never caught and that we've had a scandal or two in the last few years."

"We've weathered bad press before," Pickering protested. "We can do it again. Tomorrow this will be old news. We've done nothing to protect Inspector Nivens. Good God, the murder only happened last night. There hasn't been time for a cover-up even if we'd wanted to do such a thing."

"Is there any credence to the story?" Barrows drummed his fingers on the desk. "That's the important question. They didn't come right out and say it in the article, but they certainly hinted that there was a relationship between the victim and Inspector Nivens. They spent two paragraphs on the O'Dwyer trial and how it was Santorini's testimony that convicted the three brothers."

"We'll not know why or who killed Santorini until Inspector Havers begins a proper investigation," Pickering pointed out. "Until then, let's just tell any reporters that show up we're treating this like any other homicide investigation."

There was a knock on the door, and a second later, a young constable stuck his head inside. "Sorry to interrupt, sir, but we've just had a letter delivered by messenger from the Home Office."

Pickering, who was closest to the door, took the envelope. The constable retreated, closing the door softly as the sergeant handed it across the desk to Barrows. "It's addressed to you, sir."

"Oh, blast." Barrows stared at the elegant script on the front of the cream-colored envelope. "It's the Home Secretary's handwriting. This isn't going to be good news." He plucked a brass letter opener from his top drawer and slit the top of the envelope. He read the contents and then sighed. "It's what I expected. The Home Secretary claims he doesn't wish to interfere, but he strongly suggests that we mustn't allow Inspector Havers or anyone else from the Leman Street Station to head the investigation."

"But why, sir? There's no love lost between Havers and Nivens. He'll do a proper investigation. It's only one article in the gutter press," Pickering pointed out.

"And by tomorrow there will be half a dozen more," Wadsworth argued. "There are political implications if this isn't done properly, and having anyone from Leman Street head up the investigation could end in disaster for the force. We need someone from the outside, someone who is known to have the highest level of integrity."

"It'd be good if they were known to loathe Nigel Nivens as well," Pickering muttered.

Barrows' mouth was set in a grim line. "I knew I should have sacked Nivens when I had the chance. But instead I let his family's influence pressure me into keeping him on the force."

"Sacking him wouldn't have been easy." Wadsworth shrugged. "We all know he withheld evidence in the Starling case, but in any formal hearing Nivens would claim he was pursuing a different line of inquiry that entailed holding on to the evidence until the proper moment."

"Different line of inquiry my foot." Barrows snorted. "What you really mean is the evidence statements of a number of police constables and even a formal complaint from one of our best officers might not have been enough to get him off the force. Not with his family's power."

Neither of the other two men contradicted him. Barrows stared off into space with a bemused expression on his face. Finally, he smiled. "Pickering, can you step out into the hall and call a constable for me? I want to send two important telegrams."

Nivens was so stunned, he was momentarily speechless. He couldn't believe this was happening. Not to him. When he finally found his voice, he forced his gaze away from the dueling pistol and looked at the two men on the other side of the desk. "Surely you don't think I had anything to do with Santorini's murder?"

Havers said nothing; he merely stared at Nivens. It was Chief Inspector Boney who broke the silence. "We've made no assumptions as yet, but it was your weapon that was used to kill him. It's well-known amongst the criminal classes that Bert Santorini was one of your informants."

"All detectives use people as sources for information. I'm no different from any other inspector," Nivens protested.

"True, but that's not a fact the general public understands," Boney explained. "Now, let's start at the beginning. You say the last time you saw the gun was when you brought it home from being repaired. Where in your house do you keep it?"

"On a bookshelf in my study."

"You don't have it under lock and key?" Havers exclaimed.

"Why would I?" Nivens retorted. "My house is securely locked, and I trust the people I invite to social occasions."

"What about your servants?" Havers asked. "Would one of them have taken it without your permission?"

"They wouldn't dare. Besides, I'm a bachelor and my household is small. The only person who lives in is my housekeeper, Mrs. Vickers. She takes care of me, and once a quarter, the heavy cleaning is done by a domestic agency. But we've used the same one for years, and none of them would dare touch my things."

"Well, if your servants wouldn't dare touch it, and you trust all your friends, that leaves only you," Boney said softly.

"Don't be absurd," Nivens blustered. "Obviously the killer managed to get inside and take the weapon. I've no idea how, but I assure you, I'll get to the bottom of this. I'll find out who is trying to frame me, and I'll bring Santorini's murderer to justice. I'll personally see to it that they hang."

Boney sat back in his chair and stared at Nivens. "Are you under the assumption that you're going to have anything to do with the Santorini investigation?"

"But of course. Santorini was murdered in this district, and by rights I should get the case," Nivens argued. "I've had more experience with homicide than Inspector Havers. I caught the O'Connell murderer."

"You found the killer standing over O'Connell's body moments after they'd had a shouting match about splitting up the cash from a robbery," Havers snapped. "I've solved half a dozen murders. God's truth, Nivens, are you completely delusional? No one in their right mind would think it appropriate that the man whose gun was the murder weapon be in charge of finding Santorini's killer."

"But just because it was my gun doesn't mean I had anything to do with Santorini's death." Nivens now had a hollow, sick feeling in his stomach. He'd noticed that Havers hadn't bothered to address him by his proper police rank; he'd said "Nivens," not "Inspector Nivens." Fear snaked up his spine, his throat went dry, and he clenched his fingers tight to keep his hands from shaking as he finally realized that he might be in serious trouble.

He knew he wasn't a popular officer; his ambition and his disdain for friendships with both his fellow officers and the rank and file were now working against him. There wasn't anyone on the force he trusted to prove he was innocent. He was far too hated for that. "But you must let me investigate this case. Both of you know there are many in the force who resent me, and I'm not sure that even the local lads will examine all the evidence properly. You must believe me, I'm innocent. For God's sake, I'm a police officer, sworn to uphold the law!"

"Just like you upheld the law when you withheld evidence in the Starling case," Boney reminded him. "Let's be realistic, Nivens. If it hadn't been for your family's influence with the Home Secretary, you'd have been sacked then. The last thing we need now is for the press to find out about *that* as well as the fact that you own the gun that killed Santorini."

"But the press doesn't have wind of either of those things yet, and we can make sure they never find out," he pleaded.

"It's too late for that." Boney pulled a newspaper off his lap and slapped it against the desk. "Take a look at the lead article." He shoved it across to Nivens.

Nivens read the headline and felt the blood drain out of his face. Shaking his head, he frantically tried to think of something to say, some way to defend himself.

There was a sharp knock on the door and then a constable stepped inside. "I'm sorry to interrupt, sir, but you've had a telegram from the Yard." He directed his comment to Chief Inspector Boney as he stepped inside, gave Nivens a wary glance as he moved past him, and handed over the telegram.

Boney opened it as the constable hurried out. He read it and then gave it to Inspector Havers, who also read it. Havers smiled as he looked at Nivens. "I shouldn't worry about us local lads not examining the evidence if I were you. The case has been handed off to another station, one I'm sure you're familiar with."

Nivens ignored Havers and directed his question to the chief inspector. "Which one, sir?"

"Ladbroke Road. Inspector Gerald Witherspoon has been put in charge."

"The post office just delivered a telegram from the Yard, sir," Constable Barnes said as he returned to the duty inspector's office. He'd taken the witness statements to the sergeant and had been at the front counter when the lad arrived. When he saw the telegram was for Witherspoon, he'd immediately guessed what it was about. "I've a feeling you're going to get handed the Santorini case," he commented as he handed over the message.

The inspector ripped open the slender envelope, pulled out the paper, and read it quickly. "Gracious, how did you know?" He looked at Barnes.

"The article in the *Sentinel*, sir." Barnes chuckled. "Chief Inspector Barrows doesn't want there to be even a hint of a scandal about this investigation, not with the press finding out the murder weapon is owned by Inspector Nivens."

"True, but that doesn't mean he had anything to do with Santorini's murder. Guns are frequently stolen."

"Agreed, sir, but this isn't the first time Nivens has been accused of disreputable behavior. Remember why he ended up at the Leman Street Station. By rights, he should have been sacked rather than transferred, and I imagine our chief superintendent is concerned about the press getting wind of that information."

Witherspoon nodded and rose to his feet. "We'd best get cracking, then. Drat—the murder was last night and by now the body has been moved to a morgue." He frowned. "This is most unsettling. Taking over a case after the victim's been moved is the worst possible way to begin a proper investigation. I do like looking at the murder scene. One learns so very much from seeing the details of how the body lies and where the weapon was found."

"I'm sure whoever was in charge last night took care to note all the details, sir," Barnes replied. "Your methods have become standard procedure." The constable was well aware that many of the techniques used by Witherspoon had been in place for a number of years. But the implementation of their use had been somewhat haphazard from one police district to another until Inspector Witherspoon's phenomenal success in solving murders.

For ambitious officers, the fastest road to promotion in the Metropolitan Police Force was an ability to decipher a homicide and bring the killer to justice; the successful inspector's name was always prominently mentioned in newspaper articles. Once Witherspoon began solving one murder after another, every district in the force followed the same methods. He'd popularized them.

"I do hope so." Witherspoon started for the door. "The first thing we'll need to do is speak to whoever was in charge last night."

"That would be Inspector Havers." Barnes followed him. "He's probably waiting for us at the Leman Street Station."

They stopped at the sergeant's desk, signed out, and left. Stepping outside, Barnes shivered in the cold wind; Witherspoon buttoned his coat and pulled on his leather gloves. The sky was overcast, gloomy, and the air damp.

Barnes looked up and down the street but didn't see any cabs. "We'll have more luck getting a hansom on the High Street."

"Good idea. There are usually street lads on the High Street looking to earn a few pence carrying ladies' shopping parcels or taking messages. We need to let our households know we might be very late tonight."

Davey Marsh loved going to the Witherspoon household. Inspector Witherspoon always gave more than most when he wanted you to take a message to his home, and, even better, Mrs. Goodge always gave you something to eat. He wasn't disappointed this time, either.

"Ta, Mrs. Goodge." Davey, a slender, fair-haired lad grinned

broadly as the cook put a plate with two jam tarts and three slices
of buttered brown bread in front of him. "This is ever so good. Uh,
do ya mind if I take one of the tarts home for me little sister?"

"Phyllis is wrapping up your sister's tart as well as some bread
for you to take home," the cook replied. "Now, are you certain the
only thing the inspector said was that he'd caught a case and would
be home late tonight?"

"That's all he told me." Davey started to grab a tart but then
reached for a slice of bread instead.

"I wonder where he was going." Mrs. Jeffries sat down at the
head of the table.

Davey quickly chewed and swallowed the food in his mouth. "I
know. They was goin' to Whitechapel. I 'eard his constable tellin'
the hansom driver to take 'em to the Leman Street Police Station
and that's in Whitechapel." He shoved another bite in his mouth.

Mrs. Jeffries glanced at the cook, who was frowning. "Are you
certain?" the housekeeper asked.

"Heard it plain as day, ma'am. They was on their way to Leman
Street Station."

The cook shoved the plate closer to Davey. "Go on, then. Eat
up, Davey."

Phyllis, who had heard the whole exchange, moved closer to the
housekeeper and whispered, "Should I get Smythe and Betsy?"

Mrs. Jeffries nodded. "Yes, and if you can manage it, stop and
have a word with Ruth as well. As soon as Wiggins comes downstairs, I'll send him to fetch Luty Belle and Hatchet."

"Right, I'm off, then." Phyllis rushed to the coat tree, grabbed
her coat, and with a quick smile at Davey, raced down the corridor
for the door.

As soon as the lad finished eating, Mrs. Goodge handed him a brown-paper-wrapped parcel of food and bundled him out of the back door. She hurried to the kitchen. "You don't think our inspector has the Santorini murder, do you?"

"You read the article in the *Sentinel*. Why else would he be going to the East End?" Mrs. Jeffries said.

It was a newspaper they didn't generally read, but today Wiggins had picked up a copy at the newsagents when he'd spotted the headline earlier this morning on his way back from getting Mrs. Goodge her rheumatism medicine from the chemist.

Mrs. Jeffries plopped into her chair. "But I'm not sure how I feel about this situation."

The cook stared at her for a moment before taking her own seat. "Don't be ridiculous, Hepzibah. If our inspector has a case, then we're on the hunt."

"I know, but it will be strange to work on a case involving Inspector Nivens. I'm not sure I'm up to it." She shook her head. "He's tried so hard to hurt our inspector and, even though that newspaper article didn't come right out and say it, the writer hinted that Nivens is the prime suspect."

Mrs. Goodge hesitated, not certain how to say what she thought. "Hepzibah, I understand Nivens has acted like a swine, and I've no great liking for him, either. But whether he is innocent or guilty shouldn't have anything to do with our commitment to justice."

"I know," Mrs. Jeffries said. "But, on the other hand, why should we help someone who has spent years undermining Inspector Witherspoon?"

"How do you know we'd be helping Nivens? Maybe we'd be helping someone innocent, maybe we'd keep someone from being hanged for a murder they didn't commit. What's more, we've already sent Phyllis for Smythe and Betsy as well as Ruth. What are we going to tell them? That we're not even goin' to look at this case because it *might* involve Nigel Nivens?"

"Of course not," Mrs. Jeffries protested, but in truth, she had no idea what she was going to say or do about this situation. What's more, she knew the cook was right, but somehow the thought of working on this case and possibly helping that odious man seemed wrong. Simply wrong. "First of all, we don't know his being called to Leman Street Station has anything to do with the Santorini murder, and second, finding out anything will be very difficult. Santorini was killed in Whitechapel, the East End, the roughest part of London."

"We've gone into rough places before." The cook crossed her arms over her chest and stared at her friend. "And if you'll recall, Betsy spent most of her life there. She knows her way around, as does Wiggins, and even our Phyllis has learned a few tricks about taking care of herself when she's on the hunt."

"But Ruth certainly won't know anyone from the East End and, and . . ." Her voice trailed off as she realized how foolish she was being. Closing her eyes, she sighed. "Forgive me; I'm being an idiot. Let's just find out what the facts of the case might be."

Thirty minutes later, Betsy and Smythe arrived. Smythe was Inspector Witherspoon's coachman. He carried their three-year-old daughter, Amanda, in his arms. Betsy, a slender, blonde young matron with lovely features and blue eyes, had been the household maid before marrying the coachman. They now lived a quarter mile away in their own flat. Smythe was a good fifteen years older than his wife. He had brown hair graying at the crown and temples, a tall, muscular build, and a hard face that was saved from being harsh by the smile in his brown eyes. He put his daughter down. "Blast a Spaniard. Even for this time of the year, it's still ruddy cold outside."

Mrs. Goodge held out her arms. "Come see your godmother, and we'll take off that heavy coat and hat," she called. She, along with their friend Luty Belle Crookshank, and the inspector were the three godparents to the child. Amanda raced toward her, squealing in delight.

The cook scooped the child up and sat down at the table with the toddler on her lap. She untied the ribbons holding the warm woolly hat on the little one's head and then began unbuttoning her heavy winter coat.

"Do we have a murder?" Betsy sat down across from the cook. But just then, they heard the back door open and the sound of footsteps.

A moment later, Luty Belle Crookshank, a small-statured, white-haired American, scurried into the kitchen with Hatchet, her butler, on her heels. Wiggins brought up the rear.

"I hear we got us another murder." Luty skidded to a halt as she spotted Amanda on the cook's lap. "Nells bells, my baby girl's here."

Hatchet stopped abruptly to avoid crashing into his employer, causing Wiggins to stumble to a halt to avoid running into him. "Really, madam, don't stop so suddenly. We might have had a most distressing accident." He was a tall, white-haired man with a spine as straight as an admiral's and a manner that was equally comfortable with a beggar or a duke. He was supposed to be Luty's butler, but in truth, they were far more than that and very devoted to each other.

Luty ignored him, flew across the room, and plopped down in

the chair next to the cook. Amanda giggled happily as Luty chucked her gently on the chin.

"Is Lady Cannonberry coming?" Hatchet asked as he took a chair next to Luty.

"I'm not sure." Phyllis put a pot of tea on the table. "She wasn't home, but I left a message with Everton, her butler, that she was needed. He wasn't sure when she'd be back, so I told him to ask her to stop in if she arrived back before lunch. If she isn't back, I told him to make sure she knew to be here this afternoon."

"Then we'll get on with it now that everyone else is here," Mrs. Jeffries announced. She told them what little they knew thus far. "So you see," she concluded, "I'm not really sure the case has anything to do with the murder of Bert Santorini."

"What else could it mean?" Luty declared. "Our inspector was sent there because he's got a good reputation, and if he's in charge of that murder, the police can't be accused of covering anything up to protect one of their own."

"Yes, it does seem that way," Mrs. Jeffries agreed. "But perhaps before we do anything, we ought to be sure of the facts."

Smythe shook his head. "Luty's right, Mrs. J.—it's the Santorini killing. I think Wiggins and I need to get to the East End right quick." He glanced at the carriage clock on the pine sideboard. "If we take the train, we've time to get there before the pubs close for the afternoon."

"Why should you two get to go?" Betsy frowned at her husband. "I'm the one that knows that neighborhood."

"I know where Felix Mews is and Wiggins and I can get there fast." Smythe grinned and dropped a kiss on his wife's cheek. "And the little one is goin' to need 'er nap soon."

Wiggins was already on his feet. "We'll be back as soon as we can," he said as the two men disappeared toward the back door.

After leaving Whitechapel Station, Smythe had gone into the Kings Arms, a big, crowded workingman's pub on the Commercial Road, while Wiggins headed for the quieter streets in search of a smaller, more local place. It didn't take him long to find the Crying Crows Pub.

He opened the door, stepped inside, and then knew he'd picked the wrong place. For the East End, the pub was too fancy for most of the locals. Crimson wallpaper with an intricate gold fleur-de-lis pattern covered the walls, the bar was polished oak, and the planks on the wooden floor gleamed. There was a mirror running the length of the bar, and the keg taps visible over the top of the counter were a pale cream ceramic instead of wood. But worst of all, the place was empty save for one old man sitting at a table by the window.

The barmaid was drying a tray of whisky glasses while a barman with a receding hairline was picking up empty pints and cleaning the tables. It was close to closing time, but Wiggins had hoped there'd be a few more people in the ruddy place. He almost turned and walked out, but just then the barmaid saw him. "You've time for a quick one if ya want," she called.

Feeling stuck, Wiggins went to the bar. "I'll 'ave a pint of bitter, please. I 'ear there was a killin' around these parts last night."

"You a reporter?" The barmaid picked up a glass, stuck it under the tap, and pulled the lever. She put the drink in front of Wiggins.

"Nah, just visitin' my auntie. I live in Chelmsford. My auntie told me there was someone murdered near 'ere."

"Yeah, it 'appens from time to time." She went back to her task.

"Guess it 'appens everywhere from time to time." Wiggins took a sip. "Mind you, me auntie said the poor bloke was killed with a copper's gun."

She stared at him a moment and then shrugged. She was an attractive young woman with brown hair piled high on the top of her head and held together in an elaborate twist with a trio of pale gray combs; her eyes were blue and her face long and narrow. "Don't believe everything you hear. We get lots of police in here and most of 'em are a decent sort. You sure you're not a reporter?"

Wiggins wished he'd worn his old jacket and flat cap instead of the new one he'd bought at Christmas. "Do I look like a ruddy reporter?"

"You're dressed like one." She looked him up and down. "That coat costs more than I earn in a month."

"I make a good livin'," he retorted. "And this coat was a present from me auntie. Cor blimey, what's wrong with the people in this part of town? Last I 'eard, it wasn't a crime to be curious about a murder. I was only makin' a bit of conversation."

"Sorry. I didn't mean to sound rude. You're a customer, and we pride ourselves on treatin' our customers right." She flushed slightly and glanced toward the other end of the long counter. He followed her gaze and saw that just beyond the mirror was a closed door. "It's just that the owner knew the man that was killed. To be honest, we all did."

"Was they friends?"

"You could say that." She managed a brief smile. "He stayed here for a few months, but then the two of 'em had a falling out, and he moved to a lodging house. But still, even if they did have words, it's not nice to know someone who was murdered. Mrs. Callahan told us not to talk about him, especially if any reporters come around asking questions."

Wiggins realized he'd already made some headway here. She was talking about the murder, and he'd even picked up a tiny morsel of information. "Well, you can rest easy, miss." He gave her his best smile. "I'm just a simple workingman. I'm in charge of the Inbound Department at Pierce and Son, not a newspaper reporter."

"Pierce and Son? They're over by Liverpool Street Station, right? I walk right past there on my way home." She gave him a long, assessing look. "You're in charge of a whole department? You look awfully young for such a position."

Wiggins knew then he might have made a mistake. He wasn't conceited, but he knew he was attractive. The last thing he needed was her dropping into the Pierce warehouse and having a look for him, but he couldn't retreat now. As the saying went, "In for a penny, in for a pound." He laughed. "Why, thank you, miss. That's the nicest thing anyone's said to me in a long time."

"My name is Janice, Janice Everly." She smiled flirtatiously.

"Christopher Carrow," he lied. He never used his real name when he was on the hunt. "It must be terrible for all of you, I mean, seein' as how you knew the man. Is your Mrs. Callahan afraid the killer will come after her?" Wiggins dropped his voice to a conspiratorial whisper and leaned closer as he spoke.

"Nah." She laughed. "She's scared that if any of us talk to the newspapers, she'll lose half her customers. We get a lot of business from the local constables and detectives. The Leman Street Station is close by, and Mrs. Callahan doesn't want them upset and thinkin' we're talkin' out of turn. Mrs. Callahan has worked hard to fix this place up and make it nice, you know, so that we attract the right sort of customers."

"She'll have your guts for garters if she hears you." The barman came from the far end of the bar and put a tray of dirty glassware on the counter. "Good Lord, Janice, she's in a bad enough mood today"—he cast a quick glance at the door behind the bar—"and if she hears you, she'll have your head on a pike and probably mine as well."

"Oh, for goodness' sakes, Alex. What's wrong now?" Janice frowned at the barman and picked up the tray. She put it on the shelf behind her and then pushed it neatly down to the far end.

"It's the ruddy gin. We're almost out of it," he muttered, "and of course, she's blaming me. But you know that I told her we weren't just low on it, but that we were almost completely out. I told her to add it to today's order, but when the brewery wagon came this morning, it didn't bring much of anything except the whisky."

"I know you told her. I was standin' right next to you when you yelled up them stairs on Saturday night that we needed more," Janice agreed.

"Now she's sayin' that she never heard me and that I should have made sure she knew we was almost out." He tossed his cleaning rag onto the counter.

"She had to have heard you—you was shoutin' loud enough to raise the dead. Besides, she doesn't like either of us goin' upstairs to her quarters. Remember how she yelled at me when I went up to tell her that one of the keg handles broke." Janice turned back to Wiggins. "You see what I'm on about, don't ya? No matter what we do, if something goes wrong here, it's our fault."

"Can't you work somewhere else?"

"We could, but Mrs. Callahan, for all her faults, pays better than most around here," Alex interjected.

"But still, if you get blamed for every little thing that goes wrong, that don't seem right."

"For the most part, she's not as bad as some I've worked for. I think she's just upset because she was once friends with Bert Santorini, and she feels bad he was shot. Still, she shouldn't take it out on us."

"That's the trouble with bein' a workin'man." Wiggins took another sip of his beer. He tried to think of a way to keep them talking, but he suspected he was running out of time.

"You'd best drink that up." Alex nodded at the pint of beer that was still almost full. "It's closing time, and Mrs. Callahan won't let drinkers dawdle any later than the law allows."

CHAPTER 3

Barnes yanked open the front door of the Leman Street Station. He and Inspector Witherspoon stepped inside and straight into a wrestling match between three constables and a black-bearded giant. They stopped inside the doorway.

One of the constables managed to get the flailing man onto his back and promptly sat on him while the other two grabbed at his arms. "Get your bloody 'ands off me." The giant flung one of the constables to one side as three more police rushed in from the corridor. "You can't treat me like this." He began kicking his legs into the air, trying to dislodge the constable sitting on his chest. One of the newcomers grabbed at a leg, managed to snag it, and held it down, while the other two flattened themselves onto all four of the prisoner's limbs. Finally, they got him subdued, but it took five of them to hoist the fellow to his feet.

"He's a big one, sir," Barnes muttered.

"Indeed, Constable," Witherspoon agreed. "He's at least six and a half feet tall."

"And he's a ruddy troublemaker," the constable who'd been tossed to one side snapped as he got to his feet and joined the others surrounding the prisoner. They shepherded him toward the hallway.

"You coppers are the troublemakers; I weren't doin' nuthin' but mindin' me own business when your lot set upon me like a pack of mad dogs," he shouted.

"Mind you search him properly," the desk constable called as they disappeared into the corridor. "He carries a knife in his left boot." He broke off and gave the new arrivals a faint smile before turning his attention to Witherspoon. "Welcome, sir. You must be the inspector from Ladbroke Road. We don't normally greet guests like this, but, as I'm sure you know, it happens."

From the hall, they heard a keening and then a horrible, sad sob. "Why'd she do it, why'd she leave me like this?"

"Oh, for God's sake, Henry—she'll be back," an irritable voice replied. "She always comes back."

"She won't, not this time. My Sophie is gone for good."

They heard who they assumed to be the giant begin to cry in earnest, his sobs wrenching and heartfelt, so much so that the inspector gave a sympathetic glance in his direction.

"Sorry, sir." The desk constable frowned toward the corridor. "Henry's a big one and not a bad one, but he gets drunk whenever Sophie takes it into her head to run off with someone else."

"Yes, well, that must be dreadful for the poor fellow. He sounds heartbroken. I'm Gerald Witherspoon," he replied, "and this is Constable Barnes. We're here to see Inspector Havers. Is he available?"

The constable's eyebrows rose in surprise. "They didn't say it was you two who was expected." His broad face split into a welcoming grin. "I'm right pleased to make your acquaintance," he said to Witherspoon before turning to the constable. "Come on, Barnes—don't you recognize me? The hair's a bit grayer and I've put on a pound or two, but I haven't changed that much."

Barnes stared at him curiously.

"For goodness' sakes, man, you and I patrolled these streets together twenty-five years ago."

"Ye gods, as I live and breathe—you're John Rhodes. I'd have thought you would be retired by now." Barnes laughed, extended his hand, and the two of them shook.

"I could say the same about you," Rhodes replied, "but I like my work, and this district suits me. I've had mainly desk duty for the last ten years. I've got to tell you, Barnes—you've made some of us old coppers right proud. You and your inspector have solved some of the most complicated murders this city has ever seen."

"It's not just the two of us, John." Barnes chuckled. "We have a lot of help from the other lads on the force. Everyone does their part."

"It's good to see you again, Barnes"—Rhodes nodded—"but I expect you don't have time to stand about and talk about the old days. Now that you're here, I *do* expect you to let me buy you a drink when you've time for a pint. Inspector Havers is waitin' for you in the duty inspector's office. It's the second door on the right."

They headed toward the office, Barnes knocked, and they entered. Inspector Havers rose from his chair and came around the desk, his hand extended. "Inspector Witherspoon and Constable Barnes, welcome to Leman Street." He shook hands with both of them and then pointed to two straight-backed chairs in front of the desk. "I'm all ready for you, so please sit down. Would you care for tea?"

"No, thank you." Witherspoon took his seat. "We're fine. I appreciate your taking the time to see us. I know how busy you must be." He glanced at Constable Barnes and saw that he'd taken his notebook and pencil out of his pocket.

"True, this station does see a lot of activity"—he gave them a rueful smile—"as I'm sure you've just seen. Henry Spangler is as big as they come and, for the most part, a decent sort. He works down at the docks loading freight, but he can't hold his liquor, and when he drinks, he generally gets into terrible mischief. Usually that only happens when his lady decides to hunt for greener pastures."

"That sort of thing happens at Ladbroke Road as well," Witherspoon said. He cleared his throat. "Inspector Havers, I want you to understand that I've no idea why Constable Barnes and I were called into your district and given the Santorini case. I assure you—"

Havers interrupted. "Don't feel awkward, Inspector, I know exactly why. First, it's because one of our officers appears to have some connection to Santorini's death—Inspector Nigel Nivens' gun was used to kill the man—and second, the press already have that story."

"Yes, I know. I saw today's *Sentinel*." Witherspoon unbuttoned his heavy overcoat. "Still, it's odd that they'd call us in so quickly."

"Not really." Havers shook his head. "No one, least of all the police commissioner and the Home Secretary, want even a hint of scandal on this case. If someone from this district were to investigate and found evidence that Nivens *didn't* kill Santorini, the public could well think we were covering up for one of our own. The

Metropolitan Police have had enough nasty publicity in the past ten years, but public faith in us has finally been restored, and the Home Secretary wants to keep it that way."

"I see." Witherspoon was relieved that Inspector Havers didn't seem to resent their coming here. "Well, in that case, we'll get to work."

"Excellent." Havers pushed the box file, which was on the side of the desk, toward the inspector. "Here's the file and what few witness statements we were able to obtain. I had a word with the victim's landlady, Mrs. Frida Sorensen. She was shocked and distressed, but she had no idea who Santorini's next of kin might be, so we've not been able to locate any family members. Mrs. Sorensen thought Santorini had come originally from Turin in Italy. Unfortunately, you'll need to visit the lodging house again. It was quite late when we got there last night, and frankly, the lighting in the room was so bad I decided to wait until today to do a proper search. Mrs. Sorensen assured me she'd keep it locked."

"He had a room to himself?" Barnes looked up from his notebook.

"He did. Santorini did quite well; he owned his cart outright, so all the money he made was his to keep. For the most part, he delivered ice, but he'd expanded his business to include evening deliveries of flower bouquets. He took them to the restaurants in the theater district," Havers explained.

"Where is Santorini's body, sir?"

"He's been taken to the morgue at London Hospital. Dr. Robert Stapleton is doing the postmortem. He'll be sending his report along today. Are you going to headquarter here or back at Ladbroke Road?"

"We don't want to be in the way, but it would be far more con-
venient for us to stay here," Witherspoon said.

Havers grinned. "Good. You can use this office."

"I don't want to put you out," Witherspoon protested.

"You won't be. The chief inspector will be gone for a few days,
and he says the duty inspectors can use his office." Havers pointed
at the file box. "That's the official information we have on the deceased, but if you'd like, I can give you the unofficial version." He
paused, and when both Witherspoon and Barnes nodded, he continued speaking. "As I've said, Bert Santorini was an iceman and
has had his own cart for several years now. However, there was
gossip that he was more than just a small businessman trying to
make a living. He was often seen throwing a bit of cash about, and
he had an eye for the ladies."

"What kind of gossip?" Witherspoon asked.

"That he was involved in fencing stolen goods; supposedly, he
used his ice cart to move stolen items from one place to the next.
But we never found any evidence that Santorini was a fence,"
Havers warned him. "Nonetheless, I think it's a line of inquiry you
might want to pursue."

"Especially as Inspector Nigel Nivens was and is considered one
of the force's experts on housebreaking," the constable murmured.

"True, and just so you'll know, we've already interviewed Inspector Nivens. He claims he has no knowledge about this matter." He
shrugged. "But then again, that's exactly what I'd expect him to say."

"When did Santorini come to England?" Witherspoon wanted
as much information as he could get. In so many of their previous
cases, it was often some tiny fact about a victim's past that pointed
to the killer.

"I'm not sure, but one of the constables said he thought Santorini had come here as a child. He didn't have a foreign accent."

"He testified at the O'Dwyer trial, didn't he? Wasn't he Inspector Nivens' source?" The inspector tried to recall all the details of the case. But the only fact he could remember was that it involved three brothers.

"He was. As a matter of fact, it was Santorini's testimony that convicted them." Havers sat back in his chair. "Unfortunately, in this part of town, some of the local people don't see anything wrong in dealing in stolen goods. For the most part, these people are dreadfully poor, and there's a bit of resentment toward those that are better off. The O'Dwyers had a reputation for handing out a bit of cash when people were desperate. Some of the townsfolk were furious with Santorini for testifying against them."

Witherspoon thought for a moment. "The O'Dwyers gave money to people who were destitute? Really?"

"Sounds like one of them silly myths that spring up about crooks," Barnes scoffed. "Most criminals are just that—criminals that have decided it's easier to rob, steal, defraud, or even kill instead of working for a living."

"I agree, Constable. I don't know if the gossip about the O'Dwyers is true or not. I'm simply telling you what my lads have reported hearing from the locals."

"It doesn't really matter if it's true or not," Witherspoon speculated. "What matters is that they had a reputation for reaching into their pockets to help those less fortunate."

"Exactly." Havers nodded. "This might be important, because it could well be that someone took revenge on Santorini for testifying. All of the brothers are now in Pentonville Prison."

"Revenge is a pretty potent murder motive." Witherspoon frowned thoughtfully. "Perhaps it will be useful to find out who benefited from their generosity."

"That won't be easy," Havers warned him. "People around here don't like telling the police anything. You should also know that the O'Dwyers have a lot of family and friends here. None of them had any love for Humberto Santorini. About the only place he was welcome these days is the Thistle and Thorn Pub on Nickels Street. That's here in Whitechapel."

"Was Santorini ever arrested?" Barnes asked.

"Not that I know of—at least there's no record of him being arrested here in London," Havers replied. "You've got his address, and the file also contains the O'Dwyers' family address as well as a list of Santorini's customers. Do you have any other questions?"

"Can you show us where he was killed?" Witherspoon rose to his feet.

"Of course. I'll take you there now. But you'll not find much. My lads searched the area thoroughly."

"I'm not questioning the competence of your constables," Witherspoon explained. "I like to see where the murder occurred. I find it very helpful."

"Oh dear, I think I've made a dreadful mistake," Mrs. Jeffries said. "I shouldn't have called you all here until I had more information. I'm so sorry to have wasted everyone's time."

"Don't be silly." Luty grinned and shot to her feet. "We've got the name of the victim, the supposed name of the killer, and we know where he was murdered. Felix Mews. That's plenty to start with. I've got a source in that part of town, and I'll bet he knows something."

Alarmed, Hatchet stared at her in disbelief. "Madam, just what do you think you're doing? I hope you're not intending to race to Whitechapel and make contact with that disreputable—"

"That's exactly what I'm goin' to do," she interrupted. "And he ain't disreputable; he's reformed. Brockton's done his time. Like I said, he knows plenty about what goes on in the East End." She glanced at the clock on the pine sideboard. "If we use the carriage, we should be able to git there and back by four o'clock. Maybe by then Smythe and Wiggins will be here."

"Who are you going to see?" Phyllis asked curiously.

"Brockton Bellingham," Hatchet muttered. "He's nothing more than a confidence trickster and flimflam man."

"I told ya, he's reformed." Luty glared at Hatchet. "Now you can either come with me, or you can sit on your backside doin' nuthin'. Which will it be?"

"Don't be ridiculous, madam. Of course I'm going with you." He stood up and fixed her with a steely stare. "And just to be clear here: It will be a cold day in the pits of Hades before I let you anywhere near that dreadful person without me. He's quite likely to steal your purse."

"Come on then—let's git goin'." Luty laughed and then looked at the others. "We'll be back for our afternoon meeting."

Phyllis suddenly leapt up. "Take me with you? You're right—we do have enough information to start our investigation." She was still smarting over Wiggins and his theft of her idea; she'd never heard him mention becoming a private inquiry agent until *she'd* confided her own ambitions to him. "I can speak to some of the shopkeepers in the neighborhood. I might be able to find out all sorts of useful information."

"But Phyllis, the East End isn't like Holland Park or Putney," Mrs. Jeffries warned. "You'll need to be very careful. It's a rough place, and you might find it difficult to get anyone to tell you any-thing." Wiggins and Smythe could take care of themselves, and Luty would have Hatchet with her. But Phyllis was a lovely young woman, and Mrs. Jeffries didn't like to think of her on her own in that part of the city.

"She'll be fine, Mrs. Jeffries." The cook crossed her arms over her chest and stared at the housekeeper. "Our Phyllis knows how to take care of herself, and, what's more, she's not daft enough to get herself into any situations that might hurt her."

"I'd go, too," Betsy announced. "But I've got to get Amanda home for her nap." She also had to make arrangements for their upstairs neighbor to take care of the toddler for the next few days. She wanted to be on the hunt as well.

"I'll get my coat." Phyllis hurried to the coat tree.

"Good, that's settled then," Luty announced. "Let's get crackin'. It's already a quarter past one."

Frida Sorensen's lodging house was in a better part of the East End, on a shady street off the Mile End Road. The three-story brown brick house was decent and well-kept, with the window frames painted a pale ivory and a black wrought-iron fence surrounding the tiny front garden.

"Santorini has done well for himself," Barnes commented as they approached the front door. "A private room in this kind of lodging house costs a pretty penny." He lifted the polished brass knocker and let it fall. A moment later, the door was opened by a red-haired young woman with a feather duster tucked under her arm. "You the police, then?"

"Yes. We'd like to speak to Mrs. Sorensen," Witherspoon said.

"She's been expectin' you lot." She cocked her head to one side and looked them both up and down. "You're not the ones that were here last night."

"That's correct, but we're the ones that are now in charge of the investigation into Humberto Santorini's murder," Witherspoon explained.

"If you say so." She waved them inside and closed the door. "Wait here. I'll let 'er know you're back."

"Thank you," Witherspoon said as she disappeared past the staircase.

Barnes turned slowly, studying the foyer. The faint light of an overcast winter afternoon filtered in through the fanlight above the door. The walls were painted a pale yellow and hung with paintings of wildflowers. The small space was furnished with a walnut entry table holding a vase of decorative dried flowers, and opposite that was a yellow and green ceramic umbrella stand.

A tall middle-aged woman with blonde hair piled high in an elaborate chignon appeared in the hallway. Buxom, yet very much in proper proportion to her height, she was what many would call a handsome woman. Her eyes were blue, her cheekbones high, and her complexion unlined save for a few brackets around her eyes and mouth. She stared at them for a few moments. "You're not the same police who were here last night."

"No. I'm Inspector Gerald Witherspoon, and this is Constable Barnes. We're now in charge of this case," Witherspoon replied. "I take it you're Mrs. Sorensen?"

"I am."

"May we speak with you a few moments?"

She frowned in confusion. "But why? I've already told that other inspector everything I know."

"It's common procedure when the case gets passed to another

inspector, Mrs. Sorensen," Witherspoon said quickly. "This won't take long."

She sighed heavily. "Alright, let's go into the parlor."

They followed her down a short hall and through an open doorway. This room, like the foyer, was painted a pale yellow. It was furnished with a gray horsehair three-piece suite, a curio cabinet filled with figurines and knickknacks, and two side tables, both of which were covered with neatly stacked magazines and newspapers. At the far end of the room was a fireplace, over which hung a painting of the sea.

She waved them toward the sofa. "Have a seat."

"Thank you." Witherspoon sat at one end and Barnes settled down on the other. Mrs. Sorensen sank into one of the overstuffed chairs. "I know this must be very shocking for you, Mrs. Sorensen, but we'll try to be as quick as possible. Can you tell us how long Mr. Santorini has lodged here?"

"Let me see." She frowned thoughtfully. "He came in September. That's right, September tenth. I remember now because it was just the day after Mr. Pomfret left."

"Where did he lodge before he came here?" Barnes asked.

"He had a tiny room at the Crying Crows Pub. But he got turfed out when the landlady needed his room for extra storage."

"Do you know if he had any enemies?" Barnes asked.

She turned her attention to the constable. "I'm not sure what that means."

"I mean, did he ever mention that there was someone in his life who wished him harm?"

"Why would he tell me that? I'm his landlady, not his father confessor."

"He was a Roman Catholic?"

"I don't recall him ever going to church, but I do remember that he once told me he'd been baptized in Turin. That's in Italy."

"Did he get along with everyone here at the lodging house?" the constable asked.

"As far as I know, he got along with everyone just fine." She shrugged. "But he wasn't here much. He worked long hours—left right after breakfast and didn't get in until late in the evening."

"He did deliveries late at night?" Barnes asked.

"No, but he spent a good bit of time in pubs. He used to go to the Crying Crows, but after he got turfed out, he switched to the Thistle and Thorn."

"I see. That's very helpful, Mrs. Sorensen." Witherspoon stood up. "May we have the key to his room, please?"

Barnes hastily tucked his pencil in his pocket, closed his notebook, and got up as well.

"It's unlocked. Santorini's room is the first one on the left at the top of the stairs." She rose and led them out into the hallway to the bottom of the staircase.

"His room is unlocked?" Witherspoon frowned. "But Inspector Havers said you told him you'd keep it under lock and key until it could be searched."

"I unlocked it when I heard Marianne letting you in."

"Where did he stable his pony and cart?" Barnes put his hand on top of the newel post of the bannister. He knew the Leman Street constables had taken both the animal and the ice cart to a commercial stable near the docks.

"At Dartman and Sons. They're just off Hanover Lane."

"Thank you, Mrs. Sorensen," Barnes said as he and Witherspoon started up the stairs.

They reached the landing and stepped into the dead man's

room. The drapes were closed tight. The constable crossed to the window and pushed the heavy, old-fashioned navy blue and gold patterned paisley curtains aside. He turned and took a good look around the room.

A thick blue and gray carpet runner lay on the oak floor between the end of the iron bedstead and the wardrobe. A nightstand with a pitcher and bowl stood in the corner next to an overstuffed brown horsehair chair. A chest of drawers was on the far side of the bed.

"Perhaps carting ice and flowers about London pays well," Witherspoon murmured.

"Or perhaps the gossip about Santorini was right, and he had more than one source of income. Shall I take the wardrobe, sir?"

"Good idea. I'll take the chest of drawers."

They each set about their assigned tasks. Barnes yanked open the door of the wardrobe. Inside, two white shirts hung on one of the pegs next to a heavy gray overcoat, and on the last peg were two pairs of trousers. A pair of scruffy boots covered in mud and a pair of black shoes were on the floor. Barnes pulled out the coat and stuck his hand into the front pocket but found nothing but a matchbox and two ha'pennies. The shirt and trouser pockets were empty as well.

There was a deep shelf at the top of the wardrobe and inside, pushed all the way to the back, was a square-shaped object. Barnes stuck his hand inside. "There's something here, sir. It feels a bit like a strongbox, only it seems made of wood, not metal."

"Excellent, Constable. The only thing in here is underwear and socks." Witherspoon closed the drawer he'd been searching.

Barnes pulled the box down, crossed the room, and waited a moment for the inspector to move to one side before laying it on the top of the chest of drawers. "It's fairly big, sir, about eighteen inches long and a good ten inches high. There's a keyhole, which means it might be locked." He tried the lid. "It is."

"There was no mention of a key in the list of the personal property found with the victim," Witherspoon said.

"Then it should be here somewhere." Barnes went back to the wardrobe and stuck his hand inside the shelf and swept it from side to side. "Nothing up here. Let's see if there's anything in his shoes." Bending down, he picked up one of the dress shoes and shoved his hand inside. Nothing. He tried the other one as well as the boots. "It's not in the wardrobe."

"I'll check these drawers." Witherspoon yanked open the top drawer and systematically searched through the undergarments for a second time, but found nothing.

For the next ten minutes, they searched for a key, checking the rest of the drawers, under the carpet runner, the mattress, and the floor around the bed. Barnes even got down on his knees to run his hands along the floor beneath the drawers. He did the same to the stand holding the water pitcher. Climbing to his feet, he dusted off his fingers and glanced around the room. "We've searched everywhere, sir. We're going to have to break the lock."

But Witherspoon was staring at the blue and white pitcher in the water basin. "Just a moment." He crossed to the nightstand. Picking up the pitcher, he angled it toward the light and peered inside. A grin spread across his face as he turned the object upside down and a key fell onto the floor. The inspector bent down, grabbed the key, and hurried back to the box. He shoved the key into the lock, turned it, and the box opened.

Lifting the lid, the two of them looked inside. There were some papers, a thin stack of bills tied together with a bright red string, a red velvet drawstring bag, and two small glass bottles with cork stoppers—one was filled with brown liquid while the other one was a dark amber.

Witherspoon grabbed the stack of bills and tore off the string. "Good gracious, these are five-pound notes." He counted them out. "There's fifteen of them, that makes"—he stopped for a moment—"seventy-five pounds."

"That's a lot of money, sir," Barnes said. "A lot more than one would think an ice vendor might have in his possession."

"You're right, of course, but he runs a business. Santorini might be one of those people who don't trust banks," the inspector said. "Let's not jump to any conclusions until we have more facts. Right, let's see what's in here." He picked up the drawstring bag, opened it, and a stream of gold sovereigns tumbled out, some clattering onto the top of the chest while the rest spilled onto the carpet runner. "My gracious!"

Barnes knelt down and scooped up the coins from the floor while Witherspoon counted out the ones on the chest of drawers.

"Here's six, sir"—the constable placed them next to the box—"and there's four here, so that makes ten. Ten sovereigns and fifteen five-pound notes. That's a total of eighty-five pounds all together. That's a lot of money for anyone, let alone a man running a business with a pony and cart."

"We'll take it into evidence." Witherspoon frowned in confusion. "But I daresay, you're correct. This is an extraordinary amount of money. Let's see what else we have here." He picked up one of the bottles. "It's got the number four written on the front as well as a date. August twenty-third. This bottle is the same way, only the number is three and date is September first."

"That looks like whisky."

"Let's see what it smells like." Witherspoon pulled out the cork stopper and took a deep sniff. "You hit the nail on the head, Constable. It smells like whisky."

Barnes picked up the second bottle, yanked out the cork, and took a whiff. "But this one smells like beer. But why would Santorini keep little bottles of alcohol under lock and key?"

"Perhaps there is more in there than just whisky or beer," Witherspoon suggested. "We'll take them into evidence along with the money and see what we can find." He put the bottles to one side and reached for the papers on the bottom of the box. "We've got some receipts here from Dartman and Sons, a couple of bills for extra oats for the horse, and two letters." He pulled one out of the envelope, read through it, and frowned. "It's written in Italian, at least I think it's Italian, but there's a bit at the bottom that's in English. *'Your loving sister, Emilia.'*"

"At least now we know who his next of kin is," Barnes said as he put the papers back inside. "Is there an address in the salutation at the top?"

Witherspoon shook his head. "No." He reached for the envelope and turned it over. "There's one here. Good, that should help. We'll notify the Foreign Office. They'll notify the local authorities in Turin to tell the poor woman her brother's been murdered. I wondered if Santorini had a will. He does have an estate." Witherspoon glanced at the stack of money. "Both that money and the horse and cart have value."

"Perhaps his sister might know. I'll send off a telegram as soon as we get back to the station." Barnes closed the box and tucked it under his arm. "Where to now, sir?"

Witherspoon grimaced. "Unfortunately, as soon as we finish at the station, we'll need to take a statement from Inspector Nivens."

"He should be at home waiting for us." Barnes started for the door. "But, knowing him, I imagine he'll make this all as difficult as possible, and we'll have to track him down."

They stopped at Leman Street to put Santorini's money as well as the box and its contents into evidence. Witherspoon had a quick word with the duty inspector while Constable Barnes sent off a constable to the post office with a telegram to the Foreign Office requesting assistance in notifying Santorini's sister about his death. They worked quickly; nonetheless, it was late afternoon by the time they made their way to the Nivens home in Belgravia.

Barnes stepped out of the hansom, paid the driver, and wished he'd listened to his wife and worn another undershirt under his uniform. The weather had turned, and the sky was darkening fast; the air smelled of rain, and the wind was gusting something fierce. Witherspoon held on to his bowler as the constable rejoined him, and they stared at Inspector Nivens' property.

The house stood at the end of a short row of three-story red-brick town houses, smaller than many other properties in this neighborhood, but so beautifully kept up that it was obvious the owner had money. The windows were encased in pristine white-painted wood, the tiny garden surrounded by a white wrought-iron fence, and the door painted a shiny black.

"I don't understand why on earth Nivens joined the force." Barnes shook his head. "Look at this place. He's obviously from money; he doesn't need the pay. Why take a decent job away from someone who really needs it?"

"Perhaps he wanted to give his life a purpose." Witherspoon shrugged. "Or perhaps he isn't as wealthy as he appears. I'm fairly sure I once heard him mention that he inherited this home from

his father. It's getting late, Constable, so let's get this over with."
Witherspoon started up the flagstone walkway to the front door.

"My money says he's not here," Barnes groused. "He knows
good and well that we'd need to take his statement."

But for once the constable was wrong, and Inspector Nigel Nivens was home and waiting for them.

Barnes knocked, and a moment later, the door opened to reveal
a tall, thin woman with gray hair parted in the middle and worn
in a severe knot at the nape of her neck. She stared at them with a
disapproving frown. "Inspector Nivens is expecting you." She
stood back and ushered them inside. "Please follow me. The inspector is in his study."

She led them out of the spacious foyer, past a carpeted staircase,
and through a set of double doors. "The police are here, sir."

"Thank you, Mrs. Vickers." Nivens stood up from behind his
desk. "That'll be all for now."

"Yes, sir." She left, closing the door quietly behind her.

"Well, it didn't take you long to get here." Nivens sat down.
"I'm assuming you're here to take my statement."

Witherspoon stared at him. "That's correct. May we sit down,
please?" He surveyed the room and realized the constable was
right. This place reeked of wealth. Heavy damask drapes the color
of burgundy wine framed the two windows, the walls were painted
in a deep forest green, and the floor was covered with an elabo-
rately patterned oriental rug in brilliant blues, greens, and reds. A
brown leather settee with a gold and red paisley pillow in each
corner faced Nivens' huge, mahogany desk. Elaborate silver candle-
sticks stood at each end of the mantel over a green-tiled fireplace,
above which was a portrait of an unsmiling man wearing a ruffled
collar of the seventeenth century.

Nivens pointed to the settee. "Sit. I won't offer you tea—this shouldn't take long at all. I've already made a statement to Chief Inspector Boney and Inspector Havers."

"But they're not in charge of the case, are they?" Barnes pulled out his notebook as he sat down on one end of the settee.

Nivens ignored him. "What is it you want to know?" He directed his question to Witherspoon.

"We understand you knew the deceased, Humberto Santorini."

"I did."

"In what capacity were you acquainted with him?" Witherspoon sat down at the other end of the settee. He decided to keep this interview as formal as possible. There were many among both the leadership of Scotland Yard as well as the rank-and-file constables who knew he had little liking or respect for Inspector Nivens. By adhering to established police procedures, Witherspoon couldn't later be accused of deliberately conducting a shoddy investigation because of his personal feelings.

"He was one of my informants," Nivens replied. "But I'm sure you already know that."

"Of course we do," Witherspoon replied. "But we need verification from you. How long had he been working for you?"

"Six months. I first heard of him and that he might be able to supply me with information last September."

"But you were still at the Upper Richmond Road Station then?" Barnes pointed out. "So how did you come to know Santorini?"

Nivens leaned back in his chair and looked at Barnes. "Really, Constable, you're asking me that? In case you've forgotten, I'm rather well-known for solving burglaries, and the reason I'm so competent is because I've always got my ear to the ground when it comes to discovering who might have information about fencing stolen goods. Santorini's name was given to me when I was investigating that series of housebreakings along the river in Putney. I made it a point to track him down. I wanted to see if he could be of assistance to us."

"Was he?" Barnes looked down at his notebook.

"Eventually. It took a month or so before he gave me anything useful."

"There's something I'm not quite clear on," Witherspoon said. "Informants generally talk to us because they're criminals themselves and need help when they go in front of the judge, or they're paid informants. Which was Santorini?"

"I paid him," Nivens admitted. "Santorini wasn't a criminal, but because of his work, the places he frequented, and the people he knew, he occasionally stumbled across information that was valuable to us."

"But we've heard that Santorini himself might have been involved in fencing stolen items," Witherspoon said.

"That was gossip. Santorini was never arrested nor was any evidence ever presented against him."

Witherspoon nodded; that's what they'd been told by Inspector Havers as well.

Barnes looked up again. "But if he wasn't involved in fencing or burglaries himself, how did he know anything? Santorini delivered ice and flowers to West End restaurants and hotels. Not the sort of establishments that your average East End burglar or fence frequents, so how would he have found out anything useful to pass along to you?"

"He didn't just deliver to the West End; he had customers in Bethnal Green and Whitechapel as well. He's lived in that neighborhood for years, and he also spent most of his evenings in the local pubs. At one time, his favorite was the Crying Crows. As a matter of fact, I believe he once had a room there. But he's not been there for some time now. It's a decent sort of place. Actually, most of the lads from Leman Street Station tend to go there when they're off duty. But Santorini also patronized the Thistle and Thorn, and that place is well-known as a meeting place for fences. Santorini was a bit of a ladies' man, and one of my other informants reported he was sweet on the barmaid there."

Barnes fixed him with a skeptical stare. "Are you implying the barmaid kept him apprised of what the local fences were up to?"

Nivens shrugged. "I don't know that for a fact, but I will say that a clever barmaid can learn a great deal if she keeps her ears open. All I know is that the information that Santorini supplied me was always useful and helped me close a number of open cases."

Witherspoon interjected. "What's the barmaid's name?"

"Alberta Miller. She's a widow."

"Thank you. Inspector Nivens, you've stated you paid Santorini for the information he passed along to you. How much would you say you've given him?" Witherspoon wanted to find out if some or even all of the money they'd found in the victim's room might have come from Nivens.

"It wasn't much. I'd give him a pound or two if he told me something that seemed pertinent."

"How much did you pay him for the information about the O'Dwyers?"

"Five quid." Nivens smiled cynically. "By that time, Santorini had realized that some bits of information were worth more than others."

"Meaning?"

"Meaning that the police were under a good deal of pressure to solve that break-in—the butler in the house had been knocked unconscious. When Santorini approached me, he demanded five pounds before he'd tell me anything."

"That's a lot of money." The constable continued writing in his notebook.

"I know, but I thought it well worth it. Those brothers almost killed that poor man."

Barnes put his pencil down and looked at Nivens. "Did he ask for more money when he testified in court?"

"No, and if he had, I'd have refused to give it to him. I don't pay for testimony, just information."

"Where were you last night?" Witherspoon asked, hoping the change of subject might move the interview along. It was getting late, and, truth be told, it had been a long, tiring day.

"Oh, for God's sake, Witherspoon. I've already told Chief Inspector Boney and Inspector Havers what I did last night. It's in my statement. Surely you've read it?"

"We have, but we'd like to hear it directly from you." Witherspoon allowed himself a small smile. "It's one of my methods, you see. I've often found that asking the same question a number of times often results in finding out a few more pertinent details."

"Alright, I'll go over it again, but I doubt you'll learn anything more," Nivens snapped. "After my shift ended, I went to Baxter's for dinner and then, as I told Inspector Havers and the chief inspector, I was at my mother's home. She wanted me to stay there as her butler, who she normally leaves in charge when she travels, had to take time off because of a family illness."

"Where does your mother live?" Barnes looked at Nivens directly, silently daring him to ignore the question.

"Number eleven Alton Place, Mayfair. I was there alone."

"So no one can confirm your whereabouts at the time of the murder?" Barnes said.

"That's correct."

"What time did you arrive at your mother's house?" Witherspoon shifted into a more comfortable position and then caught a whiff of a harsh, metallic odor. The scent was vaguely familiar, but he couldn't place what it might be.

"I left the station at half past four yesterday, as I'd come in very early to go over my notes for an upcoming trial at the Bailey. I went for an early dinner. As I've said, I went to Baxter's—that's on Oxford Street—and I made the mistake of taking a hansom cab instead of a train to my mother's house, so it took forty-five minutes or so to get there."

"I know where Baxter's is located." Witherspoon tried not to get annoyed, but Nivens' attitude was making it difficult.

"Every policeman in London knows where it is," Barnes muttered.

"What time did you leave the restaurant?" the inspector asked.

Nivens thought for a moment. "I'm not sure. I didn't look at my watch, but it was relatively early."

"Inspector Nivens, when it comes to solving crimes, I've a great deal of faith in time lines. If we're going to prove that one of our own had nothing to do with this murder, perhaps you might try a bit harder to recall the timing of your movements last night."

"At a guess, I'd say it was six o'clock or thereabouts when I left. Normally, I don't dine that early but, as I'd been too busy to eat lunch, I was hungry. After my meal, I took a hansom cab to Mayfair. My estimate is that I arrived at my mother's home at half six or so."

"When you got out of the cab, did you happen to see anyone? Any neighbors or local people?" Witherspoon asked.

Nivens gave a negative shake of his head. "No. I saw no one and, by the same token, no one would have seen me unless they were watching from their windows. But that's very doubtful—peeking out the front curtains isn't generally done by the sort of people who live in Mayfair."

"Where did you catch the hansom?" Barnes asked.

"Just outside the restaurant."

"Then we should be able to confirm your account of your whereabouts by finding the hansom driver."

"Hardly, Constable. It was a cold, busy night, and the streets were filled with people wanting hansoms. The only thing that driver cared about was getting me to my destination as quickly as he could and then getting back to Oxford Street to pick up another fare," Nivens retorted.

"He may not have looked at your face, Inspector Nivens, but he'll remember where he took you," Barnes replied. "It only happened last night."

"Possibly, but you'll have a devil of a time finding the driver. As I said, it was a cold night in the busiest part of the city, and there were dozens of cabs vying for fares."

"Did you stay in all evening?"

"Yes, I read the newspaper . . ." His voice trailed off, and he closed his eyes. "Oh drat, I stopped at the newsagents next to Baxter's and bought the evening paper. I forgot to mention that."

"Ah, so you see, Inspector Nivens, asking you the same question you'd previously answered did result in additional details," Witherspoon exclaimed. "Your stop at the newsagents wasn't in your written statement."

"I realize that. It was a simple mistake. It's hardly surprising as I'm not in the habit of having to explain my whereabouts or my comings and goings to anyone else, least of all my colleagues or superiors in the Metropolitan Police Force."

"But this is a murder investigation now, Inspector," Witherspoon reminded him, "and every detail is important."

"You don't need to remind me of *that*." Nivens face flushed in anger. "I am still a police officer. I know the importance of details. Now, to get back to your question, I read the evening newspaper—it was the *Evening Gazette* in case you're interested—then I went to bed."

"You were at your mother's home in Mayfair from half past six o'clock until you went into the station this morning?" Witherspoon inhaled softly as another whiff of that strange smell assaulted his nostrils. "Is that correct?"

"That's right."

"If you were on your own at your mother's home, where did you eat breakfast?" Barnes asked.

"At a café near the Leman Street Station." He shrugged. "I can't recall the name of the place, but the food was dreadful."

Witherspoon suddenly realized exactly what the scent was. He scooted forward and looked over his shoulder at the pillow nestled behind his back. A second later, he swung his legs to one side, turned, ducked his head to the fabric, and inhaled deeply.

"Witherspoon, just what are you doing?" Nivens asked irritably.

But the inspector ignored him. Instead, he straightened, picked up the pillow, and examined it closely.

"I asked you what you're doing?" Nivens shouted.

"Is there some reason this pillow smells like gunpowder?"

Nivens' eyes widened in surprise. "Don't be absurd—why would my pillow smell like . . ." His voice trailed off as Witherspoon held the pillow out, and there, clearly visible on the corner was a hole ringed in burned fabric.

"This looks like a bullet hole, Inspector," Witherspoon said softly. He held it to his nose and inhaled deeply. "And it smells like one as well."

CHAPTER 4

Nivens jumped up from his desk and rushed to the settee. He stared at the bullet hole with a disbelieving, stunned expression. "I've no idea how that got there. Let me speak to my housekeeper."

He moved quickly, opening the door and sticking his head into the corridor. "Mrs. Vickers, come here please," he shouted before turning and staring at the inspector. "There must be a reasonable explanation for this and I'm going to find out what it is." He nodded at the pillow. "That shouldn't be here. I tell you, it shouldn't be here."

Mrs. Vickers hurried into the room. "Is something wrong, sir?"

"What is that doing here?" Nivens demanded, pointing his finger at the inspector, who held up the pillow.

The housekeeper looked confused. "What do you mean, sir? That pillow belongs on the settee."

"I know it belongs on the settee." Nivens charged across the room, snatched the pillow out of Witherspoon's hand, and raced back. "But it's got this ruddy great hole in the corner."

"It didn't have a hole in it last Friday, sir." Mrs. Vickers still looked befuddled. "I cleaned in here and there wasn't anything wrong then. I don't know why it should have a hole in it now." Her voice trembled. "Perhaps a moth got into the room."

"There aren't any moths at this time of the year," Nivens cried. "It's wintertime."

"Get hold of yourself, Inspector Nivens," Witherspoon said softly. "Your housekeeper has no idea what's going on here."

Nivens spun around on his heel, his eyes narrowed and his face red. He opened his mouth, then abruptly clamped his lips shut and sucked in a huge, long breath through his nose. "Of course, Inspector, you're right." Turning back to his housekeeper, who had now taken several steps back from him, he said, "I apologize, Mrs. Vickers. But it's very important I find out how this pillow came to be in this state."

"I don't know, sir."

"You went to see your sister in Leicester while I was at my mother's, so the house was empty, right?"

"Yes. I arrived back on the early train this morning," she replied. "But the house was locked up good and tight."

Nivens nodded. "I'm sure it was, but nonetheless, the house has been empty since Sunday."

"Did you check for signs of forced entry?" Barnes directed his question to Nivens.

"Of course not. Why would I? I'd no idea that ruddy pillow was here." He looked at Mrs. Vickers again. "Have you had any visitors today?"

"None, sir."

"How about tradespeople?"

"Mr. Cullen's grocery boy came with a delivery, sir, but he never left the kitchen."

"Are you sure of that?" Nivens pressed.

"I go through the order, sir. I don't let the lad leave until I've checked that they delivered everything we ordered."

"Were all your windows closed?" Barnes asked.

Mrs. Vickers glanced at the constable. "In this weather, of course."

"Are you certain? Sometimes, even in the dead of winter, my wife will open a window to air out a room."

"This room didn't need to be aired out and, if it had, I'd have done it while I was in here doing the cleaning on Friday," she retorted. "There's nothing wrong with my memory, and every window in the house was closed and locked yesterday, as were the doors."

"How many doors are there?" Witherspoon asked.

"Two," Nivens replied quickly. "Front and back."

"Do you keep the household doors locked at all times?" The inspector directed his question to the housekeeper.

She nodded. "We do, sir. This is a very good neighborhood, but these days, one can't be too careful." She looked at Nivens. "Is there anything else, sir?"

"No, thank you." He waited until she'd closed the door before turning his attention back to Witherspoon and Barnes. "I know what you're thinking, Inspector, but I assure you, I had nothing to do with Santorini's murder."

"We're not accusing you, Inspector Nivens, but nonetheless, we'll have to take this pillow into evidence."

"I'm aware of that," he muttered.

"The murder weapon was left at the scene," Barnes said. "It is supposedly part of a set of dueling pistols, a set you identified as belonging to you."

"I'm aware of that as well," Nivens replied.

"May we see the box where it was kept?"

Nivens went to the bookcase and pulled down a flat box. He came back to the settee, put it on the cushion next to Witherspoon, and lifted the lid.

"You don't keep it locked?"

"The key has been lost for years. It never occurred to me that anyone would steal one of the pistols and use the ruddy thing to commit murder."

Witherspoon looked inside, noting that the gun was identical to the one they'd seen at the Leman Street Station. "But you knew both the weapons were still functional?"

"Naturally." He sighed and closed his eyes. "I don't understand any of this."

"Did Santorini tell you how he found out the O'Dwyer brothers were fencing the goods from the West End house burglaries?"

"That was the first question I asked him," Nivens said. "He told me he'd seen them moving some items from a cart and into the back door of a house on Sidney Street, a house owned by a known fence. Everything was in burlap bags, but Seamus O'Dwyer dropped one of them, and a silver teapot rolled out onto the ground."

"But the goods weren't there when you actually raided that house," Barnes pointed out. "Yet the O'Dwyers were found guilty, mainly based on Bert Santorini's testimony."

"Which is why you should be investigating them and that mother of theirs instead of wasting valuable time here with me. I had nothing to do with Santorini's murder. I've no idea why my pistol was used to kill him, nor do I know how the murderer obtained the weapon."

"Inspector Nivens, we've only just started this investigation. We'll be looking at everyone who might have a motive for the murder," Witherspoon said.

"But I didn't do it," Nivens protested. "Good Lord, man, do you think if I committed murder I'd use my own gun and leave it lying by Santorini's body? A weapon that half a dozen constables at the Leman Street Police Station saw and could identify as belonging to me. I certainly wouldn't be stupid enough to leave a pillow that was obviously used to silence the weapon in my own house. This is a nightmare, but there's one thing I do know. I'm innocent."

Mrs. Jeffries stared at the faces around the table and didn't know whether to laugh or cry. It was now half past four, and everyone was present for their afternoon meeting. None of the ones who had rushed to the East End to begin the hunt had had any luck whatsoever.

Phyllis put the teapot on the table next to the plate of brown bread and took her own seat. "In all fairness, Mrs. Jeffries, the neighborhood wasn't as rough as I thought it might be, and it wasn't that the shopkeepers didn't want to talk to me," she explained. "It was more that none of them knew anything. But I only had time to go into three shops. I'm going back tomorrow to try my luck."

She didn't mention that she'd actually gone into five establishments, but at both the greengrocer's and the butcher's the women working the counters had been so rude that Phyllis had fled rather than try to wheedle any information out of them. She felt a right coward, so much so that she'd vowed to go back and try again.

"Don't fret, Phyllis." Smythe smiled ruefully. "No one at the pub I tried knew anything, either. Maybe by tomorrow we'll 'ave a few more bits and pieces from the inspector, and that'll give us some idea where to start." He looked at the housekeeper. "Let's hope the inspector 'as found somethin' useful today."

"Davey Marsh was here quite early today, so the inspector must have had time to get to the East End and start asking a few questions," Mrs. Jeffries replied. "And we'll also have Constable Barnes tomorrow morning. Surely between the two of them there will be something useful."

"I was real disappointed that Brockton wasn't home," Luty admitted. "But his neighbor said he'd be back tomorrow, so we'll have another go at him."

"He was probably out flimflamming some poor soul out of their life savings," Hatchet muttered.

Luty glared at him. "Now you're just bein' mean. Brockton was seein' the dentist and is probably gettin' his tooth yanked out."

"So no one found out anything?" Mrs. Jeffries reached for the teapot and began to pour.

"I'd not say that, Mrs. Jeffries," Wiggins put in. "I told ya what I 'eard at the Crying Crows. Now, it weren't much, but it might end up being useful." He'd repeated the conversation he'd heard between the barman and the barmaid.

"Don't be daft. What you overheard was two people complaining about their guv," Smythe interrupted. "That doesn't count. Let's face it: we went off half-cocked and wasted our time."

"You mustn't be so hard on yourselves," Ruth, Lady Cannonberry, a slender, middle-aged woman with dark blonde hair and blue eyes, commented. "You went there because you thought you might find something to help Inspector Witherspoon solve this case."

Ruth was the inspector's "special friend" and, like the others, devoted to justice. The widow of a peer of the realm and the daughter of a country vicar, she took Christ's admonition to love thy neighbor as thyself very seriously. She fed the hungry, visited the sick, clothed the naked, and gave comfort to the prisoner. She also worked tirelessly for women's suffrage, equality for all, and most important, justice. When she was with the Witherspoon household, she insisted they call her Ruth.

"Ruth's right." Mrs. Jeffries glanced at the clock. "It's getting late. Now, I propose that we have our usual morning meeting tomorrow, and Mrs. Goodge and I will share what we've found out from Constable Barnes and our inspector."

"What do you think, sir?" Barnes tucked the pillow under his arm as they reached the pavement. It was almost full dark by now, cold and drizzling. "This isn't looking good for Inspector Nivens." He surveyed the street, hoping to see a hansom. But the only thing he saw was a uniformed telegram boy coming toward them. The lad nodded respectfully as he stepped past and went up the walkway to Nivens' front door.

"I know. Nonetheless, despite the evidence, Inspector Nivens made a good point. He's no fool, and if he'd killed Santorini, he'd not have left evidence lying around like that"—he pointed to the pillow—"nor would he have been foolish enough to leave a weapon that was clearly identified as belonging to him lying by the dead man's body."

Barnes turned and glanced at the front of the house as Mrs.

Vickers opened the door and took the telegram from the lad. Just then, a hansom turned the corner and pulled up to the curb. "There's a hansom, sir. It's dropping a fare."

They reached the cab before he drove off. Witherspoon took the pillow and stepped inside while Barnes directed the driver to take them to the Ladbroke Road Station so the pillow could be put into the evidence cupboard. They would pick it up in the morning and take it to the Leman Street Station.

The constable climbed in as the rig pulled away. He grabbed the curved, leather handhold above the window. "You know, sir, it's always possible that Nivens is playing a game."

"What do you mean?" The inspector dug his feet into the floor to steady himself as they swung around the corner.

"We had a case some time ago, sir, the Tarrant murder, where the main suspect, Thomas Witton, planted so much evidence against himself that we were sure he was innocent. Remember, sir?"

Witherspoon tapped his chin with his forefinger. "Now that you mention it, I do remember. It was the first case we had together, right?"

"It was, sir. It was just after those horrible Kensington High Street murders," he replied. It was also the only case the household hadn't helped with—mainly because it was over and done with before any of them realized there was a case. "By the time we realized Witton was guilty and could prove it, he'd done a bunk and boarded a ship for South America. Unfortunately for Witton, the ship sank less than a day after it left Liverpool. I always felt sorry for the other poor souls on that ship. None of them had committed murder."

"And you think that Nivens might be doing the same thing—letting evidence that proves him guilty be found by us in the hopes we'll think he's innocent?" The inspector's brows drew together in thought. "But one doesn't like to think of a fellow officer doing such a dastardly deed. On the other hand, we are talking about Nivens. The reason he's stuck at the Leman Street Station instead of the Upper Richmond Road is because he deliberately withheld evidence in the Starling case."

"Precisely, sir." Barnes sagged in relief. He'd made his point. To his mind, Nigel Nivens should have been drummed out of the force years ago.

Witherspoon was exhausted by the time he arrived home. He handed his bowler to Mrs. Jeffries. "It's been a long and very tiring day, Mrs. Jeffries. I do hope that Mrs. Goodge can hold dinner. Tonight, I'm going to need two glasses of sherry."

"She's made a nice beef stew, sir, and she's already put it in the warming oven." Mrs. Jeffries hung the bowler on the coat tree. "Davey Marsh stopped in this morning and told us you were going to be home late, sir. Did something happen?" She knew exactly what had happened, but for the sake of keeping their investigations secret, she had to pretend ignorance. She took his overcoat as he slipped it off his shoulders and hung it on the peg below his hat.

"Good. I wouldn't want to ruin one of Mrs. Goodge's delightful suppers," he said as he hurried down the short corridor to his study.

Following him inside, Mrs. Jeffries crossed the room and went to get the sherry while he settled himself in his overstuffed chair. Opening the cabinet, she pulled out the amber-colored bottle of Harveys Bristol Cream, yanked out the cork, and poured some into two small, elegant sherry glasses. She had no doubt whatsoever that she was welcome to drink with her employer; they'd established that custom years ago when she'd first come to work for him. She crossed the room, handed him his drink, and took her own spot on the settee. "Do tell me about your day, sir. You look positively worn out."

"To be truthful, I am. Constable Barnes and I were summoned to the East End today, the Leman Street Police Station to be precise. Apparently, Inspector Nigel Nivens is a suspect in a murder." He paused and took a sip of his drink. "But that's not exactly where the whole matter began."

"Inspector Nivens, sir? A suspect? Gracious, is it because of that article in the *Sentinel*?"

Witherspoon's eyebrows rose. "You saw it? But we don't take that paper."

"Wiggins bought a copy on his way back from the chemist's. The newsagents are right next door. He saw the headline and because it concerned the police, he picked one up. I must say, it was quite shocking."

"Indeed, it was. The article didn't come right out and accuse Nivens of the murder, nor did it actually say the Metropolitan Police would cover up a crime by one of its own, but the implication for both was apparent."

"You read it as well?"

"Constable Griffiths showed me a copy and, oddly enough, at the same time I was reading the article, one of the prisoners at Ladbroke Road was talking with Constable Barnes about this very case." He told her about the tidbit One-legged Billy had shared with the constable. "Right after that, we got the summons to Leman Street Station." He continued his narrative, occasionally sipping his sherry as he told her every detail of his day.

Mrs. Jeffries listened carefully, refilling both their glasses and asking a question when he paused to take a drink. But for the most part, she simply tried to absorb what he told her. She promised herself she'd write everything down when she went upstairs to bed. But he spoke at length, and she realized that despite her best efforts, she was afraid she'd miss a pertinent point or two. At the very least, she'd make a note of all the names of both people and places that were part of his narrative.

"So that's where we left the matter." Witherspoon put his glass down on the side table and got to his feet. "Inspector Nivens was quite upset by the time we finished taking his statement, and I, for one, am tempted to believe he had nothing to do with Santorini's murder—but nonetheless, there is a mountain of evidence against him."

"It certainly appears that way." She got up as well. "On the other hand, appearances can be deceptive. Which, I believe, is the real reason you were given the case. The Home Secretary wants to be certain the case is investigated thoroughly and that Humberto Santorini's killer is brought to justice, no matter who it may be."

Mrs. Vickers moved quietly to the study door, knocked softly, and waited for him to tell her to enter. But there was no reply. She knocked again, this time just a bit louder. Again, no response. Annoyed and more than a little concerned, she opened the study door and stuck her head inside.

Nivens was sitting on the settee, staring into space.

"Hummph." She cleared her throat and he started slightly. "Excuse me, sir. Is everything alright?"

"Yes of course it is," he snapped. "Why wouldn't it be?"

"No reason, sir, it's just that I knocked, and you didn't answer. Dinner will be served at the usual time, and a telegram has come for you." Mrs. Vickers stared at him for a long moment and then asked, "Shall I bring it in?"

"Take it to the drawing room. I'll read it there."

"Very good, sir." She withdrew, closing the door softly behind her.

He waited a moment before going to the door and pressing his ear against the wood. He listened for a few seconds and when he was sure that Mrs. Vickers had gone down to the kitchen, he stepped into the hall. He didn't want anyone, least of all his housekeeper, seeing that he was rattled by this wretched business.

Going into the drawing room, his spirits lifted as he spotted the buff-colored telegram on the silver tray. "It's about time," he muttered. He ripped it open, yanked out the message, and read it. Then he read it again and then again before dropping it onto the floor.

Stunned, he moved into the center of the room, his gaze fixed on the marble fireplace. He stood there for what could have been seconds but felt like eternity as he tried to absorb the shock of what he'd just read.

One short telegram shifted his entire world.

He didn't believe it, but it was right there, in black and white. It had to be a mistake. She couldn't possibly mean what she'd written. Shaking his head in disbelief, he walked across the carpet to the marble-topped liquor cabinet, lifted the crystal top off the whisky decanter, grabbed one of the hand-blown glasses, and poured the liquor three-quarters of the way to the top. Taking a huge gulp, he sputtered as the brew hit the back of his throat. He forced himself to swallow and then took another, even bigger drink.

"She couldn't mean it," he told himself. "I'll send another message. Make her understand that I need her help now more than ever." He drained his glass, put it down, and started toward the

door, intending to call Mrs. Vickers and send her off with a telegram. But his steps faltered as he reached the spot where he'd
dropped his mother's missive. He snatched it up and read it again.

> *Nigel, this may sound harsh, but you must deal*
> *with this on your own. I've rescued you far too often,*
> *and it's time you learned to clean up your own*
> *messes. Teddy and I are going on a tour of Italy so*
> *please, don't pester me with your problems.*
> *Mother*

What on earth was he to do now?

He knew she was serious; she wasn't one to make idle statements, and, without her help, he was utterly doomed. The day he'd
dreaded had finally arrived. There was no going back now; he'd
have to fend for himself on this one. He started back to the liquor
cabinet and then caught himself. No, he didn't need whisky, he
needed to think.

He sucked in a deep breath and thought back to the beginning
of this nightmare. He concentrated, trying to recall the exact words
Chief Inspector Boney had used in this morning's interview. More
important, he forced himself to recall Boney's attitude toward him.
The man hadn't bothered to hide his dislike of him nor had he
given him any reason to think he was going to protect him just
because they were both police officers. The same could be said of
Chief Superintendent Barrows; there would be no help from that
quarter, either. Barrows had been giddy with delight when he'd sent
him to the Leman Street Station because of that trifling evidence
matter in the Starling case. He'd love to see Nivens permanently
out of the Metropolitan Police.

Nivens began to pace, walking back and forth in front of the fireplace as he tried to think of a way out of this mess. Someone had framed him; someone wanted to make sure he met the hangman's noose. If he didn't take matters into his own hands, whoever had done it would get their wish. Nivens refused to let that happen.

But what to do? He stopped by the hearth and drummed his fingers along the marble top of the fireplace. He couldn't count on help from the rank-and-file lads at Leman Street Station. They hated him. He didn't think any of them would deliberately hobble the investigation, but they wouldn't go the extra mile to prove him innocent, either.

He'd have to do this investigation on his own. But even as he made the decision, he was suddenly overwhelmed with fear. The truth was, he wasn't a very good investigator, and he knew it. Thus far, his path to success was based on two important factors: informants who he relied on to point him in the right direction whenever he had a burglary case, and his mother's very considerable influence with the Home Secretary and a number of other cabinet ministers.

But now one of those informants was dead and, if he knew anything about the others, they'd stay well away from him while he had this cloud over his head. Most worrying for him was the issue of money. He didn't have any. He'd not expressly been put on leave, but he knew it was coming and that meant his salary would be suspended as well.

It had never occurred to him to be frugal. There was plenty of cash in Mama's coffers, so he'd spent his policeman's salary on fine dining, good clothes, membership fees to the right clubs, and entertaining.

Nivens glanced at the telegram again. His mother hadn't expressly threatened to cut off his access to her money, but he had a feeling that might be coming next. Lord Merton, his mother's new husband, married her because she was rich, and Merton, like so many others of his class, was broke. Even before Nivens received today's dispiriting telegram, there had been signs that dear Mama was closing the doors of her bank vault to him. He couldn't let that happen. Without the ability to pay for information, he hadn't a hope in Hades of finding out anything. Not by himself. But he wasn't sure he could stop it, and without cash to pay out for information, he was doomed.

Or was he?

He closed his eyes as the strange idea settled inside him. He shook his head, hoping to dislodge the silly notion, but it clung to him tighter than a barnacle clings to a piling. No, he told himself, don't even consider that course of action; the very thought of it is absurd.

He stood there for a few minutes, playing about with the notion, and then realized as insane as it appeared, it might be the solution to all his problems. It could well be a way to both prove his innocence and to prove he'd been right about that other matter and had been for years.

The ornate French carriage clock struck the hour, jerking him out of his thoughts. He saw that it was already too late to do anything this evening. He'd have to make his next move tomorrow morning, and he'd have to be very, very convincing if he was to succeed.

The next morning, Constable Barnes put his mug on the kitchen table and got up. "You've done well to remember everything, Mrs. Jeffries. Yesterday we learned so much so quickly that if I didn't have my notebook, I'd be a bit lost."

As was his usual custom when they had a homicide, the constable called at Upper Edmonton Gardens; supposedly it was because he and the inspector often went to parts unknown rather than the station when they were on a case. But the second and, to his mind, most important, reason was to have a quick word with Mrs. Jeffries and Mrs. Goodge before going upstairs to the inspector.

On one of his early cases with Witherspoon, he'd realized that the inspector was getting information from a source outside the investigation itself. It hadn't taken him long before he realized the source was right here in the Witherspoon household. At first, he'd been alarmed. He hated the idea of a bunch of amateurs sticking their collective noses in police business because they'd all read too many of Mr. Arthur Conan Doyle's stories in the *Strand Magazine*. But then he'd realized that not only was the information useful, but that Mrs. Jeffries and her band of sleuths could get people who wouldn't give a policeman the time of day to tell them all sorts of things.

More important, Barnes had come to learn that all of them in their own way had resources that were simply unavailable to the average policeman. Mrs. Goodge had colleagues up and down the breadth of the land, and she'd stayed in contact with most of them; Smythe had a source at the docks that was privy to the most sensitive of information, while Wiggins, Betsy, and Phyllis could cover a whole neighborhood and get everyone from the local shopkeepers to the street lads to talk their heads off. Luty Belle Crookshank ruthlessly used her connections to the rich and powerful to track down clues, while Hatchet had friends in the art, theater, and—he suspected—the criminal world. Like the others, Lady Cannonberry helped as well. She had a vast network of friends and acquaintances who supplied her with useful bits and pieces. Mrs. Jeffries had the most difficult task of all: She was the one who took every little morsel of information and put it all together. Quite simply, she was the best detective he'd ever known.

Mrs. Jeffries laughed. "To tell you the truth, Constable, I cheated. Before retiring last night, I wrote down most of what I'd learned from our inspector, and you very kindly supplied us with a bit more information. I'm sorry that we had so little to give you."

"It's early days yet, and your lot will do your share." He started toward the back stairs. "I'll see you two tomorrow morning."

Ten minutes later, they heard the front door open as the two policemen left. A few minutes after that, the others began to arrive for their morning meeting. Betsy and Smythe were the last to arrive. Betsy's eyes were slightly red and her mouth set in a flat, grim line as she crossed the room and took her usual spot at the table. For once, neither Luty nor Mrs. Goodge asked where Amanda was.

Smythe, his face set in a frown, pulled his chair out and flopped down next to his wife. "The little one was fussy today, so we've left her with our neighbor," he muttered. He didn't look at Betsy nor did she so much as glance in his direction.

It was obvious to everyone that this morning, something had gone badly wrong between these two. But Mrs. Jeffries didn't have time to worry about the state of their marriage; that was their business. "We've much to cover this morning," she announced. "If no one objects, I'll tell you everything we've found out from the inspector and Constable Barnes." She repeated each and every detail they'd learned, and when she finished, she sat back in her chair. "I don't think I need to tell any of you what you must do. You know that already."

"I'll try Mrs. Sorensen's lodging house." Wiggins got up. "I've already been in the Crying Crows, for all the good it did."

"Don't say that," Phyllis objected. "We've only just started and, from what Mrs. Jeffries told us, Inspector Nivens drinks there when he's off duty. I think it's worth having another go at it."

"Good luck to ya, but don't be surprised if you come away with nothin'. That barman keeps his mouth closed tighter than a bank vault," Wiggins warned her. "You'd do better chattin' with the barmaid."

"But you found out a few bits from him." She grinned. "Even if it was just some complaining about their guv."

"Right then, I've a source that might be able to 'elp," Smythe offered. "After that, I'll 'ave a go at chatting up some hansom drivers."

The others, except for Betsy, volunteered to tap their various sources, and the meeting broke up. Both Mrs. Jeffries and Mrs. Goodge noticed that Betsy practically ran for the back door while Smythe took his time in leaving. When the kitchen was quiet except for the two of them, the cook looked at the housekeeper. "I wonder what's going on between Betsy and Smythe."

"I think they've had a disagreement," Mrs. Jeffries replied. "And, what's more, Betsy deliberately didn't say where she was going this morning."

Betsy stared at the spot where Bert Santorini had been killed and then turned on her heel and hurried out of the mews. Her mood was even worse now than this morning. Tears sprang into her eyes and she hastily swiped them away. She wasn't going to act like a silly schoolgirl just because she and Smythe had quarreled. He hadn't wanted her to do her part; he'd wanted her to stay home and pretend like she'd never seen or heard of the East End. But she couldn't and wouldn't do that. They'd argued something fierce and it ended only when Amanda had started to cry. They'd reassured the child they'd only been pretending to be angry with each other and had cuddled and soothed her between them. But they'd both still been blooming furious.

"How did he expect me to feel," she muttered to herself as she came out onto the Commercial Road. He'd conveniently forgotten that she'd grown up in this part of London and knew it like the back of her hand.

She'd not learned a ruddy thing by looking at the spot where Santorini had been killed, but she'd still been in such a foul mood, she didn't want to risk going directly to Mattie Mitchell's nasty little shop.

Betsy turned off the busy road and continued walking until she reached a row of shops, above which were three stories of ugly flats filled with London's poorest citizens crammed inside like rats on a sinking ship. Mattie's place was tucked between a shoe repair shop and a knife-sharpening kiosk. She stopped at the corner and waited till a brewery wagon loaded with barrels rolled past. She studied Mattie's shop and could see that the place hadn't improved since she'd last seen it, almost ten years ago. She only hoped that Mattie herself was still alive and still the same grasping, greedy cow she'd always been. But Mattie had one saving grace: She knew everything that went on in the East End, and for a few bob, she'd share that knowledge.

Betsy started across the road, dashing in front of a coal wagon, past a cockle seller pushing his cart out of a rut hole, and onto the crumbling pavement.

She paused in front of the dusty window and peered into the shop. It was supposedly a tobacconist shop, but Mattie had crammed it full of junk. Wicker baskets hung inside the doorjamb, and a row

of used trousers and shirts hung along a makeshift line on the wall
behind the counter. Along the back wall there were shelves where
the tinned goods used to be, but the window was so dusty Betsy
couldn't see if they were still there. Along the counter proper, baskets of potatoes and carrots stood next to a display of tobacco tins,
cigarette papers, and chewing tobacco.

Her hands clenched into fists as memories flooded back to her.
Mattie, standing behind the counter and cutting off the moldy bits
of day-old bread. "That's all ya get for a ha'penny," she'd said as
she'd shoved it toward Betsy. "If you find any more of the blue bits,
just scrape 'em off."

She shook herself. Now wasn't the time to let her emotions rule;
she needed information, and Mattie might be the one who had it.

Betsy frowned. The shop looked the same, but there wasn't hide
nor hair of Mattie. Maybe she'd died. But if that was the case, who
owned the shop? Mattie didn't have any family or, for that matter,
any friends. But someone was running the place.

Just then a door at the back of the room opened and Mattie, her
arms loaded with a bundle of what looked like rags, stepped into
view. Betsy opened the door, went inside, and winced as the scent
of stale tobacco, vinegar, cockles, and day-old fish assailed her
nostrils. Good Lord, the place still smelled bad.

Mattie looked almost the same. She was still thin as a rail and
her stringy white hair was still rolled into a messy bun at the nape
of her skinny neck. But her blue eyes were now watery, and her pale
skin had more wrinkles than a linen skirt on a hot summer day.

Mattie dumped her burden onto the counter next to a display of
Tinder's Best pipe tobacco. She said nothing as she looked Betsy up
and down, her sharp gaze taking in the expensive burgundy coat,

the handmade lace on the collar of the white blouse peeking above the neckline, and the elegant black kid gloves.

Betsy had worn the clothes deliberately. She was determined not to be intimidated by anyone, least of all a miserable old woman who'd once had the power of life and death over her family. But those days were long gone. She wasn't a hungry twelve-year-old begging for a few days' credit to buy a loaf of stale bread.

Mattie gave her a thin smile. "You don't look like you're from around 'ere."

"You need to get some spectacles, Mattie. I grew up 'round these parts." Betsy cocked her head to one side and smiled. "Don't you recognize me? I used to come into this shop often."

Mattie's eyes narrowed for a moment but then she shrugged. "Whoever you are, you've obviously done well for yourself. Now, we can spend the day playin' guessin' games, or you can tell me why you've come to me shop."

"I need to find out some information and, if you're still the same person as you used to be, you might be able to help me."

"What kind of information?"

"I want to know about a man named Bert Santorini."

"Him? He was murdered Monday night, but that's been in the papers so you already know it." She eyed Betsy curiously. "Why ya wantin' the goods on 'im?"

"That's my business." Betsy pulled her small, gray suede purse from her coat pocket and opened it. "But I'm willing to pay a bit if I think what you tell me is useful."

"How much?" Mattie folded her arms over her chest.

"That depends on what you know." Betsy shrugged. "Like I said, Mattie, I come from 'round here and you're not the only one that knows what's what. If you don't want to help me, I can always go see Lizzie Camber or Harry Black."

"Go ahead, try 'em." Mattie laughed. "Lizzie Camber's gone senile and Harry died last winter, but let's not split 'airs over who knows what. I know about Santorini, and the one thing I'll tell ya for free is that there won't be many mourning him at his funeral."

"He wasn't well liked?"

"Nah, the O'Dwyers hated him, but that's the least of it. He's 'ad fallin' outs with lots of people." Mattie stared at her with a cunning, speculative expression. "You'll be wantin' to know names, but that's goin' to cost a few bob."

"I've got a few bob." Betsy pulled a florin out of her open purse and handed it to Mattie. "This should buy me a few names."

Mattie's eyes widened as she stared at the coin for a moment and then tucked it into her pocket. "Santorini had his latest dustup with his landlady, Frida Sorensen."

"What kind of dustup?"

"The gossip was that she found out he was playin' about with the barmaid at the Thistle and Thorn. A night or so before 'e was killed, the two of them 'ad a right old shoutin' match."

"Where at?"

"Where else?" Mattie snickered. "The Thistle and Thorn. The barmaid's name is Alberta Miller."

"The Thistle and Thorn?" Betsy repeated. Mrs. Jeffries had mentioned it at their meeting this morning, but she'd not recognized the name and had no idea where it might be. "Where's that? I don't remember a pub with that name 'round 'ere." She caught herself as she realized listening to Mattie was influencing her own speech. She'd worked hard to learn to speak properly and she wasn't going to start speaking like a street urchin now.

"It used to be called the Hungry Badger, but one of the big breweries took a loan on it and made Horace Fielding—he's the owner—change the name."

Betsy nodded. She remembered the old pub, so finding the place shouldn't be difficult. "Did this dustup between Santorini and his landlady get violent? Did she threaten him?"

"She threatened to toss 'im into the street, but I've not 'eard that there was any fisticuffs. Just a lot of shoutin' and screamin'."

Betsy was sure she could get the rest of the details of this encounter from someone at the pub. "Who else was on the outs with Santorini?"

"Well, Harvey Macklin hated him." Mattie laughed. "He thought he had a good chance to marry the widow Sorensen, but six months ago, Santorini got kicked out of his room at the back of the Crying Crows and moved into Frida's lodgin's. Within a few weeks of his movin' in, Santorini had Harvey's room and 'is lady."

"Where does this Harvey Macklin live?"

"He's still at Frida's, but she's chargin' him a bit more rent these days. He can afford it."

"Where does he work?"

"At Stanton's over on the Commercial Road."

"Anyone else?"

Mattie thought for a moment. "He had a fallin' out with Susan Callahan—she owns the Crying Crows—but that was six months ago. I 'eard gossip that there was someone 'round 'ere that just got out of Pentonville. Supposedly, it was someone that claimed Santorini's lies put him in the nick."

"Do you know this person's name?"

"Well." Mattie scratched her chin. "The problem is, when you get to be my age, the memory gets a little foggy. I've 'eard the feller's name, but I'm not sure I can recall it . . . It's on the tip of my tongue, so to speak."

"Would another florin get it off the tip?" Betsy asked, her expression skeptical.

Mattie laughed again, an ugly sound that had nothing to do with humor. "It might. Hand one over and we'll see."

"I'm not fallin' for that old trick, Mattie." Betsy gave her a smug smile. "You tell me the name and then I'll give you the florin." She looked around the small, cramped shop and realized it was in much worse shape than it had been ten years ago when she'd left the neighborhood. Back then, the hardwood floors had been occasionally scrubbed, but now they were streaked with dirt and caked with mud in spots. The shelves behind the cash drawer, which used to be crammed full of tinned tobaccos and boxes of tea, were now half-empty, as if Mattie couldn't afford to keep them stocked, and the glass of the display case at the far end of the counter was cracked in two separate places. The case was also empty. Betsy remembered that it used to be filled with day-old pastries and bread that Mattie bought on the cheap from the bake shop.

Mattie's eyes narrowed as she watched Betsy survey her premises. "'Ere, there's no reason to say somethin' like that. I'd not cheat ya."

"You would and you did, lots of times," Betsy snapped. She couldn't control her feelings now—this place brought back too many horrible memories. Begging for a bit of onion and a carrot or two so she could make her dying mother some soup, only to have Mattie tell her she only had enough money for a half-rotten spud. "I told ya, I'm from 'ere. I've been in this miserable dump of a shop lots of times, and each and every time, you had your thumb on the scales when you were weighing out those disgusting vegetables that you sold to us. You know, awful stuff the greengrocer was throwin' out. You sold me moldy bread and bacon that wasn't fit to eat and charged a pretty penny for it because you knew my family didn't have the means to shop anywhere else. You'd cheat me, Mattie, over and over again, but this time I've plenty of coin, and I'll be passin' it around someplace else." She turned on her heel and stomped toward the door.

"'Ere, 'ere, don't get all huffy on me. I was only tryin' to make a livin'. For God's sake, I was poor, too. Come back. I'll tell ya what I know. You'll regret not 'earin' me out."

But Betsy kept going to the door.

"Don't be daft. I know somethin' that can 'elp you. It's only a bloomin' florin. From the way you're dressed, you can bloody well afford to pay me."

Betsy ignored her.

"At least tell me who ya are," Mattie cried.

Betsy reached for the doorknob, grabbed it, and then turned to look at her old enemy. She started to say her maiden name and then stopped. She'd love to see the look on the old witch's face when she found out that the poor, struggling young girl was now a wealthy woman who wore a coat that was worth more than all the inventory in Mattie's shop. That would be sweet revenge. But even sweeter revenge would be to leave her in the dark. Mattie hated not knowing.

"I'll leave you to figure that out. You always thought you were so much smarter than the rest of us." With that, she pulled the door open and went outside.

The Dirty Duck Pub wasn't open for business yet, but that didn't stop Smythe from stepping inside. He'd come to see the owner,

Blimpey Groggins, and he wasn't in the mood to waste time. It had been a bleeding bad morning. He'd had words with Betsy, which was rare for the two of them, and those words had Amanda in tears, which upset both of them even more. But, blast a Spaniard, why the Hades couldn't the woman understand that he didn't want her going back to the East End?

He understood that she was a proud and independent woman, but, blooming Ada, she'd known nothing but pain and heartbreak when she lived there, and he didn't want her going down that road again. But instead of understanding that he was trying to protect her, she'd gotten a bee in her bonnet that he was trying to keep her off the case. Women! He'd never understand them. He stalked down the short corridor to the public bar, stopped, and surveyed the room. Blimpey was sitting in his usual spot in front of the fireplace, reading a newspaper, and Eldon, Blimpey's man-of-all-work, was shoving a keg onto a shelf below the bar.

Blimpey, a portly man with a ruddy complexion and sharp blue eyes, put his paper down. He was a buyer and seller of information, and he knew everything that went on in southern England. He had sources at every newspaper, police station, magistrate's court, the Old Bailey, insurance companies, hospitals, shipping lines, and Parliament; and there were whispers he even had a source at Buckingham Palace.

He charged a pretty penny for his services, but Smythe could well afford them. He'd come back from Australia a wealthy man and, because of the circumstances of the Witherspoon household, had kept his financial situation a secret from everyone except Betsy. Mrs. Jeffries had figured it out, of course, but he'd never told the others; and now so much time had passed, he was worried that if he did tell them, they'd resent him for keeping it a secret.

"Nice to see ya, Smythe. 'Ave a seat." Blimpey nodded toward the empty stool opposite him. "I wasn't expectin' you quite so soon."

"And I didn't expect to be here this fast, either, but ya know 'ow it is—sometimes life moves a bit faster than you think it will." He sat down. "What do ya know about that murder in the East End?"

"Bert Santorini?" Blimpey shrugged. "Not much, but one thing I do know is that Santorini 'ad more than 'is fair share of enemies."

"He testified against them Irish brothers, the O'Dwyers," Smythe muttered, thinking back to what Mrs. Jeffries had told them this morning. "But who else 'ated him?"

"Before we get on to who else might 'ave wanted the bloke dead, there's somethin' ya need to know about the O'Dwyer brothers," Blimpey said. "Now, I'm not tellin' ya they are pure as driven snow—they're not. The lads are thieves, but they're not violent."

"But they coshed that butler on the head and left 'im for dead," Smythe argued. He'd read the reports of the burglary in the papers.

"No. Whoever burgled that 'ouse coshed the butler on the 'ead," Blimpey insisted. "But it wasn't the O'Dwyers."

"'Ow can you be so sure?"

Blimpey's eyes narrowed. "Don't be daft, Smythe. It's my job to know such things. The O'Dwyers never, ever enter an occupied 'ouse, and, as the butler was there that night, they'd 'ave not gone inside."

"Maybe they didn't know 'e was there?"

"But they would. Seamus O'Dwyer— 'e's the eldest—always takes a look before they hit a place, and that night, there were lights on in the kitchen. Seamus wouldn't 'ave missed that and 'e'd 'ave called the burglary off. Someone else robbed that place, not the O'Dwyers."

"So you're sayin' the O'Dwyers know that Santorini lied in court and now have a motive for killin' him," Smythe said.

"Course they do, but they couldn'a done it—they was in the nick when 'e was shot."

"But they have family and friends that might 'ave done it." Smythe leaned forward.

"True, but think on this: Santorini was more useful to the O'Dwyers alive than dead," Blimpey explained. "If they could prove the fellow lied under oath, they'd get out of jail."

"But 'ow could they prove that Santorini lied? He'd never admit it."

"Because Fiona O'Dwyer, the boys' mother, 'ired me to find some evidence that does prove it, and that's exactly what I'm goin' to do."

CHAPTER 5

Witherspoon stared at the front of the Crying Crows Pub as he waited for Barnes to pay the hansom driver. The building was just off the Whitechapel High Street on a short road that dead-ended at the back of a derelict flour mill. It was a two-story brown brick structure with a huge, brilliantly painted sign showing two crows, their mouths wide-open and their wings spread in flight, mounted over the double doorway. The pub was separated from the other buildings on the road by a narrow passageway filled with cast-off broken junk on one side and a larger, paved walkway leading to a side door on the other. Along the very top of the building was a crimson sign with gold lettering that read *Bryson's Ales and Stouts,* one of the largest breweries in southern England.

He and the constable had debated whether to start here or at the Thistle and Thorn. They'd settled on this pub because it was connected to both Nivens and Santorini. It also had the advantage of being the closest one to the Leman Street Station.

Barnes joined the inspector, yanked open the door, and they stepped inside. "No wonder the lads like coming here. It's not just decent, sir—it could give a pub in Mayfair or Belgravia a run for their money." He shook his head. "It didn't look like this twenty-five years ago."

In the center of the room hung a five-branch brass chandelier with pale pink globes covering the gas burners. The floors were polished oak and the walls covered in a red and gold fleur-de-lis wallpaper. The pub was shaped like an L, with the bar facing the door and a row of private booths enclosed in wood partitions and topped with delicately etched glass running along one side. Tables with curved wooden chairs, potted plants on brass stands, and several padded love seats were strategically placed to maximize the number of people that could be served.

"You've been here before?" Witherspoon asked.

Barnes nodded. "Yes. Back then, the walls were whitewashed, the floors just plain old planks, and there wasn't a fancy mirror behind the bar. But as they say, times change."

It was only a few minutes past eleven o'clock, opening time, so the place wasn't full. A dark-haired young man dressed in a neatly pressed white shirt with the sleeves rolled up and black waistcoat stood behind the bar, polishing glasses. He glanced at them as they crossed the floor. "What'll it be, sir?" He directed his question to Witherspoon.

"We'd like to speak with Mrs. Callahan," the inspector said.

He put the glass down on the counter tray. "She's in her office, but she'll not thank me for interrupting her."

"This is police business, lad." Barnes gave him a hard stare. "And we'll not thank you if you waste our time. Please tell Mrs. Callahan we're here and that it's important."

The barman blinked in surprise. "Alright, alright, there's no need for threats. I'm just tryin' to 'ang on to my job here. There's many of your lot that comes in 'ere and we always treat 'em right. Keep your shirt on and I'll get 'er." He tossed his towel on top of the polished glasses and disappeared through a door at the far end of the bar.

Barnes turned to the inspector. "In this part of London, sir, you've got to show 'em that we're not to be trifled with. Take my word for it, most of the people here would just as soon spit on a constable's shoes rather than tell him anything."

"I quite understand, Constable." Witherspoon knew Barnes wasn't one to use his position to intimidate or bully others. Furthermore, his knowledge of the East End far surpassed Witherspoon's own. "The barman appeared to be more frightened of his employer than of us."

"He probably is—jobs in this part of the city are hard to come by. I expect this one pays pretty well."

The door opened and a middle-aged woman with dark red hair and thick spectacles emerged. She wore a cream-colored blouse with a high collar and puffy, leg-of-mutton sleeves. A blue and cream striped skirt topped with a wide blue sash circled her thick waist, and a ladies' timepiece dangled from a gold chain around her neck.

"I'm Susan Callahan," she announced. "My barman claims you want to speak to me."

"We do, Mrs. Callahan. I'm Inspector Witherspoon and this is Constable Barnes," he replied. "Is there somewhere we can speak privately?"

She crossed her arms over her ample bosom. "What's this about, then?"

"Bert Santorini," Barnes said.

"Oh, him." She looked at the barman. "We'll be in the snug, Alex. Call Janice to give you a hand when we start filling up. We'll start getting busy when the lunch hour comes 'round," she explained as she lifted the wooden top of the counter and stepped through. "And half our customers will be your lot. It's this way." She led them around the bar to the row of private booths and into the first one. She slid onto the leather seat and nodded toward the opposite side. "Make yourselves comfortable."

They took their places and Witherspoon waited till Barnes pulled out his notebook before he spoke. "Mrs. Callahan, as Constable Barnes said, we're here to ask you a few questions about Bert Santorini."

"He was murdered night before last, but what's that got to do with me? I didn't kill him."

"We're not accusing you of murder, Mrs. Callahan. We're merely trying to learn what we can about the victim. Now, may I ask you how long you've known the deceased?"

"I'm not sure. I think it's been around five or six years."

"He was a customer here?"

She nodded. "Yes—that's when I first met him. He came in most evenings and had a drink or two, but in the last few years, he delivered ice when I needed it. We don't use it often, just when the weather gets hot."

"You became acquainted with him as both a customer and a supplier?" Witherspoon wanted to make sure he understood the relationship the victim had with members of the local community.

"A customer first—it was only later that he started making deliveries. Santorini got the ice cart and horse about three years ago. Before that, he did odd jobs and, if he could get it, day labor at the docks. He also did a bit of translating for some of the local trades-people, especially the importers. Italian was his mother tongue."

"He must have done quite well to be able to afford to buy the cart and horse. That's a good business," Barnes commented.

"He was always a hard worker," she replied. "But he was a lucky sod as well. Santorini bought the ice cart and the pony on the cheap. The owner was arrested for stealing and had to sell fast."

Barnes glanced at Witherspoon before he spoke again. "What was the name of the man Santorini bought it from?"

"Philip Graves. He got sent to Pentonville but he's out now"— she smiled wryly—"and from what I hear, he's been looking for Santorini."

"Do you know where we can find Graves?" Barnes asked.

"I don't know his address, but I've heard he's got a bed at Tilson's over on Clouston Road. He shouldn't be hard to find—your lads have their eyes on him. They helped me toss him into the street when he showed up here last week."

"What do you mean?" Witherspoon asked.

"He walked in just after evening opening and swaggered up to the bar like he owned the place. Started bothering poor Alex about where I was and where Santorini was, and when Alex told him it wasn't any of his business where either of us might be, he got rough. That's when a couple of your lads told him to get out."

"You mean police officers," Witherspoon clarified. When she nodded, he continued. "I understand why Graves might threaten Santorini, but why did he make threats against you?"

She smiled slightly. "Because I'm the one that had him arrested."

Wiggins walked past Frida Sorensen's lodging house for the third time and hoped that no one had noticed him. The people in this

part of London were a sharp-eyed lot; they had to be if they wanted
to survive.

His steps slowed as he reached the corner. Stopping, he wondered if he ought to try finding someone at the Thistle and Thorn.
That was the pub Santorini frequented before he was killed. Wiggins' luck here was downright miserable, his feet were cold, and
he was afraid of being spotted. But just as he made up his mind
to move on, the front door of the lodging house opened, and a
clean-shaven tall, lanky man with thinning brown hair stepped
outside. He came down the short walkway, turned, and set off at a
brisk pace. Wiggins waited a few moments and then followed in
pursuit.

The man moved quickly, dodging past two grim-faced women
carrying shopping baskets and a cluster of skinny children squabbling over a ball. When his quarry reached the crowded pavements
of the Commercial Road, Wiggins moved closer. He followed him
for a good five minutes until the man turned a corner and stepped
inside a building.

It was a pub called the Pig and Ale. Wiggins hesitated; at their
meeting this morning, no one had mentioned this pub and he might
be wasting his time. But he'd not learned anything today, and this
fellow had come out of the lodging house. There might be a chance
he knew something useful. Wiggins yanked open the door and
went inside.

The place was small. There were two tables in front of the
benches along the wall next to the door; a short, old-fashioned
curved bar; and a couple of rickety-looking chairs in front of the
empty fireplace at the far end. He inhaled sharply to catch his
breath and then wished he hadn't, as the sour scent of spilled gin,
stale beer, and greasy mutton hit his nostrils.

The man he'd been following stood at the bar. Wiggins slid into a spot next to him just as the barman said, "You're here earlier than usual, Harvey. You get sacked?"

"Mr. Stanton's closed the shop for the day so he can go to a funeral. His wife's sister passed away and she's bein' buried today. You know my guv—if he's not there, he'll not open up, so I lose a day's pay. But what can you do? I need to work, especially now."

"You want your usual?" the barman asked.

Harvey nodded.

The barman glanced at Wiggins. "What'll you have?"

"A pint of bitter."

It took a few moments for both of them to get served. While he waited, Wiggins glanced at Harvey, who was staring morosely at the wooden counter. The man's shirt was fraying at the collar, his shoes were scruffed, and there was a hole in the sleeve of his coat. But then again, that wasn't surprising. Almost everyone in this part of London was poor, even the ones that had work.

As soon as they'd both been served, the barman said, "Hey, Harvey, give us a shout if anyone else comes in. I've got to go to the back and count out the kegs." He stopped long enough to see Harvey nod and then he disappeared through a narrow doorway at the end of the bar.

Wiggins took a sip, sighed, and then smiled. "I'm hopin' this'll make up for a misery of a day."

"It'd take more than one pint to end my misery." Harvey took a sip from his beer, put it down, and continued to stare at the wood as if it held the secret to life.

"It sounds like you've had a right awful day as well." Wiggins grinned. "Sorry, I wasn't eavesdroppin', but I couldn't 'elp overhearin'. Losin' a day's pay is 'ard."

"Tell me about it." Harvey shook his head. "Seems like nothin' is going right for me these days."

"I know that feelin'." Wiggins hoped the misery-loves-company ploy would keep the man talking or, even better, get the fellow drinking more. The more beer that went down a throat, the looser the tongue. "I was supposed to do another run out to the docks, but when I got to the warehouse, the bloomin' goods had already been moved. I'm out of half a load and it's too late to pick up another one." He was making it up as he went along and hoping he sounded believable.

Harvey nodded in a gesture of understanding. "Life's hard, in' it. Mind you, mine's been a bloody mess for months now, and before you know it, the police'll be 'round pesterin' me with stupid questions."

"The police?" Wiggins stared at Harvey with an expression of what he hoped was surprise. "Why'll they be questioning you?"

"Because of Bert Santorini."

"Who?"

"Don't you read the papers? He's the bloke that was murdered just down the road from here." Harvey took another gulp. "And he lived at my lodgin' house. They've already been there talkin' to Frida—she's the owner—and I know she told 'em there was bad blood between me and him."

"Cor blimey—you and the dead feller didn't get along?"

"We hated each other." He snorted. "Santorini got tossed out of the Crying Crows when the woman who owns it found out he was playin' about with one of the barmaids from the Thistle and Thorn, so what does the blighter do? He moves into Frida's and starts workin' on her."

"Workin' on 'er?" Wiggins repeated. "What does that mean?"

"You know—sweet-talkin' her and complimentin' her cookin' and tellin' her how pretty she looks." He lifted his glass and took a gulp of his beer.

"What's wrong with that?"

"Everything's wrong with it," he exclaimed. "You don't do that to another fellow, and I made it real clear when he first started flirtin' with her that Frida and I had an understandin'. We was together. But Santorini was a smooth-talkin' bastard, and he had the sort of looks that women likes—leastways, Frida liked them well enough. Before I knew it, I was out in the cold, and he had the best room in the house." He took another swig of beer, put his glass down, and closed his eyes. "And despite what one of the newspapers said about the gun that killed Santorini belongin' to a copper, that'll not do me any good. The police stick together, and they'll have me in their sights quick enough."

"But just because you didn't like the man doesn't mean they'll think you killed him. I mean, why would they?" Wiggins picked up his beer and took a sip.

"Because a few nights before Santorini was killed, I had a right old shoutin' match with him. We was at the Thistle and Thorn, and I'd had too much to drink. I don't usually drink there—I generally go to the Crying Crows—but part of me was just itchin' for a set-to with Santorini. I'd 'eard gossip that he was playin' about with the barmaid there. Sure enough, the bastard swaggered in and started chattin' her up like she was the ruddy Queen. But then he saw me, and he knew why I'd come—he knew I was goin' to go back to Frida's and tell her what I'd seen. He started in on me, tellin' me to mind my mouth and keep my nose out of his business. But this time

I didn't back down; this time, I was ready for 'im. I let my temper loose and told 'im that I was goin' to tell Frida everything and that I'd get her to believe me." He closed his mouth and looked away.

But Wiggins wasn't going to let him stop there. "What happened then?"

"He started laughing. He said she'd never believe me." Harvey smirked. "Odd thing was, she believed me right off when I told her. She wasn't surprised, so I think she'd already suspected he was playing her for a fool. Still, that's small comfort. I'm in a world of trouble; I know the coppers will think I did it."

"You didn't come to blows, and you'd 'ad one too many; that 'appens all the time. The police know that," Wiggins commented.

"But that's not all I said. I threatened him, ya see. In front of a dozen witnesses, I told him I'd kill him."

"You had Philip Graves arrested?" Witherspoon hoped he understood her correctly.

"He took ten pounds out of my cash drawer, so I set the law on him. There's nothing wrong with that. I won't let anyone steal from me," Susan replied. "Life's tough enough without one of your suppliers turning on you to line his own pockets."

"What were the circumstances of this theft?" Barnes asked.

The inspector noticed the constable was staring at her intensely.

"As I told you earlier, I didn't often need ice, but it was a hot day and I'd asked Graves for a bushel of ice. Some Russians had started coming in, and they'd complained that the vodka was too warm. It was hard to keep it cold, given the heat we'd had, so Graves got me the ice. I paid him and asked him to carry it into the back room for me. Then he came back out front here. Now, I'd gone with him so that I could get the bottles into the ice, and when I came out here,

Graves was gone. A few minutes later, I opened the cash drawer and saw that I was short ten quid."

"You counted out your drawer right then?"

"Yes, we were getting ready to close for the afternoon. I always took the cash to the bank before we open for the evening licensing hours."

"Was the pub empty when Graves was out here alone?" Witherspoon asked.

"No, Bert Santorini was here. He's the one who saw Graves taking the money out of the till."

Barnes raised an eyebrow and glanced at the inspector. He could see that Witherspoon was also surprised. "Was Santorini the only one who witnessed the theft?" he asked.

"The room was empty—that's why Graves felt like he could help himself," she explained. "Bert walked in just as he was slamming the drawer shut and shoving the money in his coat pocket. What's more, Graves ran out of here like the devil himself was after him."

"I see," Witherspoon murmured. "Can you think of anyone else, other than Philip Graves, who might have wanted Mr. Santorini dead?"

She shrugged. "He wasn't a popular man, Inspector. He considered himself quite charming, but he had a knack for making enemies."

"Can you give us the names of these enemies?" Barnes cocked his head and studied her.

She laughed. "Well, me for one, but I certainly didn't kill him." She paused, her expression puzzled as she looked at the constable. "Is there something on my nose, Constable? You're staring at me in a very rude manner."

"My apologies, Mrs. Callahan." He smiled ruefully. "I didn't intend offense, but you look familiar to me. I worked around these parts years ago—it was my first assignment as a constable. I'm wondering if we have met before?"

"I doubt it," she replied. "I've only been in the area for six years. Before that, I lived in Leeds."

"Back to Mr. Santorini," Witherspoon said quickly. "Why did you dislike him?"

She gave Barnes one more glance before turning her attention to the inspector. "As I said before, Santorini could be very charming. I was so grateful to him for catching Graves when he tried to steal from me that we became friendly. Santorini started coming in regularly, and sometimes he'd even bring a bouquet for the bar. Occasionally, one of the hotel dining rooms he supplied with ice and flowers wouldn't need everything he'd put on the cart. He'd bring the extra flowers here."

"For your bar?" Barnes clarified.

She shrugged. "Or me—as I said, we were friendly at that time, and I thought he was just being nice. I've prided myself on making my customers, even the local police lads, feel welcome here, and he was no exception. But I realized he wasn't to be trusted when I let him stay in a room at the back."

"You gave him free lodging?" Witherspoon asked.

"Don't be daft," she retorted. "I made him work for his keep." She raised her arm and gestured at the surroundings. "I've spent a fortune on this place, fixing it up right and proper, and I was worried about someone breaking in. At that time, several businesses in the neighborhood had been broken into at night and burgled. I was a widow and alone. I live upstairs. I wanted to make sure that I was safe and that my premises were watched properly. Bert Santorini offered to stay here at night to keep an eye on out."

"How long did he stay?" Witherspoon asked.

"More than a year." She smiled wryly. "He was a bit of a sweet talker, was our Bert, and for a long time, I didn't keep a close watch on him. But then one of my customers complained about the beer."

"Complained in what way?" Witherspoon asked.

"That the beer didn't taste right. That it tasted watered. So I started watching him and realized he was drinking my stock." She jabbed a finger toward the bar. "Helping himself to my beer and whisky. I wouldn't have minded him taking a nip every now and again, but he did something far worse. The bastard was drinking so much of my stock that he was adding water to both the beer and the whisky to keep me from knowing how much of it was going down his throat. Do you know what would happen to me if the brewery caught wind of that? They don't take kindly to their alcohol being watered down. It could have cost me everything. They hold the loan on this place. I told Santorini he had to go. He wasn't happy about it, and we had a terrible argument."

"Is that when he moved into Frida Sorensen's lodging house?" Barnes looked at her.

"That's what I heard." She shrugged. "And as far as I was concerned, good riddance."

Witherspoon realized time was getting on, and they needed to move along. "Who else disliked Santorini?"

"Fiona O'Dwyer—she's the mother of the lads Santorini testified against—but, then again, she would hate him, wouldn't she?" Behind her spectacles, her eyes narrowed thoughtfully. "And I've heard that one of the other tenants at Frida's place had words with him a few nights before he was killed."

"Do you know his name?" Barnes pressed.

"No, but if you stop by the Thistle and Thorn, someone there ought to know who he is. Supposedly the two of them got into a shouting match a night or so before Bert was murdered."

"What time do you open for the evening?" The constable looked up from his notebook.

"Half six, that's what my license allows."

Barnes nodded. All the pubs in the area were licensed for evening opening at that time. "Were you here all afternoon on the day Santorini was killed?"

She opened her mouth to speak just as a loud crash banged against the building. Startled, she jerked, as did the two policemen. Barnes and Witherspoon both scrambled out of the snug and raced to the front of the pub. Susan Callahan was right behind them.

The three of them reached the front just as Alex pulled the door open and charged outside. He reappeared a moment later, holding a stone the size of a bulldog's head. "At least this time they didn't break the windows." He held the door open. "But it looks like it made a right nasty dent in the wood."

"Did you see who it was?" Susan demanded.

"Sorry, Mrs. Callahan, but they'd scarpered by the time I got around the bar and opened the door."

"Bloody hooligans." Susan Callahan grabbed the stone out of Alex's hand and glared at it. "I'll have their guts for garters when I get my hands on whoever did this." She pointed to her damaged door. "This is the second time in six months the blighters have done this."

"This has happened before?" Barnes examined the wound in the wood.

"Once before, only then it was the window."

Barnes leaned closer to the door and studied the gash in the wood. "This is a bad one. It's going to take more than a bit of sanding down to fix it properly."

"Did you report the previous incident to the police?" Witherspoon asked her.

"There was no need to. There was half a dozen of your lot in here when it happened, and even then, the bastard who did it was able to get clean away."

"When was that?" Barnes stood up straight.

"Three, four months ago." Susan shrugged. "I don't recall the exact date."

"It was in the middle of December." Alex went back behind the bar. "The same day that the fellow from the brewery come by to see you."

"That's right. Mr. Morland was here the same day it happened. Luckily, he'd gone before the stone come flying in."

"Do you know why you're being harassed in this manner?" Witherspoon was a tad embarrassed that a roomful of policemen hadn't been able to apprehend one stone thrower.

"Isn't it blooming obvious?" She waved her arm in a circle. "I've made this pub into a showplace, something to be proud of and not just a gin hole for the local scum that used to drink here when my husband owned the place. But when he died and it became mine, I wanted it to be bigger and better than any pub in Whitechapel. Despite having to take a loan from the brewery, I've succeeded. But there's some 'round here that resent anyone who wants to make themselves or the neighborhood better."

"Have you had to raise your prices?" Barnes asked.

"Of course." She snorted faintly. "But I've attracted a much better class of clientele. Not everyone around here is a pauper.

There's plenty of businessmen from the tea trade and shipping companies as well as the local police that want to drink in a clean, decent pub, and that's what I've given them."

"And it appears it's causing you a bit of worry," the constable remarked. "Well, as Santorini was still alive when the first incident happened, today's incident doesn't appear to have anything to do with his murder."

"Let's hope so, Constable," Witherspoon agreed. He turned to Susan Callahan. "I'm sorry for your door getting hit, Mrs. Callahan, and very glad that no one was harmed. That's quite a large stone. If you'd like, we can report this incident when we get back to Leman Street."

She shook her head. "Don't bother. Whoever did it is long gone, and the street ruffians 'round here won't turn in one of their own."

Witherspoon nodded in understanding.

"I'll just nip back and get my notebook and pencil." Barnes hurried back toward the snug.

As soon as he returned, Witherspoon turned to the publican and said, "We'll be back if we have any other questions."

They said nothing until they were outside the pub with the door closed. "What do you think, sir?"

"I think the attacks on the place are exactly what Mrs. Callahan said: locals who resent what she's done to the pub."

"That's probably right," Barnes said. "And it seems as if her relationship with Santorini ended six months ago. Where to now, sir?"

"Let's go to the Thistle and Thorn. I'd like to find out more about the confrontation that occurred there the night before the victim was killed."

*   *   *

Betsy had calmed down by the time she walked into the kitchen for their afternoon meeting. Everyone, save for Ruth Cannonberry, was already there. Mrs. Goodge was putting a plate of scones on the table, Phyllis was pouring boiling water into the teapot, Mrs. Jeffries was putting the butter and jam next to the scones, and Hatchet was pulling out Luty's chair.

Betsy gave her husband a tremulous smile as she took her seat next to him.

Under the table, Smythe grabbed her hand and gave it a squeeze. Leaning close, he whispered, "I'm sorry, love."

"Me, too. I know you were only trying to protect me, and I should have listened to you." She kept her voice low, hoping there was enough background noise to mask her words.

He gave her a sharp look. "Did something 'appen?"

"Nothing bad. I'll tell you when we get home," she said. But she wasn't sure she would tell him the whole of it. After she'd stomped out of Mattie's miserable shop, she'd given up on finding out anything more about the case. Instead, she'd walked the streets of Whitechapel, going past the ugly tenement where she and her family had lived before death and indifference had split them apart; past the now-closed church where she'd once been part of a stone throwing mob that broke the windows of that particularly heartless institution; past the boarded-up house where a local pimp had tried to force her into the game and she'd barely escaped with her life and her virtue. She walked until she was finally so exhausted, she waved down a hansom cab and headed here, to the West End, to her home.

Mrs. Jeffries took her seat. "Are we ready to start?"

"Shouldn't we wait for Ruth?" Wiggins asked.

"She sent Everton over with a message," Mrs. Jeffries said. "She told us to go ahead and get started. Apparently, she's on the hunt, so to speak, and she'll get here when she can." She paused a second and when no one objected, continued speaking. "Now, who would like to go first?"

"Let me. Mine won't take more than two seconds," Luty said. "Accordin' to Brockton Bellingham, Bert Santorini had a bit of money and lots of enemies."

Hatchet snorted. "Fingers crossed the man was telling the truth."

"He wouldn't lie to me," Luty retorted.

"He'd lie to the Almighty himself if he thought it would give him an advantage," Hatchet replied. "He's a confidence man, and I, for one, do not believe he's reformed. He's simply old and a bit more tired now. But you mark my words, he's still in the game."

"Enemies?" Mrs. Jeffries repeated. She didn't want the meeting delayed by these two having one of their never-ending arguments. "You mean other than the family and friends of the O'Dwyers?"

Luty nodded. "Brock claims that Santorini had a habit of usin' people and then tossin' them aside when he couldn't git anything else out of them. But Brock wouldn't give me any names when I pressed him. Just said that everyone knew to watch their backs if they was around Santorini."

"I heard something like that as well," Betsy added. She smiled apologetically at the elderly American. "Sorry, Luty. I didn't mean to steal your thunder. I'll wait my turn."

"Don't worry about it," Luty said. "I only heard one more tidbit and that's that Santorini had taken up with a pickpocket named Dickie Stiles."

Again, Hatchet snorted.

Luty frowned at him. "Don't be mean, Hatchet. Brockton's changed and you know it. People can change—you know *that* as well as I do. I don't know why you're so set against the fellow."

"I'm not set against him," Hatchet replied. "I'm simply reserving judgment as to this supposed 'change' in his character."

"Humph. I think you're just jealous," Luty declared. "You don't like havin' to play second fiddle to someone you think is beneath you."

"That's absurd," Hatchet argued, but before he could say any more, Mrs. Jeffries interrupted him.

"Did your source know why Santorini had taken up with this pickpocket?" she asked.

"No, he just said that he was standing right next to Santorini at the Thistle and Thorn Pub on Saturday evening and that he'd seen Santorini give Stiles a note." Luty reached for her teacup.

"I'll have a go at finding out," Smythe offered. "I've a source that might be able to 'elp with that information."

"Good. That might be very useful. Did you find out anything today?" Mrs. Jeffries looked at the coachman.

"Not too much, but I found out a bit about the O'Dwyers." Smythe repeated everything he'd heard from Blimpey Groggins. When he'd finished, the others were silent.

Wiggins frowned in confusion. "Let me make sure I understand. Mrs. O'Dwyer is 'irin' your source to 'elp her prove that Santorini lied in court? Is that what you're sayin'?"

Smythe wished he'd kept that specific bit to himself. He didn't want to call attention to the fact that his source was someone who could be hired for cold, hard cash. That might lead to some very uncomfortable questions. "Yeah. It's 'ard to explain, but my source 'as a lot of connections in London. Mrs. O'Dwyer knew this and that's why she went to him for 'elp."

"If what your source says is true," Betsy murmured, "then she knows her boys are innocent. Watching your children go to prison for a crime they didn't commit must be dreadful."

"We don't know that they are innocent," Hatchet pointed out.

"But it makes sense," Phyllis argued. "That's probably why Santorini was killed. He lied under oath and three people were sent to prison. Why else would someone kill him?"

"But there could be another reason he was killed. According to my source, Santorini was good at making enemies," Betsy said. "Oh, sorry." She gave her husband a rueful smile. "I've done it again, haven't I? Jumped in instead of letting you finish."

"No, go ahead—I'm done." Smythe squeezed her hand again. "It sounds like you found out a few bits today."

"Just a few." Betsy told them about her encounter with Mattie Mitchell. She left out the part where she paid for information and also where she'd given in to her memories, lost her temper, and then stormed out. "As you can tell, there were a lot of people who hated Santorini," she concluded.

"One of them is right scared 'e's goin' to be blamed for Santorini's murder," Wiggins put in. "Oh, blimey, now I'm doin' it. Sorry, Betsy. Finish your bit."

"That's it, I'm afraid. I only managed to speak to one person today and that's all I was able to get out of her."

"You've found out more than I did," Phyllis muttered glumly. She looked at Mrs. Jeffries. "I don't think talking to the local shopkeepers is going to be very useful. None of the people I spoke to today knew anything about the man except that he'd been murdered."

Just then, Fred stood up, and a moment later, they heard a knock on the back door.

"I'll get it," Phyllis offered. "Perhaps it's Lady Cannonberry." She hurried out of the kitchen and disappeared down the hall. "Oh, Ruth, we've been waiting for you . . . Good gracious, you've brought a visitor."

"Please don't be annoyed with Lady Cannonberry. I stopped her in the communal garden and insisted she hear me out," a loud, male voice said.

"Cor blimey." Wiggins half rose from his chair. "That voice sounds right familiar. Is that . . ."

But by that time, everyone knew who'd come calling with Ruth Cannonberry as she and her guest came into view, followed by a confused-looking Phyllis.

Nigel Nivens bowed toward the group gathered around the table. "I know I'm not particularly welcome here, but please, listen to me."

"Please, everyone. Inspector Nivens claims he's the victim of a dreadful miscarriage of justice," Ruth explained. "I think we should hear what he's got to tell us."

"Inspector Nivens?" Shocked, Phyllis gaped at him.

There was a moment of silence as they all stared at Nigel Nivens. Finally, Mrs. Jeffries said, "Inspector Nivens, what are you doing here?"

"Do forgive me for barging in like this. But Lady Cannonberry took pity on me when I said I had to see you." He gave Ruth a quick, grateful smile. "It's quite literally a matter of life or death." He darted a quick look at the empty chair next to Hatchet.

"Would you care to sit down?" Mrs. Jeffries offered. "We've tea as well. You're most welcome to join us."

"Thank you, Mrs. Jeffries." He moved quickly to the empty spot, almost as if scared she'd rescind the invitation.

Ruth took her usual seat. Phyllis gave herself a small shake and got another teacup and a plate from the sideboard. The room was eerily quiet as she poured a cup of tea and placed it and the plate in front of Nivens.

Mrs. Goodge pushed the scones toward their unwanted visitor. "Help yourself," she muttered.

Nivens nodded politely and took one of the pastries. "Thank you. You're all being very kind to me. I know you're well aware of the fact that there has been some tension between myself and Inspector Witherspoon."

"Not really." Mrs. Jeffries gave him a polite but cool smile. "Our inspector doesn't comment on police business nor on his assessment of his colleagues." That, of course, was a bold-faced lie, but she knew Nivens couldn't prove her words one way or another. Besides, she was rather annoyed at having to be civil to the man. "Now, Inspector Nivens, if you'll be so good as to tell us why you've come here."

"And what's all this about something being a 'matter of life or death,'" Mrs. Goodge scoffed. "That sounds like something out of one of Mr. Conan Doyle's stories."

Nivens, who'd shoved a huge bite of scone in his mouth, chewed rapidly and swallowed. "But it is a matter of life and death. Mine. I'm in terrible trouble, and if I can't find assistance, I'm going to hang for a murder I didn't commit."

"What on earth are you talking about?" Mrs. Jeffries knew good and well what he referred to, but it was essential to keep up the pretense. She was pleased that Mrs. Goodge had seemed to get what she was trying to do, and she only hoped the others would either keep silent or, if they spoke, not give the game away. "Why would you hang for a murder you didn't commit?"

"I'm being framed for the murder of Bert Santorini."

"Isn't that the murder our inspector is investigating now?" Phyllis looked at Mrs. Jeffries, her expression innocent.

"I believe that's the name I overheard him and Constable Barnes discussing," she replied before turning her attention back to Nivens. "But what's that got to do with us?"

Nivens looked down at his plate and then lifted his chin. "I've heard rumors that you and the household assist the inspector in his inquiries," he murmured. "And I'm hoping you'll help me."

Mrs. Jeffries said nothing for a moment. She merely stared at him with what she hoped was an expression of shock on her face. "You've heard rumors about us? Inspector Nivens, I don't know what on earth you're talking about."

"I'm talking about how you and the others"—he waved his arm around, indicating all of them—"help Inspector Witherspoon. It's no secret, Mrs. Jeffries. Everyone on the force knows he has assistance."

"Blast a Spaniard, what's 'e on about?" Smythe exclaimed.

"Have you gone daft?" Mrs. Goodge added. "Help our inspector? Well, I never heard of such nonsense. I'm a cook, not a policeman."

Mrs. Jeffries shook her head, again with what she hoped was an expression of stunned disbelief. "I don't know what to say to such a statement, Inspector Nivens. What you're suggesting is absurd. We're merely servants in the inspector's household. I've no idea how or why such rumors might have started, but I assure you, it simply isn't true."

"Do you expect me to believe that?" Nivens looked skeptical. "You honestly expect me to believe that Gerald Witherspoon has solved more murders than anyone in the history of the Metropolitan Police Force?"

"Whether you believe it or not, it happens to be true," she replied calmly.

"Please. Not that many years ago he was just a jumped-up clerk in the records room, and then all of a sudden, he's the great hero who solved those horrible Kensington High Street Murders." Nivens' eyes narrowed speculatively. "That was just about the time you came to work for him, wasn't it, Mrs. Jeffries?"

"It was."

"And from what I recall, your late husband was a policeman, wasn't he?"

"He was, but I fail to see what that has to do with anything. My husband was a village constable, which is hardly comparable to what Inspector Witherspoon does."

"Nonetheless, I'm sure you learned something about police procedures before you came to London. It's hardly surprising that, given Inspector Witherspoon's remarkable rise from clerk to homicide detective, I'd think he had help."

"He wasn't a clerk," Ruth interjected. "He was in charge of the records room and a fully-fledged police inspector. How dare you imply that he isn't capable of solving murders on his own."

Nivens seemed to realize he wasn't making any friends with this approach. "I'm sorry. Please, I meant no disrespect—it's just that I'm desperate. If I don't get help, I'm going to hang for a murder I didn't commit."

"Nonsense," Mrs. Jeffries scoffed. "You should have more faith in your colleagues. The Metropolitan Police will do a thorough investigation and catch the person responsible for Mr. Santorini's murder."

He stared at her with a frightened, disbelieving expression.

"You don't understand, Mrs. Jeffries. They all hate me. No one is going to go out of their way to see that justice is done."

"Are you saying that everyone on the force will deliberately seek evidence that you're the culprit and ignore evidence that proves your innocence?"

Nivens felt the blood drain out of his face as her words hit home. For a moment, he couldn't respond, but finally, he managed to speak. "That's exactly what I'm saying. I'll admit that I've never sought friendships within the force, and I'll admit that I'm driven by ambition and not personal relationships. That, perhaps, was a foolish choice on my part, but nonetheless, it shouldn't condemn me to hang."

"But the newspaper said the gun that killed that poor fellow was yours," Phyllis blurted. She wanted to hear what he had to say, wanted to find out as many details as possible before they went back on the hunt.

He looked at her. "That's true, and I've no idea how the killer got the weapon; but, just so you know, my house was empty the night before the murder as well as the night of the murder."

"Was there any evidence of a break-in?" Hatchet realized what Phyllis was up to and decided to help.

"No, but picking locks isn't an unknown skill in the East End. That's probably how the killer got inside my home."

"Then I suggest you give the police a chance to prove that very thing," Mrs. Jeffries said quickly. "They're not fools, you know."

"No, they're not fools, but I've a feeling you know as well as I do, that once the police have made up their minds that someone is guilty, they stop looking at anyone else. Take my word for it— they've already made up their collective minds that I'm guilty. But despite what anyone thinks, despite the false evidence laid against me, I'm not a murderer. You must believe me. Please, I'm begging you. I need your help. You're my last hope."

For a brief moment, Mrs. Jeffries felt sorry for him, but then she pushed that feeling aside. This was the man that had twice betrayed Inspector Witherspoon for his own self-interest. "It's not that we don't believe you, Inspector. It's that we're powerless to assist you." She waved her hand at the people seated around the table. "For some strange reason, you have it in your head that those of us here have helped Inspector Witherspoon. But I assure you, that simply isn't true. We're only his servants and Lady Cannonberry is his friend. She's merely come by to gain our assistance in planning a surprise for Inspector Witherspoon's birthday. I don't know what you want us to do, but I certainly don't think we'd be of any help to you whatsoever."

Nivens knew when he was beaten. He got up from the table. "I'm sorry to have intruded upon you. Thank you for listening."

CHAPTER 6

The Thistle and Thorn was a far different pub from the Crying Crows. There were no potted plants, private booths, or fancy mirrors. Instead, the oak floor was blackened with age, the bricks around the small hearth were chipped, and the gas lamp globes were grimy and discolored. Yet even though it was almost time for afternoon closing, the pub was crowded. Workingmen and -women swathed in coats and shawls stood two deep at the bar. A row of bread sellers, their baskets stacked next to the hearth, had taken over the benches. Half a dozen people squeezed around each of the three small tables in front of the unlighted fireplace. Those that couldn't find a place to sit or lean stood clustered in small groups.

The noise dimmed as Barnes and Witherspoon stepped inside. The inspector stood by the door while Barnes made his way through the crowd toward the barmaid working the counter. Two elderly women, their faces openly curious, made a space for him between them. The constable nodded his thanks as the barmaid slid a pint to her left, where it was deftly caught by one of the women.

"Looks to me like you're in the wrong pub." The barmaid stared at him. "The coppers around here usually give their business to the fancy place up the road. But as you're here, what can I get you?"

"Nothing, ma'am. I'm on duty." Barnes studied her for a moment. She was an attractive dark-haired woman with smooth white skin; even, unremarkable features; and brown eyes that were red rimmed as if she'd been crying. He guessed she might be in her mid-thirties. "I'd like to speak to Alberta Miller. Is that you?"

"Hang on, Pete," she yelled at a patron at the far end of the counter who was banging his glass against the wood. "That's me, but, as you can see, I'm the only one here, and we're busy. It's almost time for last orders, so if you want to talk to me, you'll have to wait."

Barnes started to remind her that he was here on official police business but then thought better of it. This wasn't the Crying Crows, which had been almost empty when he and Witherspoon had gone inside, nor was it some elegant saloon bar in Holland Park or Putney. This was a busy workingman's East End pub, and if he pushed the woman too hard, he'd find out nothing. "Thank you, ma'am," he said politely. "We'll wait, then." But she'd already dismissed him and moved farther down the bar.

"She's asked us to wait until she closes up," Barnes told the inspector when he rejoined him. He glanced around the crowded room. "And I think we'll get more out of her if she's not trying to do two things at once."

"Did you tell her why we were here?" Witherspoon also surveyed the area.

"No, sir, but I'm sure she knows. She didn't look surprised that I knew her name."

Witherspoon nodded. "Right, then, we'll wait."

No one said a word until Phyllis returned from escorting Nivens to the front door. But as soon as she took her seat, everyone spoke at once.

"He's got a bit of nerve, showin' up 'ere." Wiggins shook his head in disbelief. "Does he think we're all stupid and that we can't remember some of the mean things 'e did to our inspector?"

"Nivens always had plenty of nerve," the cook commented.

"That's because he always thinks that he's better than everyone else," Betsy added. "And that the rest of us should be grateful just to be breathin' the same air as him."

"Arrogant, upper-class sod," Smythe muttered.

"That varmint's got more nerve than a bobcat in the henhouse," Luty declared.

"I don't understand." Phyllis looked at Mrs. Jeffries. "Are you saying we're not going to investigate this case?"

"Not at all," Mrs. Jeffries replied calmly.

"I'm confused." Phyllis frowned and crossed her arms over her chest. "What does that mean? You flat out told him we wouldn't lift a finger to help him."

"That's not true. I told him we were nothing more than servants in Inspector Witherspoon's household, which is absolutely correct. What I didn't admit to was that we helped our inspector with his cases and, I assure you, I have a very good reason for that."

Phyllis uncrossed her arms. "So we are going to keep help- ing him?"

"We're going to continue working on this case. But I don't consider that helping Nigel Nivens. I consider it serving justice. I'm admitting nothing to Nivens."

"But he almost 'ad tears in his eyes—he was beggin' us," Phyllis pointed out. "Mrs. Jeffries, he was pitiful, absolutely pitiful. He needed to know he had someone to help him."

"Would it have been so difficult to let him know he wasn't alone?" Ruth asked. "I agree with Phyllis—the poor man looked terrified."

Mrs. Jeffries shook her head and then looked first at Phyllis and then Ruth. "I don't think the two of you understand exactly who we're dealing with. Nigel Nivens isn't to be trusted. If he's innocent, which I suspect he is, the moment Inspector Witherspoon arrests the real killer, the first thing Nivens will do is go running to Chief Superintendent Barrows. He'd use our compassion for his circumstances and our confession that Inspector Witherspoon had assistance on his cases against our inspector."

"Surely not," Ruth protested. "He must have some vestige of honor? Doing such a despicable act after we'd helped him would be a dreadful stain upon his character."

Luty snorted. "Nivens wouldn't care as long as he got what he wanted. He's only out for himself and doesn't give a pig's ear about justice or honor or repaying a helping hand. Nells bells, the varmint's betrayed our inspector before and not just once," she reminded them. "Twice by my reckoning."

"I don't understand." Phyllis looked confused. "What are you all talking about? What's he done before?"

"That's right—he did do it twice," the cook muttered. "The first incident was so long ago, I'd forgotten it."

"What did he do before?" Phyllis asked irritably.

"He's been an ingrate," Hatchet replied. "A dreadful, despicable ingrate."

"What incident?" Phyllis asked. "What are you talking about?"

Hatchet smiled apologetically. "Sorry, Miss Phyllis. You weren't here then, but some years ago, in one of our earlier cases, Nivens withheld evidence that was important. To his credit, he did finally hand the evidence—I believe they were letters—to Inspector Witherspoon."

"If he handed over the evidence, why are you all still so sure he'd go running to Chief Superintendent Barrows?" Ruth asked.

"Because it weren't long after that investigation before Nivens was at it again," Wiggins told her. "He was stickin' 'is nose in our inspector's cases and tellin' tales about our inspector to the chief superintendent. What's more, he did it again in our last case. He 'ung on to evidence that our inspector needed, remember? That's why he ended up at Leman Street. A leopard can't change its spots. Mrs. Jeffries is right. He's not to be trusted."

"Are you certain of that?" Ruth said softly. She searched the faces around the table. "Yes, I'll admit that in the past, Inspector Nivens has behaved abominably. But this is different. This time, he's facing the hangman's noose and that alone should be enough to ensure that he behaves decently."

"Perhaps, perhaps not," Mrs. Jeffries said. "But in any case, it won't matter. We're not stopping our investigation just because none of us trusts him. Justice demands that we do everything in our power to make sure that we do all we can to see that Santorini's killer is caught."

It was almost a quarter past three before Alberta Miller had everyone gone and the front door of the pub locked. Witherspoon and Barnes sat down at one of the tables while they waited.

"Right, then. Go ahead and ask your questions." She took a seat opposite Witherspoon and stared at him belligerently.

"Miss Miller," Witherspoon began.

"It's Mrs. Miller," she corrected quickly. "I'm a widow."

The inspector smiled apologetically. "I do beg your pardon, Mrs. Miller. I assume you're aware that Bert Santorini was murdered two nights ago."

"I know he's been killed. Everyone 'round here knows he was shot. You think that just because it happened here in the East End, we've got so many killings that we can't keep 'em sorted out?"

"I wasn't implying anything of the sort," Witherspoon replied. "I was simply trying to find out if you knew why we'd come to speak with you. We hope you can help us. We've been told that you and Mr. Santorini were quite close."

"I'm not sure what you mean by 'close.' We were good friends, and I want you to catch his killer." Some of the antagonism faded as her eyes filled with tears, and she looked away.

"That's what we intend to do, Mrs. Miller," Witherspoon said gently. "Can you tell me if Mr. Santorini ever confided in you that he was frightened of someone, or that anyone had threatened him?"

"Bert wasn't scared of anyone." She swiped at her cheeks. "Maybe that's why he's dead. He trusted too many people and didn't know how to watch out for himself, even when he knew there was them that were out to get him."

"Who wished to harm him?" Barnes glanced at the inspector and could tell that Witherspoon was thinking the same thing; Santorini was neither trusting nor naive. Either this woman didn't know him very well, or she was in love with him.

"Fiona O'Dwyer, for one," she declared. "After Bert testified against her sons she told everyone that Bert lied. That he'd been paid by that fancy detective to get on the stand and lie. But he didn't lie; Bert told the truth."

"Santorini told you this?" the constable pressed. "He told you he'd not lied in court?"

"Not in so many words. But he wasn't a liar. Bert had his faults, but he wouldn't lie in court. He'd not send three innocent men to prison."

Barnes kept up the pressure. "Are you certain of that, Mrs. Miller?"

"Course I'm sure," she snapped. But she quickly looked down at the floor, and when she lifted her chin, she looked at Witherspoon, not the constable. "I said, we were friends, and I know what kind of person he was."

"Where were you on Monday evening between half five and six o'clock?" Barnes watched her carefully as he spoke.

Her eyes widened in surprise. "Where was I? You're askin' me something like that?"

"We're asking everyone who was close to Mr. Santorini."

"Where do you think I was? I was on my way here." She waved her arm around. "I don't start until half six on Mondays. The other barman and I take it in turns. That way, whoever has the late start can stay a bit later to clean up. Seems to me your lot would like to find a reason not to do your job, not to do what's right for him."

"That is not true," Witherspoon objected. "Regardless of what Mr. Santorini might or might not have done, he didn't deserve to be murdered. We will do everything we can to make certain his killer faces justice."

She smiled cynically. "You're just sayin' that 'cause the newspapers wrote that one of your people might be the person who pulled the trigger. It was that police inspector's gun, the man that Fiona

O'Dwyer claimed paid Bert to lie in court, that killed him. Why hasn't he been arrested?"

"No one will be arrested until we've finished our investigation," Witherspoon replied.

"What's there to investigate? It's obvious who killed him."

"Just because Inspector Nivens' gun was used to commit the murder doesn't mean he had anything to do with it." The inspector felt duty bound to defend a fellow officer, even one that he didn't like.

"I wasn't talkin' about him." She leaned forward, her eyes narrowed and her face flushed. "But there was someone else with even more reason. Someone who couldn't get it into her fat, thick head that Bert was just being kind."

"I'm sorry, I don't follow," Witherspoon admitted. "Who exactly do you mean?"

"I'm talking about that landlady of his. She was always throwin' herself at him and tryin' to pretend they was together. But they weren't. The only reason he put up with 'er silliness was because he didn't want to lose his room and he was a gentleman."

Barnes' eyebrows rose in surprise. "His landlady? You mean Frida Sorensen?"

"That's the only landlady he had. But she fancied she was more to him than just a landlady," she retorted, but the effect was lost as her eyes filled with tears. "If you two were any good at what you do, you'd know that, and she'd be under arrest. Everyone here heard her threaten him."

Both policemen stared at her for a moment. Finally, Witherspoon said, "Would you mind explaining that remark? Why should we have arrested Frida Sorensen?"

"Because she killed him." She swiped at her cheek as a tear escaped. "She thought he was in love with her when all he'd ever done was be nice to her. You shoulda seen her the night before he was killed—she come here rantin' and ravin', acting like some silly cow in a West End play. She threw a drink on him and told him she'd not be played about, that he'd made promises to her and if he didn't keep them, she'd make him sorry."

"This happened here? You actually saw it?" The constable wanted to be certain that she'd witnessed the event and not just heard the resulting gossip.

"Just before closin' on Sunday night." She took a long, deep breath and brought herself under control. "If you don't believe me, you can ask Jim. He was workin' that night, too, and told her to get out if she couldn't keep a civil tongue in her head. But she wouldn't leave, so Bert took her outside to try to calm her down, but it didn't do any good. She was screamin' at him loud enough to wake the dead."

"Is Jim here now?" Barnes rose to his feet.

She pointed to a door on the far side of the bar. "He's in the storeroom. You go ask him—he'll tell you." She turned her attention back to Witherspoon. "I know everyone thinks one of the O'Dwyers' friends done it, but it was Frida. You go and ask her where she was when he was killed—just ask her, make her prove she didn't do it."

It had started to sprinkle when the inspector and Barnes came out of the Thistle and Thorn. "Jim Reynolds confirmed what Mrs. Miller told us," Barnes said. "Apparently, Frida Sorensen did threaten Santorini, and even from outside the pub, everyone could hear her."

"At least we know she was telling the truth," Witherspoon murmured.

"Where to now, sir?" Barnes glanced up at the sky and frowned. "Those clouds are black as a widow's veil—looks like a storm is coming."

"And neither of us has an umbrella." The inspector turned up the collar of his overcoat and then pointed toward the busy corner. "There's a fixed-point constable. Let's ask him where Tilson's might be. We need to have a word with Philip Graves."

The fixed-point constable knew exactly where the hostel was located and even flagged down a hansom for them. Stepping inside, Witherspoon took his seat while Barnes gave the driver the address. By time the constable joined him, the rain was beating hard against the roof of the cab.

"What did you think of Alberta Miller?" Witherspoon asked. Despite his lovely relationship with his dear Ruth, the truth was, his general knowledge of women was somewhat limited, and he genuinely wanted to know what the constable thought.

"Mrs. Miller and Santorini weren't friends, Inspector." Barnes braced himself as the cab swung around the corner. "She was in love with him, and I'd bet my next week's pay that she hated Frida Sorensen."

"That was my impression as well," Witherspoon said. "But if Alberta Miller loved Santorini, why would she have killed him?"

"Jealousy." He shrugged. "That's been a motive for many a murder, sir. She might have feared that Santorini was going to throw her over and marry Frida. After all, Alberta Miller is a barmaid while Frida Sorensen owns a lodging house, and it sounds as if Santorini was the sort of person who looked out for himself first and foremost. But I think the most important thing we ought to find out is why Mrs. Sorensen acted like Santorini was just one of her lodgers."

"Indeed, that's precisely how she behaved. I wonder why. Both she and Santorini were adults and both of them legally unattached to anyone else." Witherspoon pursed his lips. "If we've enough time after we speak to Philip Graves, let's drop by the lodging house again. We'll have another word with Frida Sorensen. Don't you think this case is odd, Constable?"

"In what way, sir?"

"For once, we've a number of suspects. Yet I find it difficult to see how any of them could have got Inspector Nivens' gun."

"His house was empty, according to Nivens. Someone must have broken in and stolen it."

"But how would the killer have known the gun was there in his study?" Witherspoon pointed out. "And how would any of them have known where Inspector Nivens lives?"

Barnes thought about it for a moment. "He had the gun case in the Crying Crows Pub and from what we've heard, he wasn't shy about bragging about the weapons. He also had them at the station and policemen are just like anyone else—they talk to their families and friends. Someone might have mentioned it in passing; perhaps even the gunsmith talked about them. There's any number of ways the killer could have found out about the gun."

"That's true, but how would the killer have known where Inspector Nivens lives? And that his house was going to be empty?"

"Perhaps he or she followed Nivens. It wouldn't be hard, sir, not if someone was deliberately trying to make it appear that Nivens was the killer."

"You think that's possible?" Witherspoon looked doubtful. "Why go to all that trouble?"

"Simple, sir. If the killer points the finger at someone else, no one will look at him or her," Barnes replied. "Nivens had a weapon that was seen by a number of people—that fact in and of itself could be the reason he ended up our main suspect. If he's innocent, it could well be that he was simply the easiest person to frame for the murder. What's more, even in this part of London, guns aren't common, and if you can get your hands on one, it's very expensive."

The cab slowed and pulled to a stop. Barnes got out first, held the door open for Witherspoon, and then paid the driver. When he rejoined the inspector, he said, "Mind you, sir, there could be another reason that Nivens' gun was used. It could be that someone around here has a reason for wanting Inspector Nivens out of the way. He has the sort of character that makes enemies. Maybe the killer saw this as a way of getting rid of two problems at one time."

"That's an interesting idea, Constable." Witherspoon sighed wearily. "But we'd have the very devil of a time proving it. Is this the men's hostel?"

They stood in front of a narrow, four-story building so covered in soot it was impossible to determine what color the bricks had originally been. The sign over the front door read, TILSON'S HOTEL FOR WORKINGMEN.

They climbed the three wide stairs to the front door. Barnes used his fist to bang on the wood. He waited a few moments, and when no one answered, he banged again.

"Just walk in." A bearded man with longish, stringy hair and dressed in an oversized brown duster stepped between them, turned the knob, and walked inside. They followed him and found themselves in a dimly lighted foyer that smelled of carbolic soap. There was a sign on the wall that read NO SWEARING, NO SMOKING, NO FIGHTING, and bed rent must be paid every Friday by six p.m. for weekly and five p.m. for daily tenants. Below that was another sign that read BEDS 6P PER NIGHT. LIGHTS GO OUT AT 10 P.M. SHARP.

NO EXCEPTIONS. Opposite the wall, an old man wearing a once-white shirt beneath a thin black overcoat stood behind a counter. "Can I 'elp ya? I'm the evening superintendent. You two from the council?"

"No, we're the police," Barnes explained. "Do you have a tenant here named Philip Graves?"

"Oh, yeah. Graves 'as just come in. He's downstairs in the kitchen, fixin' his supper." The old man pointed to his left. "The stairs are just there."

The kitchen was a far cry from anything found in a home. The wooden floor was scratched and dented but clean. The smell of cabbage, meat pies, fish, and old sweat filled the air. Two cookers and a fireplace stood at one end of the room, and on the opposite side were two large double sinks. In between there were four rows of long tables and benches. Men milled about, some of them sitting at the tables and eating, and others either at the cookers or sitting at the closest table and waiting their turn.

Barnes stepped over to a young man eating a plate of fried bread. "Can you point out Philip Graves?"

"That's him there." He pointed to a dark-haired man sitting by himself at a table nearest the sinks.

"Thank you," Barnes murmured as he and Witherspoon moved across the large room. Graves looked up as they approached. In front of him was a mug of tea and a plate with a half-eaten cold meat pie and a hunk of cheese.

"Philip Graves?" Barnes asked.

"That's me." He had a pockmarked face and an expression hardened by three years in Pentonville. His face was long and narrow, with thin lips topped by a mustache and blue eyes that studied the two policemen warily. "What do ya want?"

"What do you think?" Barnes sat down across from him and Witherspoon quickly did the same. "Come on, now, let's not play games. You know why we're here."

Graves pushed his plate to one side. "I've lost me appetite. But then again, coppers will do that to a fellow."

"Mr. Graves, we're here about the murder of Humberto Santorini," Witherspoon began.

"What's that got to do with me? I didn't kill the bastard." He picked up his mug and took a sip.

"We know that you hated Santorini and that you were looking for him a few days before he was killed," Barnes said. "You were turfed out of the Crying Crows after harassing the barman for information about Santorini."

"Yeah." Graves grinned and put down his tea. "I was. So what? I might 'ave hated him, but I didn't kill him. From what I hear, one of you lot did that."

"Where were you on Monday evening between half past five and a quarter to six?" Barnes persisted.

"Walkin' here."

"From where?" Witherspoon asked.

"From the Commercial Road. I do deliveries for Royston's."

"The metalworks?" The constable took out his notebook and pencil.

"That's right, and on Monday evening, I finished my last run just after half past four—it was a load of screws to a factory over by Liverpool Street Station—and then I took the rig back to the stable. If you don't believe me, you can check with Royston's. They'll show you my time sheet and they'll have a copy of the delivery receipt."

"You went back to Royston's after turning the rig in?" Barnes stopped writing and looked at him.

"I had to give them the delivery chit, didn't I? Otherwise they'd not pay what they owed me. By the time I got it turned in, it was past five, so I stopped at Kerrigan's to buy a pastie for my dinner and came on here." He glanced around the room, his expression glum. "It's not much, but right now, it's home. Anything else?"

"Mr. Graves, we understand that you blamed Santorini for your, er, incarceration," Witherspoon said.

"I did. He set me up so he could get me horse and cart. He told that stupid cow that owns the Crying Crows that I 'elped myself to her cash drawer and stole ten quid. I never touched that cash. He took it. But she set the law on me, and I got three years in that hell-hole of a prison and he got my business."

Barnes eyed him speculatively. "That's a very long sentence for a rather small theft."

Graves flushed. "It weren't my first time. I'd been sent up once before."

"You'd been imprisoned previously?" Witherspoon asked. "For what?"

"I was accused of stealin' a toff's purse," he admitted. "Picking his pocket, so to speak."

"Were you sent to Pentonville?"

He shook his head. "No, the Scrubs."

"How long were you at Wormwood Scrubs?" Witherspoon asked.

"A year. At the time I thought it was the longest year of my life, so when I got out, I vowed I'd never go into a place like that again. But thanks to Santorini, I ended up somewhere even worse."

"How did you come to get the ice cart and the pony?" Barnes asked.

"From my uncle. He owned them, and he left 'em to me when he passed away," Graves explained. "I was makin' a good living, too, saving a bit of cash and thinkin' about emigrating to Australia or Canada. But then Santorini told his lies and I ended up in Pentonville."

"You must have hated him," Witherspoon said softly.

"I did, and I was happy when I heard he'd been shot. But I didn't kill him. If I'd done it, I wouldn't have used some fancy gun, I'd have used my bare hands."

By the time Inspector Witherspoon arrived home that evening, Mrs. Jeffries had spent several hours thinking about Bert Santorini's murder. But despite her best efforts, despite her analyzing what little information they had from every possible angle, she simply couldn't make heads or tails of it. The one conclusion she had reached was that she was sure Nigel Nivens was innocent.

She'd arrived at this deduction for one very simple reason: Nivens wouldn't have shown up at their back door unless he was desperate for help in proving his innocence. She agreed with everything Nivens had told them; mainly, that he was so loathed by practically everyone in the Metropolitan Police that they wouldn't work overly hard to prove his innocence. She disagreed with him about one very important point: Gerald Witherspoon wasn't like anyone else, and he would do *everything* in his power to catch the real killer.

She reached for the inspector's overcoat and hung it below his bowler. "I'm glad you're not too late tonight, sir. Mrs. Goodge has done a lovely Lancashire hot pot for your supper and an apple crumble for pudding."

"That sounds delightful. Do we have time for a sherry?" He started down the hallway.

"Of course, sir." She followed the inspector into his study, went to the liquor cabinet, and poured them both a drink.

"Here's your sherry, sir." Mrs. Jeffries handed Witherspoon his glass, took her own, and sat down.

"Thank you, Mrs. Jeffries. I don't mind admitting that I've looked forward to this all the way home." He took a sip. "The traffic was dreadful and it took ages to get across town."

"Did you come home by train?"

"We took a hansom cab," he replied. "We had a very busy day, and after we'd finished our last interview, we stopped back at Leman Street. By the time we finished up there, we'd missed the express train, and Constable Barnes wanted to pop into Ladbroke Road. But I'll tell you about that later."

"It sounds as if you're making progress on this case." She took a sip from her own glass.

He frowned thoughtfully. "I'd like to think we are, but frankly I'm not sure. We took statements from a number of people today, but I'm not certain that anything we heard will help us find Santorini's killer."

"Now, sir, you always feel that way at this point in a case and yet, you always solve it. Remember what I told you, sir. Your 'inner voice' is listening to every statement, assessing your suspects, and making certain you come up with the right answer." She could see he needed a boost to his self-confidence. Though he'd solved one homicide after another, he still had moments of terrible self-doubt.

He smiled gratefully. "You always say the right thing, Mrs. Jeffries. It's just that this is such an odd case that I am fearful that whoever killed Bert Santorini will get away with the crime."

"You don't think Inspector Nivens might have done it?"

"I don't." He sighed. "Yet I've no real reason for why I think he's innocent. He's someone who will bend the rules when it suits his purpose, but I don't think he's a murderer. Besides, there seems to be a number of people who had reason to hate the victim. To begin with, Susan Callahan, the owner of the Crying Crows Pub, disliked him intensely." He repeated everything Mrs. Callahan had told them about her association with Santorini.

"So this Mrs. Callahan had asked Santorini to leave because she caught him watering her liquor stock," Mrs. Jeffries murmured, "and she was afraid the brewery would catch wind of it and call in her loan?"

"That's right. She considered herself lucky that it was a customer and not a representative of the brewery who realized the liquor was being compromised. But the strangest thing that happened while we were there was someone heaved a huge stone at the pub door. It was quite disconcerting—" He broke off with a frown. "Oh dear, I've just remembered that it happened right when we asked Mrs. Callahan where she was at the time of the murder."

"I take it she didn't answer that question."

"Indeed, but we can easily rectify that mistake." He shrugged. "I suppose a huge stone hitting the door was a bit of a distraction. But as it wasn't the first time her pub was the target of vandals, we don't think it had anything to do with Santorini's murder." He continued with his narrative. When he'd finished, he took another sip and Mrs. Jeffries quickly asked a question.

"This man that she caught stealing from her, Philip Graves, he got three years in Pentonville for stealing ten pounds. That seems a very long sentence."

"There's a reason for that, and I'll get to that when I tell you about our meeting with Graves, but before we interviewed him, we

went to the Thistle and Thorn." He described the interview with
Alberta Miller. "She seemed quite put out that we asked where she
was at the time of the murder. Honestly, Mrs. Jeffries, it's a standard question, yet people always seem to be so offended."

"At least you should be able to determine if she's telling the
truth or not," Mrs. Jeffries pointed out. "If she was walking to
work that day, surely someone will have seen her. Was anyone at
the pub able to verify what time she arrived?"

"Constable Barnes asked the other staff member, and he said she
arrived a few minutes before half six."

"How old is Alberta Miller?"

Witherspoon tapped his finger against his chin. "I'm not very
good with estimating someone's age, but I'd say she was in her early
thirties."

"Was she attractive?"

Again, he thought before he answered. "Indeed, I'd say she was.
She wasn't the sort of beauty that would stop people in the street,
but she was quite pretty." He blushed slightly. "Of course, I'd never
say such a thing in front of my dear Ruth. I'd not want her getting
the wrong impression."

"No, of course you wouldn't, sir."

He looked at her curiously. "Why are you asking about her ap-
pearance?"

"Because, sir, from what you've told me, it sounds as if Mrs.
Miller and the victim were far more than friends."

"That's what Constable Barnes said. He thinks she was in love
with Santorini."

"And did he also think that jealousy could be the motive for
Santorini's murder?"

"He did, but I don't see how Alberta Miller could have got her

fingers on Inspector Nivens' weapon. How would she even have
known it existed? Nivens didn't patronize the Thistle and Thorn."

"Perhaps she found out some other way, sir? People talk in
pubs—perhaps she overheard a conversation. I'm not saying she
did such a thing; I'm only saying it's possible."

She had no idea if Alberta Miller had overheard anyone talking
about anything; she only wished to get the inspector thinking along
some different lines of inquiry.

"Yes, that's what Constable Barnes says. I suppose anything's
possible. Once we finished at the Thistle and Thorn, we interviewed Philip Graves." Witherspoon took another sip. "Graves
wasn't very cooperative at first, and that men's hostel where he lives
is positively dreadful, but nonetheless, it's a roof over one's head."
He told her the particulars of the interview, ending with Graves'
assertion that if he'd murdered Santorini, he'd have done it with his
bare hands.

"Gracious, sir. It appears as if half the East End had a reason to
want Bert Santorini dead."

"It does seem that way." He drained his glass. "Do we have
time for another one?"

She took his glass and rose to her feet. Her mind worked furiously as she crossed the study, refilled his drink, and topped off her
own glass. Susan Callahan's description of her relationship with
the victim didn't ring true. She thought it far more likely that the
woman let him stay because the two of them were romantically
involved. Tomorrow, she'd have a word with Constable Barnes and
get his opinion.

"Do you believe Philip Graves?" she asked as she handed the
inspector his sherry. She'd no idea why that had popped into her
mind, but nonetheless, she'd learned to trust her own "inner voice."

Witherspoon cocked his head to one side. "Actually, I do. There was something about him that made me think he was being truthful."

"And he did have a point about the access to Inspector Nivens' dueling pistol." She sat down again. "But, again, like Alberta Miller or even Frida Sorensen, he could easily have found out that information."

"And Nivens' house was empty the night before and the night of the murder. Graves was an admitted pickpocket, so it's quite possible that he also knew how to pick locks. I do believe both activities require one to be good with one's fingers."

Mrs. Jeffries nodded. "When do you think you'll be able to speak to Mrs. O'Dwyer?"

"Tomorrow. We simply didn't have time today. I know everyone thinks she has the most motive for wanting Santorini dead, but I'm not so certain about that." He gulped the rest of his sherry and stood up. "I'm starving. I'm so glad Mrs. Goodge cooked Lancashire hot pot. That's one of my favorites."

Mrs. Jeffries got up as well. She started to ask why Constable Barnes wanted to stop at Ladbroke Road and then decided she'd ask him herself tomorrow morning.

Betsy closed Amanda's bedroom door and went into the parlor. She stood in the open doorway and gazed at her home. The floor was covered with an oriental carpet in red, blue, and gold; the walls painted a pale blue; and the overstuffed sofa and chairs covered in a vibrant blue cotton. Blue and white striped curtains draped the windows; there was a hexagonal table with three matching chairs with embroidered, padded royal blue seats; and on the mantel over the white stone fireplace there were half a dozen photographs of her family in silver frames. She and Smythe could have afforded a much grander home, but compared to where she'd come from, this was the lap of luxury, and she was very, very content.

Smythe was in his overstuffed chair reading the newspaper. She moved into the room, closing the door quietly behind her. He put the paper down on the side table and smiled at his wife. "Do you want to tell me about what 'appened today? You were upset when you got to Upper Edmonton Gardens."

"I was." She crossed the room and sat down on the end of the sofa. "You were right: I should never have gone back to the East End. It brought back too many awful memories." She told him about her confrontation with Mattie and how she'd stormed out before learning everything she could and then walked for what seemed miles, forcing herself to visit every place that had been part of her life then. When she'd run out of words, she took a deep breath and slowly let it out. "I'm not going back there. Not for this case, not for any case. It's too hard."

"I know, love, I know." He reached across and patted her arm.

Her eyes filled with tears as she recalled the last place she'd gone. "I went to the cemetery, the one where my mum was buried. Dear Lord, Smythe, she was put in a pauper's grave. There's not even a rock or stone to mark where she was laid to rest, and when I'd got there, I'd no idea where she was. I couldn't find her. I couldn't remember the spot where they buried her. It looks so different now." She started crying in earnest, shoving her hand over her mouth to keep her sobs from waking up Amanda.

Smythe moved out of his chair and onto the sofa. He pulled her into his arms and held her, letting her cry it out. Finally, when the tears had stopped, she drew back, pulled a handkerchief out of her sleeve, and blew her nose. "I'm not sure what I'll tell the others, but I'll come up with something."

He stared at her for a moment. "Sweetheart, you should have told me that your mum's not having a proper grave was so upsettin' for you."

"I didn't know it was until today." She smiled awkwardly. "I had no idea that I'd react the way I did when I went back there. Once I got away from the East End, I suppose I pushed it out of my mind. But it all came back today. I remember never having enough to eat and in the winter we were always cold. That's what killed my baby sister—the cold getting into her lungs, drowning her so she couldn't breathe." She closed her eyes and shook her head. "That was horrible—it was all horrible—and the final horror was watching my mother waste away with that awful sickness."

"Don't think about it anymore, my love. Don't think about it. You're here now and I'm going to make sure you never go hungry or have to face anything like that again." He lifted her chin and kissed her lightly on the lips. "I'm glad you're not goin' back there again. It's too hard on you and it worries me 'alf sick."

"I'm sorry, my darling. I didn't do it to worry you—I just wanted to help. But there's plenty I can do without going back to White-chapel."

"Good. I'm glad you told me about your mum and her grave. We'll have her grave found and make sure she's properly buried."

"Smythe, that'll cost the earth."

"Don't be daft. You know good and well we can afford it. I came back from Australia a rich man and that was over ten years ago. We've made wise investments, and we've plenty of money. I'm sorry I didn't get to know your mum, and I'm sorry you didn't get to know mine. We didn't ask to be born poor—that's just the way it was. But we've enough now to buy ourselves comfort for our bodies and for our feelings. We'll get your mum a proper coffin, grave, and headstone."

"I don't even know where they put her," Betsy protested. "Like I said, it all looks different now."

"You let me worry about that," he promised. "I'll find her, and I'll handle everything."

Constable Barnes was a tad earlier than usual the next morning, but both Mrs. Jeffries and Mrs. Goodge were up and had the tea ready. They spent a good fifteen minutes discussing what the inspector and the constable had learned thus far.

Mrs. Jeffries looked at Barnes. "What did you really think of Susan Callahan's assertion that she only invited Santorini into the back room of her pub because she wanted protection?"

"I didn't believe it for a moment, but I didn't want to say anything to the inspector." Barnes grinned. "He's a bit naive when it comes to relationships between males and females. Mind you, I'm not just saying that Mrs. Callahan wasn't telling the truth. I had a quick word with one of the constables in Leman Street when the inspector and I stopped in to see if the postmortem report was ready. He said there *hadn't* been a series of break-ins in that part of Whitechapel at the time she invited Santorini into her back room. I think she was just a lonely widow."

"You think she had feelings for him?" Mrs. Goodge asked curiously.

Barnes glanced at Mrs. Jeffries. He knew that the "Mrs." in the cook's title was a courtesy and that the lady had never been married. He didn't want to be crude, but he thought it important to be as specific as possible. "Well, I'm not sure I'd say she had 'feelings' for the man, but I do think she liked being with him. According to what we've heard, Santorini was a handsome fellow."

Mrs. Goodge stared at him for a moment before she burst out laughing. "Gracious, Constable, you're being so very delicate, but at my age, you needn't bother. I may never have been married, but I do understand that some relationships between men and women are rather, how shall I put it, 'carnal' in nature. Is that what you're trying to say?"

"That's it exactly." He laughed.

"But you think Alberta Miller really was in love with him?" Mrs. Jeffries asked.

"She was far more emotional about his death than Mrs. Callahan appeared to be, so, yes, I think she genuinely cared about him. Mind you, that could mean we ought to take a closer look at her. Murder is often committed by people who profess to love each other. On the other hand, Susan Callahan simply seemed to see Santorini as someone who ended up being a mistake in judgment and a terrible nuisance." He glanced at the clock on the sideboard. "Time's getting on. Is there anything you need to tell me?"

"Not very much." Mrs. Jeffries told him what Smythe, Betsy, and Wiggins had discovered the previous day. "Unfortunately, you know most of this already, but I did think it prudent to repeat what they'd found out."

"What about that pickpocket Dickie Stiles?" Mrs. Goodge tapped her on the arm. "Luty said she'd found out that Santorini gave him a note on Saturday night. That might turn out to be important."

"Dickie Stiles?" Barnes frowned as he repeated the name.

"Luty's source said he was in the Thistle and Thorn on Saturday night and that Santorini had given Stiles a note," the cook explained. "The important thing to remember here is that Stiles was standing right beside Santorini, so the note must have been for someone else. Now I ask you, who do you think that note was for? None of the people you've interviewed have said he contacted them in that manner, so who was it for?"

"I've no idea," he admitted. "But we'll definitely have a word with Mr. Stiles. Mind you, considering that Santorini was playing about with more than one woman at a time, maybe he was sending it to one of his ladyloves?"

"The only way that makes sense is if he had a new lady that we don't know about," Mrs. Jeffries said. "He was at the Thistle and Thorn, so Alberta Miller was right there. Why send her a note? And he lived at Frida's lodging house, so why send her one?"

"You're being too practical, Hepzibah," Mrs. Goodge countered. "From the way you describe him, Bert Santorini was a philanderer, and the one thing they never want to do is anger one of their conquests, unless they're wanting to be rid of her. Santorini could easily have intended that note for Frida Sorensen. Perhaps he sent it with an excuse as to why he wasn't home that night. He might have realized she was beginning to suspect he was playing about with Alberta Miller and was hoping to throw her off the scent. After all, we know that on Sunday night, the night before his murder, Mrs. Sorensen confronted him at that very pub."

Mrs. Jeffries wasn't sure what surprised her the most, that the cook's analysis made sense or that she knew so much about how a philanderer behaved. "That's very possible," she finally said.

"Nonetheless, we'll have a word with this Dickie Stiles," Barnes said. "Let's just hope he knows how to read."

"And that he actually read the note," the cook added.

The constable chuckled. "Take my word for it, Mrs. Goodge. If he's a pickpocket, he read the ruddy note. They're not known for honor, honesty, or integrity."

CHAPTER 7

"Morning, sir, Barnes," John Rhodes called as Witherspoon and Barnes stepped inside the Leman Street Station.

"Good morning, Constable. Has the postmortem report arrived?" Witherspoon inquired as they crossed the short space to the counter.

"The messenger brought it a few minutes ago. The witness statements are here, too." Rhodes pushed a flat envelope and thin stack of papers across the reception counter.

"Excellent." Witherspoon picked them up and turned toward the duty inspector's office. "I'll go through the witness statements first. Someone must have seen something on Monday night."

Barnes glanced at Rhodes and smiled wryly. Rhodes merely raised an eyebrow, each man silently acknowledging what they both knew to be true. In this area of London, it was usually "See no evil, hear no evil, and speak no evil." But Barnes didn't want to depress the inspector, so he said, "I'll be right there, sir. I'd like to have a quick word with Constable Rhodes."

"Good idea. Perhaps he'll know where we can find Dickie Stiles." Witherspoon disappeared into the office.

"I know exactly where and *when* you can find the little rotter," Rhodes announced as Barnes turned back to him. "The Pig and Ale—that's on Newcomb Street. Dickie shows up there at a quarter to one every day. Stiles likes that pub because it's cheap and a bit dirty. None of us police frequent the place and Stiles, being a pickpocket, finds that adds to the charming character of the establishment."

"I'd forgotten what a wit you are, John." Barnes laughed and leaned against the counter. "Ta. That'll give us time this morning to interview Mrs. O'Dwyer."

"Good luck getting anything out of her," Rhodes warned. "She's convinced that Santorini lied on the stand. She'll not have any reason to help find his killer."

"I know, but we've got to try. I'd best get moving." He pushed away and started toward the corridor, stopped, and turned back to Rhodes. "John, have you ever been inside the Crying Crows Pub?"

"A time or two. Most of the men from here stop in for a pint or a whisky, but I like to go home when I get off work. The missus worries."

"But you've been there. Have you ever seen the owner, Susan Callahan?"

"Buxom, red-haired woman with thick spectacles?" Rhodes asked. He continued speaking when Barnes nodded. "I've seen her a time or two. Why?"

"I'm not sure how to put this, but she seems so familiar to me. Did she look familiar to you, too?"

"Really? Maybe I didn't look closely enough, but I didn't recognize her."

"I'm probably getting her mixed up with someone else." Barnes shrugged and resumed walking toward the duty inspector's office.

"Wait a minute," Rhodes called. "I just remembered something. Inspector Nivens asked me the same thing."

Barnes went back to the reception counter. "When was this?"

"A couple of weeks after he was assigned here. He asked me how long I'd been at this station, and I told him I'd been here for over twenty-five years, then he asked the same question: Did Mrs. Callahan look familiar to me?"

"Did he say that she looked familiar to him?" Barnes asked.

Rhodes thought for a moment. "I believe he did."

Barnes nodded and then thought of something else he needed to ask. "I know that Inspector Nivens isn't popular with the lads, but is there anyone here that he was close to, anyone he might have had a drink with?"

"The only person I've seen him with is one of the newer recruits. His name is Clyde Donner, and he's a bit of a bootlicker, if you know what I mean. I've heard that he goes to the Crying Crows with Nivens."

"Is he on duty now?"

"He's on fixed-point duty outside Whitechapel Station. But his shift ends at half past three, so he should be back here by four o'clock at the latest."

"Good, maybe we can have a word with him before he goes home. But if we miss him, can you tell him that we'd like to speak to him?"

"Will do," Rhodes said.

"Ta. I appreciate it. It's amazing how some things never change. Nivens is doing the same thing here as he's done everywhere else.

No one likes the man, but he always finds someone young and stupid to do his bidding."

"That would be Donner," Rhodes agreed. "Mind you, we were hoping to have a few days without Nivens' presence, but he's still showing up."

"Nivens comes into the station?"

"Not every day, but he's been here twice to get his post and water that stupid plant his mum gave him." Rhodes lowered his voice and leaned across the counter. "Seems his nibs is corresponding with a couple of detectives in New York and in Paris, and he's having their letters sent here."

"What on earth for?"

"What do you think? He's trying to impress everyone and hoping that someone will mention his initiative and foresight to the brass at the Yard. Nivens is desperate to prove he's a good detective and even more desperate to get away from here."

"And he thinks that will do it for him?" Barnes shook his head in disbelief. "He's just fooling himself. A batch of letters from overseas isn't going to get Nivens promoted. Maybe he should concentrate on doin' his job a bit better if he wants to move up in the force."

Rhodes laughed. "That'll be the last thing he thinks of doin'."

Barnes chuckled. "True. Thanks for everything, John."

"Before you go, I just remembered some gossip that might come in useful when you're talking to Mrs. O'Dwyer. It's just hearsay, bits and pieces, but, like I said, it might help to loosen her tongue a bit."

It took less than five minutes for Rhodes to pass along what he'd heard. Barnes listened carefully, thanked his old friend, and then went to the duty inspector's office to meet Witherspoon. The inspector looked up as the constable stepped into the room. "Sorry that took me so long, sir. Constable Rhodes wanted to pass along a few bits he'd heard."

"Not to worry. It took me ten minutes to find the Santorini file, and I wanted to make certain today's witness statements and the postmortem report gets added to it. I don't know why people won't put files away properly."

"Any luck with the witness statements, sir?"

Witherspoon pursed his lips. "Not as much as I'd hoped. Most of the witnesses claim they heard and saw nothing. But the constables did a very thorough job. They interviewed the shopkeepers and clerks near the mews, as well as several locals who were on the scene. One of these witnesses stated that he saw Harvey Macklin in the crowd that gathered when Santorini's pony and cart ran out of the mews."

"So that means Macklin was there." Barnes nodded. "And he was the one who had words with the victim outside the Thistle and Thorn."

"Let's see him right after we speak with Mrs. O'Dwyer."

"What about Dickie Stiles?"

"We can interview him tomorrow," Witherspoon replied.

"Did the reports say anything else that might prove useful?" Barnes asked.

"Not much—simply that none of the hansom cabdrivers in the area reported picking up or dropping a fare near the mews at the time Santorini was killed."

"That might mean the killer is a local," Barnes speculated. "Which would let Nivens off the hook. On the other hand, Nivens knows the neighborhood, and he wouldn't have been foolish enough to take a hansom. He'd have walked."

Witherspoon rose to his feet. "It's a puzzle, isn't it? But one which I'm sure we'll solve if we're given enough time."

Barnes' brows drew together. "What does that mean, sir?"

The inspector drew a telegram from his pocket. "This arrived while you were talking to Constable Rhodes. It's from Chief Superintendent Barrows—he wants to see us tomorrow morning."

"But we've only had the case for two days," the constable protested. "Surely he's not expecting us to have caught the killer this quickly."

From the coat tree in the corner Witherspoon grabbed his overcoat and put it on. "I sincerely hope that's not the reason we've been summoned, but what else could it be?" He looked at Barnes, his expression troubled. "Frankly, I'm worried about the situation. We both know there's no love lost between our chief superintendent and Inspector Nivens, but I won't be a party to an investigation that isn't completely thorough, and we're nowhere near that point as yet. We've not even interviewed Mrs. O'Dwyer."

"That's not our fault, sir. This has been a complicated case from the start, and we've had to cover a lot of territory in a very short time," Barnes pointed out. "But I don't think the chief superintendent would have us do anything untoward in the investigation. Despite his dislike of Nivens, he's a police officer first and foremost."

But Barnes wasn't as sure of that as he sounded. He knew that Barrows' political instincts were as finely honed as a surgeon's scalpel, and the chief superintendent might see this situation as a way of getting rid of Nivens once and for all.

"You're probably right, Constable." Witherspoon grabbed his

bowler. "It's just that this case is so very, very odd. Let's get cracking, then, and if we're lucky, Mrs. O'Dwyer will be home."

The O'Dwyer residence was on a short street between Whitechapel and Mile End. The houses were a cut above the rest of the neighborhood in that they were set back from the street a few feet with front doors that had a proper stoop. Witherspoon stopped in front of number 3. It was a two-story brown brick structure that was far enough away from the local factories to avoid being covered in soot. The door and the trim around the windows were painted white, and the brass knocker in the center was shined to a high gloss.

"Let's hope she's here," Barnes muttered as he banged the knocker against the wood.

The front door was yanked open, and a middle-aged woman stared at them sullenly.

She was short and stocky, with black hair streaked with gray, a thin mouth, and blue eyes. "What do you want?"

"Are you Mrs. O'Dwyer?" Witherspoon asked.

"I am, but I've nothing to say to any of you lot." She started to close the door, but Barnes flattened his hand against it.

"You can either speak to us here, or you can accompany us to the Leman Street Station," the constable snapped. "But one way or another, you're going to talk to us."

Her eyes narrowed, but she stepped back, opening the door. "Come in, then, and let's get this over with." She turned on her heel, leaving them to follow her. "Close the door behind you," she ordered.

They followed her down a short corridor, through a narrow doorway, and into the parlor. The walls were papered with pink roses against an apple green background. A dark gray horsehair settee with two matching armchairs was grouped around a small, unlighted fireplace above which hung a painting of the Virgin Mary. White lace curtains hung at the two windows and a faded burgundy rug covered the floor.

Mrs. O'Dwyer eased onto the settee, crossed her arms over her ample bosom, and eyed the two policemen suspiciously.

"May we sit down, Mrs. O'Dwyer?" Witherspoon asked politely. "It's quite damp today, and my knee is paining me."

She said nothing for a moment, then she finally nodded at one of the armchairs. "Go ahead, then." She looked at Barnes. "You might as well sit, too. But don't get too comfortable—you'll not be staying long."

"Thank you," the inspector said as he and Barnes took their seats. "We're here because—"

She interrupted him, leaning forward and uncrossing her arms. "Because someone did the world a favor and murdered that lying bastard Bert Santorini."

"Well, uh, yes," Witherspoon replied. "And, of course, considering your family's somewhat unfortunate connection to the victim, I'm sure you understand why we've come to speak to you."

"I didn't kill him." She laughed. "But I'll admit, there's a big part of me that wished I had. I didn't shed any tears when I heard what happened to him."

"Where were you on Monday evening?" Barnes asked. He'd taken out his notebook and propped it on the arm of the chair.

"What time?"

"About a quarter to six," Barnes said. For once, because of Santorini's horse bolting, they had a good idea of the time of death.

"I was here fixing supper for Molly—she's my daughter. Thanks to Santorini, she's the only one I've got left home."

"How old is your daughter?" Witherspoon asked.

"Sixteen."

"Where does she work?"

"She's an apprentice seamstress at McGinley's."

"What time did your daughter arrive home that day?" Barnes pressed.

"Same time she always came home, at half past six," she replied.

"So you were here, alone at a quarter to six, the time when Bert Santorini was being murdered in the Felix Mews," the constable clarified.

"I was home alone, yes." She smiled, revealing a set of remarkably white and even teeth.

"Do you blame Bert Santorini for your sons going to prison?" Witherspoon unbuttoned his coat.

"I do. The bastard lied on the witness stand and it was your copper"—she pointed a finger at the inspector—"that paid him to do it."

"That's a very serious charge."

"Not as serious as what he did," she snapped. "Nigel Nivens paid Santorini to lie, and they was sent away for five years, five bleeding years."

"You confronted Bert Santorini about this, didn't you?" Barnes interjected softly. He'd repeated the gossip he'd heard from Rhodes as he and the inspector had made their way here. "We have it on good authority that you tracked him down at the Strand Hotel when he was making his ice and flower deliveries and threatened him in front of half a dozen witnesses."

"Bloody right I did," she yelled. "He lied about my boys. I'm not saying they was driven snow, but they didn't rob that house and cosh that butler on the head. They'd never, ever do anything like that."

"According to Bert Santorini's testimony, he saw your son Seamus shifting several large pieces of silver service, the kind that had been stolen from the house in Mayfair, out of the back of a cart and bringing them into a house on Sidney Street, the home of a known fence," Witherspoon pointed out.

"He was lying, and when the coppers searched that house, they didn't find anything. What's more, when that stupid inspector searched here, the only thing he found was two sets of andirons that belong to my family and a piece of silverware that the police planted themselves." She snorted. "But the truth didn't make any difference, did it? That copper decided my boys was guilty, and when he couldn't prove it properly, he paid Santorini to lie about it."

"You threatened to kill Santorini," Witherspoon commented. "As the constable explained, you said it in front of witnesses."

"That's a bloody lie." Her eyes flashed with temper.

"Are you saying you didn't threaten him?" Barnes shot back.

"I threatened him alright, but not with murder. Did those same witnesses tell you that he threatened me?" She smiled when she saw the look the two policemen exchanged. "No one mentioned that, did they? But Santorini wasn't one to hold his temper or his tongue. He said if I kept telling everyone that he'd lied under oath because he'd been paid by the police, he'd make sure I lost my Molly. He knew where she worked and that she was only sixteen. He threatened me daughter."

"That sounds to me like all the more reason to want him dead," Barnes pointed out.

"It was," she agreed. "But wanting him dead and killing him is two different things, and I'd not have that kind of sin on my conscience. When I had words with him, I told him I'd prove he lied on the witness stand if it was the last thing I did. I didn't say I'd kill him."

"Is there anyone who can verify that you were here on Monday evening?" Witherspoon asked. "A neighbor, perhaps?"

"I didn't speak to any of my neighbors that night. I was cookin' potatoes and cabbage along with a bit of pork belly for our supper," she said.

"Felix Mews is less than half a mile away. You could easily have gone to the mews, shot him, and then got home before your daughter," Barnes said.

"I could have, but I didn't." She stared at him. "And you're forgetting one important thing."

"What's that?"

"How would I have got my hands on that copper's fancy dueling pistol?" She smiled as she spoke, delighted to be pointing out something they ought to have thought of themselves. "That's what killed him, wasn't it? At least that's what all the newspapers are saying."

"Inspector Nivens' house was empty on the nights before the murder," Barnes answered calmly. "Both he and his housekeeper were away."

"So?" She crossed her arms again. "What's that got to do with me?"

"Someone could have easily broken into his home and stolen the gun," he explained.

"How the devil would someone like me know where Nivens lived? I was here on Sunday night, not out breaking into houses."

"Will your daughter verify that you were here all evening?" Witherspoon asked quickly.

"She would if she were here, but when Santorini threatened her, I made her quit her job and sent her to Dublin to stay with my brother. I put her on the first train to Liverpool on Tuesday mornin' and from there she caught the ferry to Ireland. I wasn't having the likes of that lecherous blackguard get his hands on her. I wouldn't have bothered sending her off if I'd known someone had killed him Monday night, but I didn't, did I? But now that he's dead, she's coming home. But she can't tell you anything. She was at work until six Monday night."

"Do you know a man named Jonny Breams?" The constable watched her face as he spoke. But her expression remained calm.

"Everyone 'round these parts knows Jonny."

"So you've met him?" Barnes pressed.

"My boys know him, and he's been here at the house."

"Then you know he's been in prison for housebreaking," Barnes continued. "As a matter of fact, he's supposed to be able to pick any lock, no matter how difficult."

"Have you gone daft?" She snorted. "Jonny's not aged well. He's only in his forties, but his hands are so crippled with the arthritis that he can barely lift a pint, much less pick a decent lock."

"True. But from what I've heard, Jonny's passed along his skills to his cousin Wally. I've also heard that Wally Breams and your lads were close friends. He's also sweet on your Molly, isn't he?" Barnes was suddenly very grateful for the gossip that he'd heard from Rhodes.

Her eyes widened in surprise. "Eh, where'd you hear something like that? She's only sixteen, for God's sake. My Molly's a good girl—she keeps herself right and proper."

"I'm sure she does," Witherspoon interjected smoothly. "When is Miss Molly coming back from Ireland?"

"Next week." She gave the constable a good glare and then turned her attention to the inspector. "She'll be home on Tuesday.

You can talk to her if you like, but, as I said, she'll not know anything about this. But go ahead, waste your time—that's the only
thing the police are good for."

Phyllis tried to make herself invisible as she stood at the end of the
bar. Compared to most of the pubs in the East End, the Crying
Crows was quite grand, but she felt very much out of place. When
she'd first arrived, the place had been crowded with lunchtime business: shipping clerks, bank tellers, a few rough sorts that looked
like they'd come from the docks, and a number of decently dressed
women that Phyllis assumed were local typists or shopgirls. It had
been so busy that it had taken a good fifteen minutes for the barmaid to take her order. But try as she might, she'd not been able to
engage anyone in conversation. Phyllis looked around, annoyed
with herself for missing her chance. The lunch hour was over, and
the place had emptied rapidly. Soon, it would be closing for the
afternoon.

The men left standing at the bar or sitting at the tables looked
rough and were giving her the kind of perusal that was just short
of insulting. Not that she was the only woman in the place, but the
other two, both of whom were sitting at one of the tables, had the
easy air of locals.

She picked up her whisky and took a sip, forcing herself not to
wince as the harsh liquid hit the back of her throat. She'd tried to
order a gin—she could at least choke that down—but the barmaid
had said they were out of that particular brew. She'd been in the
ruddy place for what seemed hours now and hadn't learned a single
thing. But that was her own fault. She'd let some of Wiggins' dire
warnings bother her, and once she'd arrived here, she'd been too
scared to do anything but make a few halfhearted attempts at con-

versation with the women standing on each side of her at the bar. That hadn't gone well at all. Even when the barmaid had taken her order, she'd been abrupt and unsmiling. It was almost as if everyone knew she was an outsider.

A red-haired, middle-aged woman wearing spectacles stepped out from a doorway behind the bar. She surveyed the room and then frowned at the barmaid. "For God's sake, can't you do anything right? If I've told you once, Janice, I've told you a hundred times to start doin' the cash before you call last orders."

"Sorry, Mrs. Callahan," the girl said. She shoved a lock of brown hair that had slipped from her topknot out of her eyes. "But we got busy and Alex isn't here and I've not had a chance—"

"I don't want to hear your excuses, girl. Just get the ruddy money ready, clean up, and take yourself off. Thank God, Alex will be here this evening." She turned and stomped back the way she'd come.

"Yes, ma'am."

Phyllis quickly looked away but not before she saw Janice's eyes flood with tears. She knew exactly how the girl felt. She knew exactly what it was like to be publicly scolded and humiliated. It used to happen to her on a regular basis before she'd found the position at the Witherspoon house.

She pushed her whisky to one side as the memories flooded back. Mrs. Bolton, her first mistress, had never had a kind word to say. The miserable woman did nothing but criticize and had delighted in pointing out Phyllis' shortcomings in front of the other servants. Yes, she knew how Janice felt, alright. The poor girl had been run off her feet, pouring last orders and trying to clean up as she went, but instead of coming in and lending a hand, her mistress had humiliated and demeaned someone who was doing her best.

"Come on, drink up, everyone," Janice shouted.

Phyllis picked up her glass and pretended to take another drink. This might be her chance. She glanced around the pub and noted that Janice had done a good job of tidying the tables and the bar. Yes, this might be the only way she'd find out anything in time for this afternoon's meeting. She put the glass down and hurried outside. Crossing the road, she eased back into a doorway and waited. One by one, the other customers filed out, some of them weaving a bit but most of them going back to work.

She'd almost given up when the door opened a last time, and Janice, wearing a jacket that had seen better days, stepped outside. Phyllis gave her a head start and then followed her. She caught up with her at the corner. "Excuse me, miss. May I speak with you?" Phyllis had decided the direct approach would be best.

Janice stopped and turned to face her. The tears she'd barely held back now poured down her thin cheeks. She sniffed and swiped at her face. "What do you want? Wait—you were just in the pub, weren't you?"

"I was." Phyllis hesitated, her sympathy for the young woman overcoming her need for answers. "And I heard the way that lady spoke to you. It was terrible. I saw how hard you were working, and she had no right to treat you that way. I just wanted to tell you that."

Janice stared at her for a long moment, then she shrugged and gave a tremulous smile. "Ta. That's kind of you. Most people wouldn't have bothered. I guess I should be used to it, but I'm not."

"I never got used to it, either," Phyllis admitted. "May I buy you a cup of tea? I could use one."

"But you just bought a whisky, which you didn't drink." Janice looked at her curiously. "You made of money?"

"No, but I would like a cup of tea to get the taste of the liquor out of my mouth."

Janice shrugged. "Alright. There's a café up the road. It's not fancy, but it's clean."

A few minutes later, they were sitting at the window of a small establishment that had all of three tables and a long counter. The floor was scarred linoleum, the chairs rickety, and the customers workingmen and -women, many of them street vendors, who popped in to warm themselves against the damp.

"My name is Isabella Morgan," Phyllis said. The name was one she'd used before and she rather liked it. She'd given up on finding out anything useful about the case and had decided to take a few minutes to cheer up someone who hadn't been lucky enough to find employment with decent people. Watching how Janice was treated had brought back painful memories of her own life, a life that could have easily seen her in even worse circumstances than this young woman's. "You're Janice, right?"

"Janice Everly. So why were you in the pub? It certainly wasn't to drink. You barely touched that whisky."

Phyllis had a fast, silent debate on how much to reveal and then realized that, as she'd used a false name, it wouldn't hurt to tell a little of the truth. "I was there because I was looking for information. I'm what you could call a private inquiry agent."

"But you're a woman," Janice protested.

"Which sometimes gives me an advantage." Phyllis took a sip of tea and then put her cup down. "The world is changing, and these days, women can do more than just be a governess or a teacher. But let's not talk about me—the case I'm working on is almost over, and I realized once I got inside the pub that there was naught to be found there."

"What kind of a case was it?" Janice stared at her, her expression a bit suspicious.

"A missing person—well actually, a missing husband," Phyllis lied. "I'm not really allowed to say too much." She leaned forward and lowered her voice. "But just between you and me, I think the husband doesn't want to be found, if you know what I mean."

Janice giggled. "Your job sounds more exciting than mine."

"Oh, I wouldn't say that. But working at a pub must be interesting. I'll bet you meet all sorts of people. Now tell me, how did you end up at the Crying Crows?"

"There's not much to tell, really. Alex Parker—he's the barman—is my cousin, and he knew I needed work so he got me the position. It was good of him, but now I'm worried that if she keeps on at me and I end up getting the sack, she'll toss him out as well." She picked up her cup, cradling it in both her hands. "Though it won't be so hard on him; he seems to have plenty of extra money these days. Still, he did get me the job and I'd not like to see him out of work."

"She'd sack you just because the pub got busy and you didn't have time to do whatever it was she was shouting about?"

Janice shook her head. "No, it's not that. She screams all the time. Oh God, I don't know what I'm goin' to do. It's a right mess, and it's all my fault. I wish to God I'd never stuck my nose into that stupid storage room."

"What happened?" Phyllis asked gently.

"I can't tell ya, I can't tell anyone—you'll think me a thief and I'm not. I'm not." Janice kept her voice low but didn't look up.

"I won't think you're a thief," Phyllis said softly. "Because if you were, you'd not be in such a state now. You wouldn't care. Come on, then, get it off your shoulders. You'll never see me again, so whatever it was, your words will be safe with me."

"You promise?"

"I do," Phyllis agreed.

Janice finally raised her head. "It was this past Sunday, just after morning closing, and I was taking the last of the cleaning rags out to the laundry basket by the back door. When I got to the hall, I saw that the door to the storage room, the small one that Mrs. Callahan uses, was ajar. I've always been curious. I mean, she's so secretive that it's only natural to wonder why she keeps everything under lock and key. So I had a peek inside. Everything was covered in dust. It looked like no one had been in there for years. I started to leave, then I saw an overcoat hanging on a peg. It was dusty as well, and I thought it had probably belonged to Mr. Callahan."

"Mr. Callahan?"

"Mrs. Callahan's late husband—he's been dead for years." She snorted slightly. "Probably died to get away from her. I don't know what came over me; it's just that we've so little money, and I knew that coat might fit my grandfather. His is so thin, he can't even go out on some days when it's too cold. So I went over to have a closer look at it. I was thinkin' I might ask her if I could buy it off of her, you know, for a reasonable sum, something not too dear. Anyway, it was a right nice coat, still thick and wearable. I checked the pockets, and there was a really decent set of leather gloves. I pulled them out to have a closer look and then I heard the upstairs door open, the door to her flat, and I knew if she caught me, she'd sack me on the spot."

"Really? Just because you were in an old storage room?"

"*Her* storage room and I've just told you, she's very sensitive

and particular about her privacy," Janice said. "She doesn't like
answering questions, and no one that works for her has ever seen
the inside of her flat. If you have to go up there, she'll make you
stand on the landing until she comes out to see what you want. I
tell you, she's a strange one. Look at how she treated Bert Santorini. They was right close, so close that everyone thought they were
goin' to tie the knot. But she caught him cadgin' a bit of liquor and
tossed him out on his ear. What's more, I don't think she really
caught him doin' that. I think she was angry about something else
and lookin' for an excuse to be shut of him."

"Why do you think that?" Phyllis asked, taking care to make
the question as casual as possible. But this was the first mention of
Santorini, and she wasn't going to ignore her chance to find out
something useful.

"Because Bert liked wine, not whisky or beer. She kept a bottle
of decent red wine behind the counter when he was livin' in that
lower room. If you ask me, I think she found out he was messin'
about with Alberta Miller, the widow that works at the Thistle and
Thorn, or she had some other reason to want to be rid of him."
Janice sighed. "But as I was sayin', there I was in the storage room,
holdin' them gloves, and the only thing I could think to do was
make a run for it before she got downstairs."

"Did it work?"

"Barely. I made it to the back door of the pub just as she come
downstairs, and I stuffed the gloves in me pocket. Then I saw her
yank the storage room door shut and lock it."

"So why are you frightened she'll sack you?" Phyllis thought it
a reasonable question.

"Because of the gloves. I took 'em and now I can't get in there
to get them back in the pocket of that ruddy coat." She closed her

eyes and sighed heavily. "What am I goin' to do? Once she finds them gloves gone, it's over for me and Alex. She's a hard one, is Mrs. Callahan."

Phyllis took another sip of tea. She didn't believe in giving false hope, but really, the poor girl was worrying about nothing. Still, she understood: When you were terrified you were going to lose your job, thinking clearly could be difficult. "I think you're worrying about nothing. First of all, how will she know you were ever in the room? Second, why would she bother to check the pockets of an old coat; and third, even if she discovers them gone, why would she think you took them?"

Janice's eyebrows drew together. "I'd not thought of it like that." Her face cleared and she smiled. "Good Lord, you're right— she's no idea I was in the room. If she did, she'd have already sacked me. Mind you, I do hope she doesn't go back in for a few months. That should be long enough to cover any footprints I might have left."

Phyllis laughed. "Footprints—goodness, that floor must have been really dusty."

"It was. That room hadn't been opened in years, probably since Mr. Callahan died. There were streak lines on the floor where Mrs. Callahan had drug out an old trunk. She'd pulled it across the room and then shoved it back. When I went inside, I walked on the lines, but when I heard her flat door open, I wasn't as careful. I just ran out of there, and I might have smudged into the dust on the floor."

"I shouldn't worry about that." Phyllis took a sip of her tea. "Even if she goes in again, all she'll see is a smear off one of the streaks, and she'll probably assume she made it herself."

"I hope so. Mind you, at least now I've satisfied my curiosity. I once asked Alex what she kept in there, and he said that when her husband died, she made him carry some of Mr. Callahan's clothes down there. It was mainly old stuff she couldn't sell. Alex said that when Mr. Callahan died, she started selling everything the old man owned." She frowned. "I wonder why she didn't sell the coat. It's a nice one."

"Maybe she was sentimental about it," Phyllis suggested.

"I doubt that." Janice looked disapproving. "You're talking about a woman who tossed her widow's weeds in a trunk the day after her husband's funeral. I know that for a fact, because Alex saw her do it when he was carrying down poor Mr. Callahan's chamber pot. The only reason she didn't sell the pot was because it was cracked."

"Why didn't she throw it away?" Phyllis mused.

"She doesn't like throwing things away," Janice replied. "She's an odd one, she is. But, then again, she's a woman facin' the world alone, so I expect she keeps her life private so people won't try to take advantage of her."

"You mean like this Bert Santorini did?"

"Exactly. She felt like he'd played her for a fool, and she isn't one to take that sort of thing lightly."

"Would she have been angry enough about it to have killed him?" Phyllis asked. "I mean, after all, the man was shot."

Janice looked surprised by the question. "I doubt it. It happened six months ago. But she didn't let him get off easy, either. She told everyone that he was a thief and that she'd banned him from stepping inside her pub."

"I see," Phyllis murmured. She wished she could think of something else to ask, something that might actually be useful in solving this case, but if Santorini hadn't been inside the pub in months, there wasn't anything else for Janice to tell her.

Once again Witherspoon and Barnes found themselves at Frida Sorensen's lodging house, but this time, Frida was nowhere to be found.

"Sorry, but she's gone." The voice belonged to an older middle-aged man with reddish-brown thinning hair, a long face, and the palest complexion Barnes had ever seen outside of prison.

"She didn't say when she'd be back." The man started to close the door, but the constable blocked it by shoving his arm against the wood. "And who might you be?"

"I'm one of her lodgers." Again, he tried to close the door and again, Barnes pushed hard against the wood.

"What's your name, sir?" the constable asked.

"Harvey Macklin."

"Good. If we can't see Mrs. Sorensen, then you'll do. We've been wanting to speak to you."

Macklin's long face seemed to grow even longer. "What for? I've got nothin' to do with you coppers."

"Oh, but you do, sir," Witherspoon said quickly. "We understand you had a terrible disagreement with Bert Santorini a few days before he was murdered. We'd like to speak to you about the incident."

Macklin eyed them speculatively and then stepped back, holding the door wide. "Alright. Come in, then. We don't need to have our chat out here in front of God and everybody. Frida lets us use the parlor, so come inside."

They followed him and when they were all seated, Witherspoon said, "Mr. Macklin, we have it on good authority that you and the victim had a dreadful argument a few days prior to the murder."

"I wasn't the only one who quarreled with him," he insisted. "Most people who knew Santorini ended up squabblin' with him. He was that kind of person, always swaggerin' about and tryin' to bully people."

"What was the reason for your dispute with Santorini?" Barnes asked. He knew what it was, as Wiggins had told Mrs. Jeffries, who'd passed the information to him. But he needed the inspector to hear it.

"If you know we had a dustup, you must know what it was about." Macklin's cheeks turned red as he blushed. "It was about Frida. Santorini moved in here after he'd been turfed out of the Crying Crows and started sweet-talkin' Frida. I told him that Frida and I had an understanding and that she weren't for him. But that didn't matter to a man like Santorini. He started workin' on her, sweet-talking her and bringing her flowers. Before I knew it, I'd been tossed out of my room and given a miserable one at the top of the attic, and she'd raised my rent, while he had moved in and taken over."

"Surely if you'd genuinely had an 'understanding' with Mrs. Sorensen, that wouldn't have happened," Barnes pointed out. He was deliberately trying to rile the fellow; lots of information comes out when people lose control of their tempers and their tongues.

"That's not true," Macklin cried. "We was goin' to get married as soon as Mr. Stanton gave me a raise in my wages. I told Santorini we were almost engaged, but he just laughed at me and said that if I couldn't hang on to my woman, I wasn't much of a man. I'll not be spoken to like that, and I told him so to his face."

"Did the dispute between you and Santorini end in a physical confrontation?" Witherspoon asked.

"Huh?"

"Did anyone throw a punch?" Barnes stopped writing and glanced up. "Did you use your fists to get your point across?"

Macklin shook his head. "Nah. Santorini took off like the coward he was—told everyone he had deliveries to make, but he was just tryin' to hang on to a bit of pride."

Barnes glanced at Witherspoon. From the skeptical expression on his face, Barnes could tell that the inspector didn't believe that Santorini was the least bit scared of someone like Macklin. The constable didn't believe it, either. "Where were you on Monday evening?"

"Comin' home from work. I work at Stanton's, just off the Commercial Road."

"What time does the shop close?" Witherspoon asked.

"Five o'clock."

"Do you walk home?" Barnes asked.

"Most nights. Sometimes I stop in for a pint at the Crying Crows or the Pig and Ale, but that evening I come straight home."

"Do you come along the Commercial Road?" Barnes kept writing as he spoke. "That would be the fastest way here."

"Usually, but sometimes I don't," Macklin admitted. "Santorini was killed on Monday evening, and that night, I went along Lower Chapman Street. I had nuthin' to do with Santorini's murder. I didn't like the bloke, but I'm not a killer."

"But you threatened him with physical bodily harm," Witherspoon reminded him. "We've spoken to several witnesses, and they all say the same. What's more, if you were walking home, you'd have gone right past Felix Mews about the time the murder was committed."

"That's stupid." Macklin leapt to his feet. "I didn't do anything,

I tell ya, nuthin'. I hated him, but I'm no killer and accordin' to the newspapers, Santorini was murdered with that copper's gun. How would I have gotten my hands on that thing? Huh, tell me that if you two are so smart."

"Sit down, Mr. Macklin," Witherspoon said calmly. "We're not accusing you of anything at the moment, merely trying to establish the facts of the case."

Macklin stared at them belligerently but sat back down.

"You work at Stanton's, right?" Barnes stared him directly in the eye. "And if I'm not mistaken, that's a locksmith."

The blood drained out of Macklin's face. "So? I work for a locksmith, so what? I'm not one myself—I just run the shop while Mr. Stanton does the rest."

"How long have you worked there?"

"Five years."

Barnes smiled slightly. "And in five years, I'm sure you've picked up a few pointers on how to open a locked door."

Macklin's mouth dropped open. "What locked door? I don't know what you're on about!"

"Inspector Nigel Nivens' home," Witherspoon said. "From what we understand, the inspector brought the dueling pistols into the Crying Crows, and we know for a fact that you were there that night." This wasn't exactly true. No one had said Macklin was there when Nivens had brought in the dueling pistols, but the inspector was hoping that Macklin wouldn't recall precisely when he'd last been there. "As a matter of fact," he continued, "you generally went into the Crying Crows because you knew you'd never run into Santorini there. He wasn't allowed inside that pub."

"Just because I was there doesn't mean I knew anything about that copper's gun," Macklin cried. "He'd not be chattin' with the likes of me, now would he?"

"Inspector Nivens is a bit of a braggart," Barnes put in quickly. "And from what we've heard, he was flashin' those pistols about and showing them off. Since you were there that night, you'd know that not only did Inspector Nivens have a weapon but that he was also going to be absent from his own home on the night prior to Santorini's murder. A night when someone clever could pick a lock and steal a gun. That would be an easy way to rid yourself of your rival. A quick stop in the Felix Mews on your way home, and with one shot, your problems were over."

"That's daft, I tell ya, daft," Macklin shouted. "You're wrong. Dead wrong. I've nothing to do with a murder. How would I know that the copper wasn't going to be home?"

"You'd know because on Friday and Saturday night, Nivens complained to several people in the pub about having to take care of his mother's home starting on Sunday night; therefore, his own house would be empty," Witherspoon explained. Again, he didn't know if Macklin overheard Nivens complaining, but it was certainly possible. Two of the lads from Leman Street, Constables Farrow and Blackstone, had both reported that they'd overheard Nivens grumbling about doing his mother this favor. As neither officer was sitting with Nivens, Witherspoon was fairly certain he'd been carping loudly enough for half the pub to overhear.

"You're out of your mind." Macklin shook his head in disbelief. "How would I know where he lived? Yes, I'll admit I was in the Crying Crows on both those nights, but that copper was across the room, and I'd no idea he had them guns with him."

"But you admit you were there."

"So what? I was standin' on my own at the back of the pub drinkin' a pint. The place was so crowded I had to lean against the wall. That policeman was sittin' up front with another copper, and I couldn't see anything, least of all that he had a set of pistols with him."

"But you knew he was there, right?" Barnes pressed. "You'd seen him?"

"I'd seen him when I went to the bar to get my pint. Everyone knew who he was—he wasn't shy about lettin' you know he was a ruddy police inspector. But that means nothing. Even if I'd seen he had a gun, how would I have known where he lived?"

"You could have followed him," Barnes said. "That sounds easy enough."

"Why are you doin' this? I've nothin' to do with Santorini's murder." He leapt up again and began to pace. "You're both just tryin' to protect that copper—that's why you're sayin' all this. But it's a lie, I tell ya, a ruddy lie."

"You're the one that's been lying, Mr. Macklin," Witherspoon said calmly.

"Lied? No, I've told ya the truth."

"No you haven't. You said that on Monday evening you walked along Lower Chapman Street."

"That's what I did," he protested.

"Then could you explain how several witnesses claim they saw you in the crowd outside the Felix Mews right after Santorini was killed?"

CHAPTER 8

"What do you think, sir?" Barnes asked as soon as he and Wither-spoon were far enough away from the lodging house to avoid being overheard.

"Well, his excuse for lying to us does make sense. Admitting he was at the scene of the crime when the murder was committed paints him in a very bad light." Witherspoon put on his bowler and glanced behind him. He smiled wryly as the curtain in the front window twitched. "I do believe Mr. Macklin was watching to en-sure we actually left the premises. What's more, I have a feeling his assertion that Mrs. Sorensen wouldn't be home until late this eve-ning was a ploy to get us out of her home and him back into her good graces."

"Really, sir?" Barnes laughed as the two men headed for the main street. "Well, I suppose that, now that his rival is dead, he thinks he might have another chance to get his old room back and

a wedding ring on the widow's finger. But I was more concerned
with whether or not you believed him."

"I'm not certain what to believe," Witherspoon replied. "The
scenario we outlined when we questioned him is plausible, but it's
also the sort of situation that would take a great deal of organizing
as well as substantial luck. Frankly, Harvey Macklin didn't strike
me as much of a planner. What's more, we've no evidence he did
know where Inspector Nivens lives or that Macklin could actually
pick a lock."

"I agree, sir. Even the way he described his relationship with
Frida Sorensen sounded a bit haphazard. But if Nivens didn't murder Santorini, then the person who did was either lucky, or they
planned it down to the last detail."

They came out onto the busy Mile End Road and stopped on
the corner. "Constable Donner goes off duty soon," Barnes reminded the inspector. "We were going to have a word with him
about Inspector Nivens."

"Let's get a hansom, then. I'd like you to take care of speaking
with Constable Donner. He might be more forthcoming speaking
to you than me." Witherspoon pulled his gloves out of his overcoat
pocket and put one on. "I'd like to read the constable's report from
Baxter's Restaurant again."

Barnes spotted a cab dropping a fare in front of a fishmonger's
shop, going around an omnibus that had just pulled in to drop off
passengers. He stepped out into the road far enough so the hansom
driver could see him and waved his arms. "Was there something
wrong with the report?" he asked as he rejoined the inspector.

"Not precisely wrong." He put the other glove on. "But there
was something about it that seemed a bit lacking."

*　*　*

Smythe stared at the five hansoms lined up outside the cabmen's shelter. The small, square green building was the closest one to where Santorini met his end. Nonetheless, it was over a mile away from Felix Mews. Smythe was cold, hungry, and thus far today, he'd not found out much. He'd had a brief stop at Blimpey's pub, but the only thing he'd learned was that one of Blimpey's people had seen a portly man wearing a dark overcoat and a bowler hat go into Felix Mews around the time that Santorini was murdered. Smythe knew that description fit Inspector Nivens, but it also fit thousands of other men in London. Still, it was better than nothing, and if his source among the cabdrivers didn't have anything for him, he'd at least have something to report at the meeting this afternoon.

The damp air turned into a drizzle, and Smythe buttoned up his coat as he walked past the row of tethered cabs, looking for a driver named Jimmy Joyner. Yesterday, he'd paid Joyner to keep his ears open. He'd told the cabbie he was a private inquiry agent, because once he'd mentioned Felix Mews and Santorini's name, it was stupid to think the fellow wouldn't have figured out exactly why he wanted information.

He spotted Jimmy heading into the cab shelter and hurried after him. Stepping inside, he was relieved that there were only three men sitting at the long, narrow table and tucking into a plate of what smelled like stewed rabbit. Jimmy was at the counter getting a cup of tea. He was a tall, wiry, balding man with a reddish complexion, high cheekbones, and a bristly handlebar mustache. Turning, he spotted Smythe. "You want tea?"

Smythe shook his head. After leaving here, he'd be going to Upper Edmonton Gardens for their afternoon meeting. Jimmy took his tea and went to the end of the table, as far away from the other drivers as possible.

Slipping onto the stool next to him, Smythe asked, "You found out anything?"

"Not a lot—there's fewer cabs in this part of London," Jimmy explained. "Most of our fares come from Whitechapel or Liverpool Street Station or the High Streets. I asked around, just like ya told me, but no one remembers pickin' up a fare to or from the Felix Mews on Monday night."

"Did anyone take a fare anywhere near that neighborhood on that night?"

Joyner gave a negative shake of his head.

"That's not surprisin'," Smythe muttered. "I didn't think you'd find out anythin'."

"I didn't say that. Ya told me to report anything peculiar that I 'eard. One of the blokes picked up a fare on Saturday night and took her to Belgravia."

"Saturday night?" Smythe frowned. "But that was two days before Santorini's murder. What's odd about that?"

"He picked up a woman on the Commercial Road and took her to an address in Belgravia, and then later that night, the same woman waved him down and he brought her back 'ere, that's what's peculiar about it. What's more, it was only an hour or so between the time he dropped her off and the time she waved him down."

"Did you ask what she looked like?"

"Course I did." Jimmy took a quick sip from his mug. "But it didn't do no good. Harry said he couldn't see her face. She was wearin' one of them widow's veils—you know what I mean—the old-fashioned kind."

"I don't suppose he remembered the exact address?" Smythe asked.

"Nah, only that it was in Belgravia."

"What time of night was it?"

"Late. The pubs had all closed, and that was another thing that was strange. There aren't too many women out on their own after dark unless they're workin' girls, if you get me meaning. When he picked her up, he was annoyed because Harry lives just off Bethnal Green, and he was sure that at that time of night, he wouldn't be able to find a fare back to Whitechapel. But he hung about the neighborhood a bit, looking for a fare, and he was right surprised when the same woman suddenly waved him down and told him to take her back to Whitechapel."

"Did he pick her up at the same spot where he dropped her?"

"I didn't think to ask." Joyner shrugged. "You never said I 'ad to find out every little thing."

"He was certain she was the same person?"

"I'm not so sure about that. Harry *thinks* it probably was—those were his words, not mine. But he said it was dark and her face was covered."

"In other words, it might or might not have been anyone to do with the Santorini case. It could just as easily 'ave been a workin' girl. There's a brothel in Whitechapel that sends them out to the West End if the customer puts enough cash about."

"Yeah. I've taken a couple of 'em myself to the fancy parts of town."

Smythe sighed heavily and got to his feet. He pulled a shilling out of his coat pocket and put it down next to Joyner's half-full mug. "Ta. This is for your trouble."

He nodded his thanks as he picked up the coin. "Should I keep on askin' about?"

Smythe considered the question. "Nah, don't bother."

*   *   *

Constable Clyde Donner was a skinny rabbit of a man with wispy blond hair slicked back with pomade, buck teeth, and a slightly receding chin. He and Constable Barnes were sitting at a table in the small interview room. The door was open and the hall filled with officers coming off or going on duty. From the looks tossed Donner's way, it was obvious to Barnes that he wasn't a popular officer.

"I don't know what I can tell you." Donner tugged at the top of his uniform. "I don't know Inspector Nivens all that well."

"But I was given to understand you were friends."

"Oh no." Donner ducked his head. "I'd hardly say we were friends. He's a senior officer."

Barnes nodded as if he agreed. "We've heard that you know him better than any of the other lads. You go drinking with him at the Crying Crows."

Donner smiled awkwardly. "Not all that often, Constable. We sometimes have a pint together."

"Did you have a pint with him last week?" Barnes asked.

"Yes."

"How many times?"

"Thursday evening and then on Saturday as well," he explained. "Generally I only drink on Saturday nights, but Inspector Nivens invited me out on the Thursday, and I didn't like to refuse."

"Thursday?" Barnes asked sharply. "Wasn't that the day Inspector Nivens brought the dueling pistols into the station?"

"Yes." Donner nodded eagerly. "He was very proud of those guns and showed them to everyone at the station. Actually, he showed them to everyone at the Crying Crows as well."

"So he had them with him when the two of you were at the pub?" Barnes asked.

"Oh yes—we were sitting at the end of the bar, and he opened the case and held them up for people to see," Donner explained.

Barnes pictured the pub in his mind. "Which end?"

"Which end of what?"

"Which end of the bar? The one by the snugs or the one at the other end?"

"Snugs?" Donner looked confused. "Oh, you mean the one by the private-like booths. It was that end. Usually Inspector Nivens likes a table, but we were late getting there and the place was crowded, so we grabbed the last two spots at the bar."

"After he showed them off, where did he put the gun case?"

Donner's thin face creased in thought. "He left them on the end of the counter."

"At any time did he leave them unattended?"

"Of course not—they're very valuable," Donner replied. "Wait a minute, I tell a lie. There was a few moments when we weren't paying attention. One of the customers had too much to drink and started a dustup with another fellow. Both Inspector Nivens and I as well as several of the other lads leapt up to put an end to it, but a customer showed the fellow the door."

"So your attention was diverted, right?" Barnes clarified.

"Only for a moment or two," Donner explained.

"Did you leave the bar?" Witherspoon asked.

"Well, yes, but it was only for a minute or two. Not long enough for anyone to have taken the gun."

"Which was it, lad?" Barnes snapped. "A moment or a minute?"

"It was a minute, perhaps two."

"Did Inspector Nivens check the case when you came back to your seats?" Barnes flipped to the next page in his notebook.

Donner bit his lip. "No, I don't recall him opening the case. But he might have done so when he got them home."

Barnes said, "You also had a drink with the inspector on Saturday night."

"That's right." Donner cleared his throat. "We had a pint after we both got off duty."

"What time did you get there?" Barnes asked.

"We got there around eight that evening, and we stayed until closing."

"Were you both drinking beer?"

"I was. Inspector Nivens was drinking whisky."

"How much did he drink?"

"I'm not sure. I wasn't keeping count," Donner stammered.

"Take a guess," Barnes snapped.

"Maybe three, maybe four," Donner replied. "Honestly, I don't think it was more than that. He wasn't drunk, if that's what you're asking. Inspector Nivens can hold his liquor."

"How did Inspector Nivens seem?"

Donner stared at him with a blank expression. "How did he seem? I'm not sure what you mean."

"It's quite simple, Constable Donner. Was he nervous or upset?"

"I don't think you could describe him like that."

"How would you describe him? Did he make any comments about the O'Dwyer trial or Bert Santorini?" There was an edge to Barnes' voice now. "Ye gods, you were with the man for almost three hours—what did you talk about? What was his mood? It's not a hard question."

"To tell the truth, he was a bit cross." Donner swallowed nervously. "Not at first, mind you, at first everything was just fine. But as the night wore on, he got more and more—" He broke off, his expression puzzled. "I'm not sure how to describe it."

"Try using English." Barnes wondered how this man had ever become a policeman. He seemed to have trouble understanding simple questions.

"Irritable," Donner said. "The inspector got irritated. He was watching Mrs. Callahan—she's the owner—and then he started in on how she looked so familiar and it was driving him insane. He couldn't recall where he'd seen her before, and so I suggested that maybe she simply looked like someone he used to know. That comment didn't go down well. He told me I didn't know what I was talking about and that he wasn't a half-wit who'd be fooled by a resemblance. Then he spotted Dickie Stiles. He's a local pickpocket—"

"I know who he is," Barnes interrupted. "How did he react to seeing Stiles?"

"Dickie got lucky there—the inspector only spotted him as he was leaving. But when he first come inside, Dickie was standing right behind us, and if Inspector Nivens had seen him, he'd have tossed him out on his ear."

"Had Inspector Nivens ever arrested Stiles?"

Donner shook his head. "No, but everyone at Leman Street knew who he was and that he was a pickpocket. Funny thing is, Stiles was one of Bert Santorini's mates. That's why it was so surprising seein' him come into the Crying Crows. Santorini and his friends weren't welcome there. But I think Dickie was looking for someone. He knows that Mrs. Callahan would have chucked him out as soon as look at him."

*   *   *

"Sorry I'm late," Smythe said as he slid into the chair next to Betsy. "But I was talkin' with a source."

"We've only just started." Mrs. Jeffries poured his tea and passed the mug across to him. "Who would like to go first?"

"Mine won't take long." Mrs. Goodge put a plate of currant scones on the table and took her seat next to Wiggins. "I finally heard from one of my sources, but she didn't have much to tell me."

Mrs. Jeffries hadn't heard anyone in the kitchen today. "Someone was here today?"

"Not in the flesh." The cook pulled a letter out of her apron pocket and held it up. "It's a note from my friend Ida Leahcock. You remember her—she's the one who owns the tobacconist shops. One of them is in Whitechapel, and, as you might recall, Ida loves gossip more than she loves breathing. I sent her a message and asked if she'd see what she could learn from her Whitechapel shop." She sighed. "It's not much. She only had two bits to share. The first, and to my mind, the most interestin', is that Frida Sorensen was seen walking down the Commercial Road, less than a quarter of a mile from Felix Mews at a quarter to six."

"That's close to the time of the murder," Betsy pointed out.

"True," Mrs. Jeffries agreed with a shake of her head. "But I don't recall that the inspector asked her for her whereabouts when Santorini was killed. He's only interviewed her once, and at that time, he'd no idea she had a personal relationship with the dead man. But now that he does, I know he hopes to talk to her again." She glanced at the cook. "We must be sure and mention this to Constable Barnes tomorrow morning. What's the other piece of information Ida sent you?"

"Just a bit of gossip—the woman who runs Ida's Whitechapel

shop says that Susan Callahan dyes her hair." She shrugged. "Mind you, she wouldn't be the only woman in London to do that, so it's hardly important. That's all I've found out. Sorry it's not more."

"Nonsense, you've told us a great deal," Mrs. Jeffries assured her. "Who wants to go next?"

"I've not got much to report," Phyllis said. "To be perfectly honest, I'm not sure it has anything to do with the murder, but as Mrs. Jeffries always says, we never know what will or won't help solve the case. I had an interesting chat with the barmaid at the Crying Crows." She told them about her encounter with Janice Everly. "The poor girl was terrified she was going to get the sack," she finished. "It was only when I pointed out that it might be months before that storage room is opened again that she relaxed. Anyway, I know it isn't much."

"Actually, it does give us insight into Susan Callahan's character," Mrs. Jeffries mused. "Though I'm not sure that has anything to do with Santorini's murder."

"I wonder why the lady is so secretive," Hatchet speculated.

Phyllis shook her head. "Janice thinks she's like that because she's a woman on her own. You know—she's wary of letting people know anything about her personal life."

Luty snorted. "Sounds to me like she's got somethin' to hide. Besides, everyone already knows she was practically livin' with Bert Santorini. Maybe he knew somethin' about her and that's why she killed him."

"But if that were the case, why would she wait six months to do it?" Betsy countered. "Crimes of passion happen in the heat of the moment, not six months after you've tossed a cheating man out of your life."

"We don't know that 'e cheated on 'er," Smythe protested. "No one 'as proven that Santorini was courtin' Alberta Miller at that time. All we've 'eard is a bit of gossip that he was sweet on the girl."

"Don't be daft," she replied. "Of course he was cheating on her. You think Susan Callahan would have shown him the door if he hadn't been? She liked him enough to make sure she kept a decent bottle of wine for him on hand, so it wasn't just a passing fancy on her part."

"Let's not get ahead of ourselves," Mrs. Jeffries warned. "Too much speculating at this point can easily lead us astray. Now, who'd like to go next?"

"I will," Smythe volunteered. He told them what he'd learned from Jimmy Joyner without, of course, mentioning that he'd paid Joyner. "Trouble is, my source wasn't sure that the woman that the hansom driver took back to the East End was the same woman he took to Belgravia only an hour earlier. What's more, even if she was, she might have been a . . . uh . . . well, I guess you'd call 'er a workin' girl, if you get my meanin'."

Betsy patted him on the arm. "We understand what you're saying." She knew her husband was slightly embarrassed to bring up the subject of prostitutes in front of Phyllis.

"I'll go next." Ruth glanced at the carriage clock on the pine sideboard. "I've a meeting with my women's group soon, and unfortunately, it's at my house so I must be there." She paused and took a breath. "It's not very much, but I might as well share what little it is. I went to a charity luncheon today, and I happened to spot Conrad Bryson and his wife."

"The man who owns Bryson's Brewery?" Betsy asked.

Ruth nodded. "That's him. It was a buffet, so when I got my lunch, I made a point of sitting at the same table as the Brysons. After we introduced ourselves, I asked him what I thought was a simple question about how pubs are financed. I thought that might lead him to saying something about the Crying Crows, which is apparently a very nice place and perhaps even that other pub, the Thistle and Thorn. I know it sounds silly, but I've not been able to contribute very much to this investigation, and as the victim seemed to have connections to both those pubs, I was hoping to find out something useful." She sighed. "But I'm afraid all I did was bore every single person at the table. It was dreadful. Mr. Bryson went on and on about how his brewery takes great pains to make sure they only make loans to fine, upstanding citizens, and they have such strict rules about how their beer and whisky is brewed to ensure it's of the best quality. Then he began talking about the loans Bryson's called in because they found out some poor publican was accused of watering down their liquor or had been arrested in their past or didn't pay their vendors promptly." She closed her eyes briefly. "Honestly, Mr. Bryson talked for half an hour, and he only stopped because his wife reminded him to eat his lunch. I'm afraid the entire experience was a terrible waste of time."

"You weren't to know that," Hatchet said. "And, as Mrs. Jeffries has mentioned many times, none of us knows what snippet of information will turn out to be important."

"Anyone else have anything to report?" Mrs. Jeffries looked at Luty and Hatchet, both of whom gave a negative shake of their heads.

"I'm hopin' tomorrow is a better day than today," Luty complained. "I tell ya, you'd think findin' out a few bits and pieces about this murder would be a darned sight easier."

Baxter's Restaurant was located on the ground floor of a busy corner on Oxford Street. Barnes pulled open the door, and he and

Witherspoon stepped inside. They stopped in the elegant, wood-paneled foyer and hovered by the archway leading to the restaurant proper.

It was a large room with more than a dozen tables covered in white damask cloths. Crystal chandeliers hung from the cream-colored ceiling. Dark wood wainscoting went halfway up the yellow painted walls, and on the street side of the room, three long windows were draped in gold and green striped curtains beneath extravagant valances. White-shirted waiters with stiff peaked collars scurried about, carrying trays of folded serviettes and putting out silver-topped salt and pepper vessels. A lad pushing a cart topped with pitchers of water emerged from the kitchen and disappeared a moment later behind an intricately carved screen at the back of the room.

"This is a fancy place, sir," Barnes murmured. "It's only a few minutes past five, but only a couple of tables have customers. Which means that if Nivens was telling the truth when he claimed he was here for an early supper on Monday evening, someone on the staff should remember him."

A waiter carrying a tray of water glasses spotted the two policemen. He stopped and put the tray down on the nearest table and hurried toward them. "May I help you?"

"We'd like to speak to the maître d' or whoever was in charge this past Monday evening," Barnes said.

"Just one moment and I'll get Mr. Caladini." He turned on his heel and rushed off, scooping up his tray as he moved between the tables and disappearing through the door on the far side of the room. A few moments later, a portly man with slicked-back black hair, a thin mustache, and dressed in a black coat, white shirt, and maroon cravat stepped into the dining room and hurried toward them. "Good evening." He smiled broadly. "I am Auguste Caladini. I understand you wish to speak with me?"

"We do. I'm Inspector Gerald Witherspoon and this is Constable Barnes."

Caladini glanced at the dining room. The customers at both tables were openly staring at them with curious expressions on their collective faces, but the maître d' didn't seem to mind the attention. He simply broadened his smile and gestured to his left. "Please, let's go into the waiting area. It's far more comfortable than standing here." He ushered them inside the dining room and toward a recessed alcove fitted with an L-shaped built-in couch and upholstered in a deep forest green velvet.

"Please sit down." Caladini gestured to the longest section while he plopped down on the short side. "Would you care for some coffee or tea? Or perhaps an aperitif?"

"No, thank you, Mr. Caladini. We're fine," Witherspoon replied.

Caladini crossed his legs and clasped his hands in front of him. "Now, how can I help you?"

Barnes reached into his pocket and pulled out his pencil and notebook. "Do you know Inspector Nigel Nivens?"

"But of course, he's one of our best customers," Caladini exclaimed. "He dines here twice, sometimes three times a week."

"So both you and your staff would recognize him on sight," Witherspoon clarified. He was surprised that the maître d' was so forthcoming and friendly. Generally, businesspeople hated the police showing up at their premises.

"Indeed we would." Caladini nodded. "As I said, he's a very good customer."

"Was Inspector Nivens here this past Monday evening?"

"He was. I served him myself, as the waiters were running a bit late in setting up the dining room for dinner."

Barnes stopped writing and looked at the maître d'. "You served him?"

"Yes. He arrived very early on Monday. Actually, we weren't really open, but, as I said, he's such a good customer, I hated to turn him away." He gestured toward the dining room. "We open at five, and, as you can see, even though it's rather early for dinner, we've guests. Most of them are from North America." He leaned closer. "Actually, that's the reason we open at such an early hour—we want to accommodate our overseas visitors. Our restaurant has been prominently mentioned in a Cook's and a Baedeker's. Those are travel guides that I was surprised to find out were available in North America. To be perfectly honest, our colonial friends provide us with a substantial amount of revenue at a time when we're generally not busy at all. The Americans, in particular, do like to dine early, and it's quite easy as most of them have very simple tastes. Now, of course, sometimes we have a bit of a misunderstanding, which is odd considering we speak the same language." He paused to take a breath and the inspector started to ask a question, but he wasn't fast enough.

"Why, just yesterday," Caladini continued, "I tried to recommend the sole meunière to a very nice gentleman from a place called Arkansas, but he kept asking if we had something called fried catfish fritters. Finally, he seemed to understand that not only did we not have the catfish, but the chef had no idea how to turn them into fritters. But as I said, he was a nice gentleman, and eventually he ordered steak and duchesse potatoes, which he enjoyed very much."

"What time was Inspector Nivens here on Monday?" Witherspoon asked quickly. He was happy that the maître d' was being so cooperative, but honestly, the fellow did go on a bit.

Caladini drew back. "But I've already told you. He arrived before we were open, and we don't open until five p.m."

The inspector tried again. "How much before opening did he arrive?"

"What time was it when Inspector Nivens got here?" Barnes added as the maître d' continued to look confused.

"Oh yes, yes." Caladini bobbed his head eagerly. "How silly of me—now I understand. Inspector Nivens arrived at a half past four."

Witherspoon and Barnes looked at each other. "You're certain of the time?" the inspector said.

"But of course." Caladini gestured toward the dining room with both hands. "He arrived just as the waiters were putting out the silverware and that always happens at half past four. Inspector Nivens banged on the front door just as Lloyd—he's the headwaiter—began setting up. Lloyd went to the door and looked out. Inspector Nivens was there, so Lloyd let him into the foyer. I happened to be passing by, and the inspector asked if it was possible to get something to eat. He said he had a very important appointment later, hadn't had any lunch, and could he get a quick meal? I told him I'd need to check with the chef, as I wasn't sure what he had ready in the kitchen." Caladini paused to take another breath.

Barnes rushed a quick question. "You're certain that Inspector Nivens said he 'had an important appointment'?"

"But of course, Constable. That's the reason I was willing to ask Bernard—he's our chef—if he could accommodate the inspector. He said he could offer him a steak or a chop with a salad. I went back to the inspector, and he said he'd have the steak and salad. He also asked for a glass of the house cabernet sauvignon. We do a very fine cabernet here."

"Did he speak to anyone while he waited for his food?" Barnes asked.

Caladini shook his head. "He read his newspaper."

"What time did he leave?" Witherspoon asked.

"Five o'clock. He was going out just as I unlocked the front door."

Witherspoon looked at the constable, who gave a barely perceptible shake of his head, indicating he had no further questions. He got to his feet, as did Barnes.

"Is that all?" Caladini asked. "Don't you have more questions for me? This is the most exciting thing that's happened to me in ages—it's just like one of Mr. Arthur Conan Doyle's wonderful stories. Though it is a pity that Mr. Sherlock Holmes does make poor Inspector Lestrade seem a bit of an idiot."

"In real life we're not quite that stupid," Barnes murmured.

"But of course you're not stupid," Caladini exclaimed. "Are you sure you've no more questions?"

"I'm afraid not." Witherspoon felt as if he should apologize. The poor man looked so very disappointed. "But you've been very helpful."

The maître d' sighed and rose to his feet. "Oh well, it's back to work, I suppose. But if you think of anything else, I'm here all evening."

"I'm sorry I'm so late," Witherspoon said as he handed Mrs. Jeffries his bowler. "But we've had a very busy day."

"You look very tired, sir." Mrs. Jeffries hung up the hat and then reached for his overcoat as he slipped it off his shoulders. "Do you want to eat right away, or do you fancy a sherry? Mrs. Goodge has made a lovely roast chicken. She's just put it in the warming oven so you've time for a drink without it being ruined."

"A sherry would be wonderful." He hurried toward his study.

Mrs. Jeffries followed him and poured both of them a drink. "Here you are, sir." She handed him his glass and took her seat. "Now, do tell me about your day."

He took a quick sip before he spoke. "As I said, it was very busy. To begin with, when we arrived at Leman Street, Constable Barnes had a quick word with his old colleague Constable Rhodes while I went over the witness statements taken by the local constables."

He took his time relating the events of the day. Witherspoon had discovered going over each and every event helped him clarify and put the information into perspective. He took care to recall every little detail. "Constable Rhodes was most helpful in that we now know that Dickie Stiles goes to the same pub, the Pig and Ale, every day at twelve forty-five."

"Did you have a chance to interview him?" She took a sip from her own glass.

"No, we didn't have time, but he is on our list for tomorrow." He continued by telling her about their interview with Fiona O'Dwyer. "She is adamant that the police planted the evidence against her sons and that they're innocent," he concluded.

"What do you think, sir?"

"One hates to think of a fellow officer doing such a thing, but we know that Nivens is capable of bending the rules when it suits him. Nonetheless, I'm going to assume he's innocent until there's irrefutable proof he isn't. After we interviewed Mrs. O'Dwyer, we tried to speak with Frida Sorensen again, but she either wasn't home or was upstairs pretending not to be home."

"What on earth do you mean?"

"I mean that I think Harvey Macklin is trying to get back into her good graces by pretending she wasn't home. I noticed him watching us from the front window as we left, and I'm fairly certain it was so he could tell his ladylove the coast was clear." Witherspoon chuckled. "We'll have another chat with her tomorrow. But going to the lodging house did give us the opportunity to speak to Harvey. He and the victim hated each other, and what's more, we caught the man in a lie." He told her about the interview and about the fact that witnesses had seen Macklin in the crowd outside Felix Mews only moments after the murder.

"So he didn't come home that evening along Lower Chapman Street as he claimed," she murmured. "But nonetheless, sir, how would someone like Macklin even know that Nivens had those fancy dueling pistols, let alone figure out a way to get his hands on one of them?"

"Because Macklin was at the Crying Crows Pub on Thursday evening, the same evening Inspector Nivens was showing off his dueling pistols to everyone. Not only that, but there were a few moments when those very guns were unattended. Additionally, Macklin has worked at the locksmith's shop, Stanton's, for the past five years." He frowned and tapped the edge of his glass with his finger. "But I must admit, Macklin didn't strike me as the type of person to be very good at planning. If Inspector Nivens didn't kill Santorini, then whoever did was either very lucky or planned every move down to the last detail."

"That is a puzzle, sir, but I'm sure you'll solve it," she said. "What did you do then?"

"When I was going over the constable's reports, I realized that no one had verified the exact time that Inspector Nivens had arrived at Baxter's Restaurant, so on our way home, we stopped there and had a word with the maître d' who was on duty Monday evening. It turns out that it was a good thing we pursued that line of inquiry. Inspector Nivens didn't arrive at Baxter's at five fifteen, as he implied in his statement; he was there at half past four."

"He lied to you?"

"Well, he implied a timeline that was a good forty-five minutes later than what the maître d' told us."

"Could the maître d' have been mistaken?"

Witherspoon shook his head. "No, he was absolutely sure because the restaurant wasn't open when Nivens arrived there." He repeated what Caladini had told them. "So you see, this is quite serious. Not only did Inspector Nivens deliberately obscure the time he arrived at the restaurant, he convinced them to fix him a quick meal because he claimed he had 'an important appointment' that evening."

"You think that appointment might have been with Santorini?"

"I don't know what to think, Mrs. Jeffries. But why else would Inspector Nivens have lied about it? Because that's what he did. He lied about the time he arrived at the restaurant because he hoped it would give him an alibi for the time of the murder. But the truth is, he got there forty-five minutes earlier, giving him ample time to eat and get back to the East End to kill Santorini."

The house was quiet as Mrs. Jeffries slipped down the back stairs to the kitchen. She put her old oil lamp on the table and sat down. It was almost eleven o'clock, and, though she'd tried, she couldn't sleep.

She glanced at the cooker and debated about whether to make herself a cup of tea but then discarded that notion. The teakettle had developed a nasty rattling, and she didn't want to wake up Mrs. Goodge. But she needed to think. Glancing at the pine sideboard, she got up and pulled open the bottom drawer. Reaching inside, she pulled out the bottle of whisky she kept on hand for medical or emotional emergencies. Grabbing a tumbler from the shelf, she went back to her seat and poured a half-inch shot into the glass.

This was most definitely an emergency.

She had no idea how this case was going to get solved.

She went back to her seat and took a tiny sip of whisky, wincing as it hit the back of her throat. It wasn't her favorite beverage, but it would have to do, and if she was lucky, it might help her sleep. Her eyes unfocused as she stared across the room in a vain attempt to find the solution to this puzzle. But after a few moments, she realized she was being foolish, and it would be best to think logically about the matter. Now wasn't the time to trust her intuition or her own "inner voice." Now was the time to think.

There was no shortage of suspects; Santorini seemed to have thrived on making enemies. It wasn't just the O'Dwyers and their friends who loathed the man. On a previous occasion, Santorini's testimony had sent another person to prison. Philip Graves claimed that Santorini's lies not only deprived him of his liberty but also forced him to sell his cart and pony, a good business for a workingman. But Graves was out of prison now, and it was possible that he wanted revenge against the man who he claimed set him up.

But there were a number of problems with Graves as the killer. As far as they knew, Graves wasn't at the Crying Crows on the night Nivens was showing off the dueling pistols. So how would he have found out about them? In addition to that obstacle, there was no evidence that Graves had an opportunity to steal one of the weapons. If he wasn't at the Crying Crows, he wouldn't have heard Nivens complaining about having to stay at his mother's house, thus realizing that Nivens' own home would be empty. But the biggest problem with Graves as the killer was even simpler: Why would he go to the trouble of manipulating the evidence to suggest that Nigel Nivens had committed the crime? There was no evidence he and Inspector Nivens had ever had dealings with each other.

She caught herself as that thought took hold in her mind. Perhaps she was wrong. Perhaps Graves did have a reason to hate Nivens.

She pulled out the sheet of stationery she'd brought down from her room, laid it on the table next to her glass, and then got up, yanked open the top drawer of the sideboard, and rummaged inside for a pencil. When she found one, she took her seat and made a note to ask Constable Barnes if Nivens had ever arrested Graves and if so, when.

She stared at the short sentence she'd just written and pursed her lips. It wasn't that she was concerned she was going senile, but she had noticed that now her memory wasn't as sharp as it once was. Well, that was something she'd just have to deal with. If she needed to write things down in order to recall them properly, so be it.

Susan Callahan had reason to hate Santorini, but, as far as they knew, had no reason to loathe Inspector Nivens. She obviously considered him a good customer and treated him decently or he wouldn't have kept going to the Crying Crows. There was the matter of Nivens thinking she seemed familiar, but perhaps that was merely an occupational hazard from being a policeman for so many years.

Then there was Harvey Macklin. He certainly had a motive. Santorini had stolen the affections of the woman he'd been planning on marrying. But, like Susan Callahan and perhaps Philip Graves, there was no indication that Macklin had ever had any dealings with Inspector Nivens. So why would he have gone to such lengths to make it appear as if Nivens was the murderer? She took another sip of whisky. Additionally, just because Macklin worked at a locksmith's shop didn't mean he knew how to pick a lock.

Frida Sorensen was furious at Santorini as well. Enough so that she confronted him at the Thistle and Thorn, the very pub where he was supposedly sweet on the barmaid. Even after Santorini had pulled Frida outside, she was screaming so loudly that everyone in the pub heard her threaten to "make him sorry" if he didn't keep his promises to her. Mrs. Jeffries was fairly sure one of those promises was to make her his wife. It was possible she decided to kill him when she realized he'd been lying to her.

Which brought up the barmaid. Perhaps that altercation between Santorini and Frida Sorensen had another unforeseen consequence. Maybe when Alberta overheard Frida's claim that Santorini had made promises, she realized that her own position was vulnerable. Frida had far more to offer than the widow Miller. Frida owned a lodging house, and if she and Santorini married, it would become his as well.

And what about the money they'd found in Santorini's room? Where had that come from? She picked up the pencil again and made another note, reminding herself to ask Constable Barnes if they'd made any headway in finding out why eighty-five pounds in cash and gold was in his locked box. Perhaps Mrs. O'Dwyer was right, and Nivens had bribed Santorini to lie in court. Mrs. Jeffries thought Nivens capable of bribery, but she wasn't sure she thought him capable of murder. She made another note, this time to ask about the beer and whisky they found in Santorini's box.

She put the pencil down and thought about everything the inspector had told her about the interview with Mrs. O'Dwyer and suddenly realized that she had the strongest reason to hate Bert Santorini, and *she* was also the only one of their suspects who had a reason for loathing Inspector Nivens as well.

Fiona O'Dwyer claimed that Nivens planted evidence in her home and that he'd paid Santorini to lie in court. But if she was going to kill Santorini herself and set the stage for Nivens to be arrested for the crime, why threaten the victim so publicly? Mrs. O'Dwyer tracked Santorini down at the Strand Hotel and, in front of witnesses, accused him of lying under oath, and then she went on to claim that she'd prove it. Why do that if you've already decided to commit murder?

Mrs. Jeffries ran her finger along the rim of her glass as another idea blossomed. Perhaps it was Santorini's threats that sealed his fate. Mrs. O'Dwyer had originally decided to prove Santorini lied in court, but when he threatened her daughter, she decided he had to die.

But was she clever enough to come up with a way of not only ridding the world of Santorini but of discrediting the policeman she blamed for taking her other children away and locking them up? What's more, even if she had come up with a plan for killing two birds with one stone, would she have had the resources to do it?

Mentally, Mrs. Jeffries began ticking off the obstacles, one by one. First, Fiona O'Dwyer would have needed to know that Nivens had a set of dueling pistols. But from what Constable Donner said, Nivens showed them off to everyone at the Crying Crows Pub, and, considering that Mrs. O'Dwyer was a local in the area, there's a good chance someone might have mentioned it. Second, she'd have needed to know that Nivens' own home was going to be empty on the nights prior to the murder. Again, she might have had someone watching both Nivens and Santorini in the hopes of finding evidence they had conspired against her sons. That someone might have overheard Nivens complaining about having to do his mum a favor. Third, she'd have had to know where Nivens lived. But she could have followed him. Mrs. Jeffries thought about what Smythe had reported at their meeting—one of the hansom drivers had taken a woman from the Commercial Road to Belgravia, where Nivens lived, and then thought he had taken that very same woman back to the East End. That woman could have been Mrs. O'Dwyer. Finally, she'd have to know how to get in and out of the Nivens house without getting caught. Nivens would have noticed a typical housebreaking, yet he claimed there was no sign of forced entry. But considering how her sons made their living, it was quite possible they learned their trade from their mother.

Perhaps Fiona O'Dwyer knew how to pick a lock.

CHAPTER 9

As soon as Constable Barnes finished adding additional details to Inspector Witherspoon's account of the events of the previous day, he put his mug on the table and started to get up.

"Just a moment, Constable." Mrs. Jeffries fumbled in her apron pocket for the note she'd written herself. "I've a couple of questions. I thought of them last night and I was afraid I'd forget, so I wrote them down." She flipped open the paper.

"I write everything down as well," Barnes replied. "In the long run, it saves a lot of grief, as everyone forgets things now and again."

"My memory isn't what it once was," she admitted. "To begin with, do you know if Philip Graves was ever arrested by Inspector Nivens?"

Barnes thought for a moment and then shook his head. "Not that I've heard, but, then again, I didn't think to ask. Why?"

"Because it seems to me as if whoever murdered Santorini also must have had a reason for hating Inspector Nivens."

"You mean because they went to such trouble to make it appear as if Nivens is guilty?"

"That's right. The killer had to have known that Nivens owned a gun—in this case, the dueling pistols—and that Nivens wasn't going to be home on the night prior to the murder."

"True, but as we've said before, Nivens bragged about them guns to anyone who stood still for ten seconds; he showed them off at the Leman Street Station and the Crying Crows Pub, so anyone in the East End could have found out about them. As to his not being home, on Saturday night when Nivens was at the Crying Crows, he complained to all and sundry about having to stay at his mother's house starting on Sunday, and it wasn't because he didn't like her home; it was because there wasn't any staff there. Which meant he'd have to take care of himself."

"That means anyone at the pub or anyone who talked to someone who'd been at the pub could have known about the guns and the empty house," the cook mused.

"But there's one other thing you're forgetting." Barnes looked at the housekeeper. "You're assuming that Nigel Nivens is innocent. Frankly, Mrs. Jeffries, I'm not so sure about that."

"I know, and my assumption isn't built on the facts of the case," she admitted. "For some reason, I just have a feeling that as despicable as he is, he isn't a killer. But let's put that aside for a moment. I've another question. Did you and the inspector learn more about the money and the alcohol you found in Santorini's box?"

"The alcohol was just that, whisky and beer," he replied. "Mind you, it wasn't particularly high quality—had too much water in it to be the best of the best. As to why Santorini had it or what those dates on the bottles meant, we've no idea."

"And the money?"

"We've not found any evidence that Santorini had a bank account, so it could just be he didn't trust banks. He had that pony and cart for three years, so it's possible the money was simply what he'd saved."

"But ten pounds of that was in gold sovereigns," the cook pointed out. "And that seems strange. No one would have paid for ice or flowers with sovereigns."

"I agree, and we're still lookin' into the matter." Barnes got up. "I'd better get upstairs. We've got to go to Scotland Yard this morning, and we want to get that over with in time to have a chat with Dickie Stiles at the Pig and Ale."

Ten minutes later, Phyllis came downstairs carrying the dishes from the inspector's breakfast. Everyone else was already at the table. She put the tray on the wooden counter by the sink and hurried to her seat. It didn't take long for Mrs. Jeffries to pass along everything she'd learned from Inspector Witherspoon and for Mrs. Goodge to add the details the constable had supplied.

"Seems to me like we know a lot of facts, but we're no closer to findin' the killer," Luty grumbled. "I'll bet that's why our inspector and Constable Barnes have to go to Scotland Yard. The newspapers haven't stopped hinting that the police are covering up for Nivens."

"Indeed, madam." Hatchet let out a long breath. "That does appear to be the case. Even the quality newspapers have begun to speculate along those lines."

"Maybe this'll be the one that we never solve," Wiggins muttered. "I can't even think of what to do next."

"Unfortunately, I don't have many sources in that part of the city." Ruth sighed. "I wish I could do more. I hate to think of poor Gerald being under such pressure."

"And the people over there can be a bit scary," Phyllis admitted. "Not all of them," she amended quickly, "but some of 'em."

"Stop it," Mrs. Jeffries demanded. "If we keep putting our minds on what we can't do or can't find out, we'll lose sight of what we have done and have found out."

"But we've not found out very much," Betsy protested.

"I disagree. We've found out a tremendous amount of information, and we can't stop now." Mrs. Jeffries was beginning to believe her own words. "You're forgetting that none of our cases has ever been easy. With each and every one of them, we've had to demand the most of ourselves when we're on the hunt. It's always hard, but it's always worth it, and I'll tell you why. It's because we demand justice, that's why. When someone has taken a human life, all of you put yourselves at risk by going into the killer's world."

"But it's not that dangerous," Wiggins murmured.

"Isn't it? When you're on the hunt, you've no idea who you might be talking to when you're out there looking for information. It could easily be the killer. Ask yourself this question: Why do you do it? You've never met the victims, so why put yourself at any risk whatsoever for someone you don't even know?"

For a moment, no one said anything, then Phyllis straightened her spine and lifted her chin. "I'll tell you why I do it," she announced. "It makes me feel like my life matters, that I'm not just a housemaid who was unlucky enough to be born poor, and that maybe because of my small efforts, some other poor person won't face the hangman for a crime they didn't commit."

"You're demanding justice for the innocent who might be unjustly hanged." Mrs. Jeffries smiled. Phyllis made her realize her own perspective had come full circle—she loved justice more than she loathed Nigel Nivens, and, despite his miserable character, she wouldn't see him hanged for a crime he didn't commit. "That's a good reason. As a matter of fact, that's the best reason of all, and I suspect it's why all of us do everything we can to find the truth when we've got a case. Not because we know the victim of the crime, but because if we don't demand justice for the dead and the innocent, we can't expect justice for anyone. Not even ourselves. Now, no more of this complaining. I, for one, don't think Nivens is a killer. But if we don't get out there and dig up what we can on Santorini's murder, Nivens is probably going to be prosecuted for a murder he didn't commit."

Chief Superintendent Barrows motioned Witherspoon and the constable into his office. "Come in, come in," he called impatiently as he waved at the straight-backed chair in front of his desk. "Take a seat, Inspector."

"Thank you, sir." Witherspoon sat, and Barnes took up a position against the wall by the door.

Barrows looked up from the papers on his desk. "I'm sure you know why I've called you here."

"You'd like a progress report, sir?"

"That's correct, Inspector." He gave Witherspoon a brief, perfunctory smile.

"The investigation is going well, sir. We've interviewed a number of witnesses and have taken statements from each of them."

"Yes, yes, proper police procedure, I'm sure you've done a splendid job. Go on, please."

"Unfortunately, there were several people in the victim's circle of acquaintances that appear to have a motive to want him dead." He gave the chief superintendent a short, but to his mind, very thorough report on their findings thus far.

Barrows listened carefully, occasionally interrupting to ask a question or make a comment. Finally, when Witherspoon finished, he said, "So what you're telling me is that there were lots of people who hated Santorini, but the only real physical evidence we have points directly at Inspector Nivens. Is that correct?"

"We're not certain of that, sir. It's still too early to come to any definite conclusions," Witherspoon replied.

"Are you sure of that?" Barrows leaned forward. "I'm not trying to interfere, but you do have substantial physical evidence against him, right?"

"That's right, but—"

Barrows interrupted. "No buts about it, Inspector—facts are facts. It was Nivens' gun that killed the man and, on top of that, it was Nivens' pillow that was used to silence the shot. That's fairly damning evidence, wouldn't you say?"

"Yes, but there are a number of people involved in the case who knew that Nivens wasn't at his home on the night before the murder," the inspector pointed out. "Some of these people might have had the skills necessary to break into the Nivens home and steal both the dueling pistol and the pillow."

Barrows stared at him for a few moments. "Are you seriously suggesting that someone framed Inspector Nivens?"

"It's not beyond the bounds of probability, sir," Witherspoon argued. "We must investigate every possible suspect to be certain that justice is done."

"Justice is a matter for the courts to decide, Witherspoon, but bad press is quite another." Barrows jabbed his finger at a stack of folded newspapers on the side of his desk. "It's not just the gutter press anymore; now the decent papers are hinting that we're covering up a terrible crime for one of our own. That isn't something that we can simply ignore, especially as there is evidence to make an arrest."

"But we have to arrest the person we know is guilty."

"Try telling that to the Home Secretary," Barrows snapped.

"I take it the Home Secretary is upset," Witherspoon murmured. "I'm sorry about that, sir."

"He is upset that we're getting bad press, and, if we don't make an arrest soon, it's going to get worse. He's not known for being a patient man, Inspector, so I expect you to do your duty."

"Are you ordering me to arrest Inspector Nivens?" Witherspoon asked.

"Not at all. What I'm telling you is that we need to get this case solved, Inspector, and sooner rather than later. I think three more days should be sufficient."

Wiggins picked up his pint and took a sip. It was his second, and generally, he never had more than one, but he was bored and more than a little depressed. He'd come to the Crying Crows mainly because he couldn't think of anywhere else to go, and he'd been hoping to learn something useful. He'd tried talking to the locals, but there wasn't more than half a dozen in the bar, and none of them were friendly.

He felt a bit foolish—he'd not contributed much at all to the solving of this case, and now he'd have to show up this afternoon with nothing.

The barman grabbed a wet cloth from underneath the bar and wiped up some spilled beer. "Oh God, no," he muttered as he looked up. "Please don't come in here. Please, please just keep on walking. She'll have a conniption fit if she sees him again."

"Hey, Alex, looks like old man Dinsworth is makin' a run for it again," a red-haired man sitting by the window called out.

"I don't care where he goes as long as it isn't in here," the barman yelled back. "She'll have my head on a pike if she finds him in 'ere."

Wiggins glanced at the window just in time to see an elderly, white-haired man wearing an old-fashioned top hat and black overcoat walking quickly past the pub. "What's he doin'?"

"That's Enoch Dinsworth. He's senile and sometimes he runs away," the red-haired man explained. "Anyone want to take bets on how long it'll be before young Rosemary comes chasin' after 'im?"

Wiggins couldn't believe his ears—these people were just sitting here making light of a poor soul who'd lost his reason. Cor blimey, he might not be a ruddy local here, but he knew what was right. He slid off the stool and slapped some coins next to his unfinished pint before racing for the door. Flinging it open, he ignored the gasps of surprise and the shouted comments from the men in the pub.

He caught sight of Mr. Dinsworth turning the corner onto the busier Commercial Road. Wiggins was after him in a flash. He'd no idea what he'd do when he caught the fellow, but common decency dictated he couldn't let some poor senile soul go wandering around on his own. He heard footsteps running behind him, but he was in such a hurry, he couldn't look around and see if it was someone from the pub.

He dodged around a costermonger whose cart was half on and half off the pavement, but even running flat out, he couldn't escape the smell of overripe fish. He spotted a fully loaded cooper's van come racing around the corner at a far faster speed than was legal. Sensing disaster, Wiggins flew past a trio of black-clad women chatting in front of a secondhand shop and finally reached his quarry just as the elderly man started to cross the busy roadway, unaware of the wagon rushing toward hm.

Wiggins hurled himself forward and, by the grace of the saint who watches out for children and fools, managed to get a grip on the old fellow's coat. Using all his strength, he pulled him backward just as the horses of the cooper's van rushed past. The two men stumbled backward, and Wiggins struggled to stay on his feet. But just then a pair of arms pushed him from behind, keeping him upright so that neither man fell.

"Are you alright, sir?" a woman asked breathlessly.

He straightened, made sure the old man was steady, and then turned. Standing before him was a dark-haired young woman wearing a green coat that had seen better days. She had blue eyes, a rosebud mouth, and skin the color of cream. Wiggins stared at her for a moment.

"Are you alright, sir?" she persisted. She glanced at the old man who was still staring at the street in front of him. "You're not hurt, are you?"

Wiggins finally found his tongue. "I'm fine, miss."

She smiled broadly. "That's a relief. I'd felt awful if you'd hurt yourself. If you'd not pulled my grandfather back, he'd have been run over by those horses. Thank God you were here, sir."

"Happy to help, miss." Wiggins took pains to speak properly. She'd not spoken many words, but he'd noticed she didn't have the same accent as most of the people here and, for some reason, he wanted her to think well of him. "I'm glad the gentleman wasn't hurt."

"Grandfather." She tugged at the elderly man's arm. "Are you alright?"

He turned to face her, a wide smile on his face. "Rosemary, girl, what are you doin' here?"

"I came to find you, Grandfather. You left the house. Remem-

ber, you're never supposed to go outside unless one of us is with
you. I know that you forget sometimes, but it's important that you
try to remember." She took his arm. "Come along now. Thank this
gentleman here; he kept you from being badly hurt. You almost
stepped out in front of a team of horses."

His smile disappeared and he looked at Wiggins. "Do I know
you?"

"No, sir. I just happened to be in the Crying Crows when you
went past. I overheard them sayin' you had a spot of trouble with
your memory, and I thought you might need a bit of 'elp."

"You were at the Crying Crows?" He laughed. "That's Millie
Slavik's place."

"No, Grandfather, it belongs to Mrs. Callahan," she said. She
looked at Wiggins. "Thank you again, sir. I must get him home now."

"Let me help you." He took the man's other arm. "My name
is"—he hesitated and then gave her one of the names he used when
he was on the hunt, "Albert Jones."

"Gracious, how rude of me. I should have asked your name and
introduced myself," she said as they started walking. "I'm Rosemary Dinsworth, and this is my grandfather Enoch Dinsworth."

"I used to work at the Whitechapel Station." He smiled at Wiggins again. "I'd still be there, but they said I was too old to work."

"Now you get to rest," Rosemary said cheerfully. "Come along,
then. Let's not trouble Mr. Jones further."

"It's no trouble, miss." Wiggins slowed his steps to keep the
same pace as his two companions. "I'm happy to escort you and
your grandfather home."

"That's very kind of you." She sighed. "Much kinder than some
around here. Thank goodness you spotted Grandfather and realized he might need help."

"Actually, miss, I didn't really notice him so much as overheard some of the comments the others at the pub made," Wiggins said honestly. "It was a bit shocking, it was."

"They don't like him in there," she explained as they maneuvered around a group of lads squatting on the pavement and playing dice. "We used to take Grandfather there occasionally as a special treat, but he kept calling Mrs. Callahan 'Millie' instead of her proper name, and she asked us not to bring him in anymore."

"Still, that's no reason for some of the comments I overheard," Wiggins exclaimed. "Them blighters were taking bets on how long it would be before you come running after your grandfather. Not one of 'em got off their backsides to 'elp." He clamped his mouth shut as he realized how he sounded.

Rosemary didn't seem to notice. "I'm not surprised. Susan Callahan has a reputation for banning people from her pub. The only people she really seems to want there are the police or the local businessmen. There's a lot of resentment against her in the community."

"That's no way to run a business."

"True, but she's successful nonetheless."

"She was always a sharp one, was Millie. Picked pockets faster than anyone in the East End," Dinsworth said. "Used to try it on at the station, but we were on to her, and we'd chase her off."

"Grandfather, you're getting mixed up again."

"I'm not. She's a smart one, she is. I saw her the other morning, too."

"Grandfather, it was still dark when you slipped out of the house—you couldn't have seen anyone." Rosemary glanced at Wiggins. "He got out last Sunday morning as well. We found him at the station. That's usually where he goes."

"It was her, too," he insisted. "The wind was blowing hard, and her veil slipped off for a good minute. I know I'm a bit daft, Rosemary, but I'm not blind. It was Millie Slavik alright."

Rosemary looked at Wiggins. "I'm sorry, he does go on a bit when he gets an idea into his head."

They had reached the Crying Crows. Dinsworth stopped and stared in through the window. "She's done well for herself—I'll give her that. Mind you, back then she was a pretty lass and smart enough to figure out that if she put on a decent dress and washed her face, she could pick the pockets of the rich in the West End. She had a tiny waist and lovely blonde curls, pretty as an angel she was."

Rosemary tugged at his arm. "Come along, Grandfather. Millie Slavik disappeared years ago. Besides, Mrs. Callahan isn't in the least pretty, and I doubt that she ever had a tiny waist."

Wiggins suddenly realized he'd done the right thing, but that once again, he'd be at their afternoon meeting with nothing to report. A bit of gossip from a senile elderly gent didn't really count. "Uh, Miss Dinsworth, if you can manage, I'll leave you here. I've just remembered I left my cap in the pub."

"I can manage, thank you, and you've been more than kind. We don't live far from here." She gave him a grateful smile. "Come along, Grandfather. Let's get you home for a cup of tea."

"I'd rather have a pint," he complained, but he let himself be led off.

Wiggins waited a moment and then stepped back inside the pub.

"I do hope that Chief Superintendent Barrows understood that I wasn't being insubordinate, but I don't believe there is enough evidence to arrest Inspector Nivens," Witherspoon said as they reached the front door of the Pig and Ale Pub. It was in a dusty, two-story brown brick building that leaned slightly to one side on the White-chapel High Street.

"In the end, he did give us more time." Barnes shoved open the heavy wooden door. "But from his point of view, this situation is perfect for getting rid of Inspector Nivens once and for all. Especially since it appears that the Home Secretary is more worried about bad press for the police rather than keeping Nivens' family happy."

"I got that impression as well." Witherspoon squinted as they stepped into the dim pub. The bar was directly across from them. The wooden floor was darkened with age and covered with scuff marks from years of heavy boots, and the glass in the one small window was so crusted with dirt that even at midday the two oil lamps hanging from the beam on the ceiling were lighted. The place was small but crowded and everyone, save for a scrawny man at the end of the counter, was watching them.

"But we might need more than three days to finish the investigation and that is essentially all the time we have," Witherspoon complained. "Today shouldn't count, as we had to waste half of it at the Yard."

"Not to worry, sir. We're making good progress." Barnes didn't like to think of what the inspector would do if Barrows tried to force him to arrest Nivens. The very idea that a fine man like Witherspoon would give up his career for someone like Nivens was too hard to bear. Instead, he forced himself to concentrate on the matter at hand. "It's a quarter to one, sir, and if I'm not mistaken, that's Dickie Stiles over there. He's the one with the black hair and pockmarked face." He pointed to the scrawny man wearing a blue, oversized jacket standing at the far end. "Constable Rhodes described him to me."

"Excellent. Perhaps he'll shed more light on this case." Witherspoon started across the floor, but Barnes pushed ahead of him and reached their quarry first. "You Dickie Stiles?" He elbowed into the spot next to him.

"I am, but I've not done anything. What do ya want with me?" He stared at them now, his expression alarmed.

"We just want to speak with you," Witherspoon said as he joined them. "It's about the murder of Humberto Santorini."

"I don't know nuffink about that," Stiles blustered.

"That's not the way we heard it." Barnes stared at him. "We heard you and Santorini were good friends—no, that's not how it was put. We were told you were one of Bert's toadies."

"I'm no one's toady." Stiles swiped at his nose.

"But you admit you knew him and that you were friends," Witherspoon said.

"Yeah, we was mates. Sometimes he'd buy me a pint and sometimes I'd buy 'im one, but that don't mean nuffink. Bert 'ad lots of friends."

"Please, Dickie, don't waste our time." Barnes laughed derisively. "We both know that Bert had more enemies than the queen has children. Now, you can either tell us the truth, or we can take a walk to Leman Street Station. Which will it be?"

"You've no cause to roust me like this," Stiles whined. "There's no law against being mates with someone. It's not my fault someone killed Bert. It's nuffink to do with me."

Several of the men at the bar grumbled, and two of the bolder ones fixed them with a good glare. But the constable narrowed his eyes and stared them down. The grumbles stopped, and all of them, a fairly old, broken-down bunch, went back to their drinking.

"Were you in the Crying Crows Pub on Saturday night?" Witherspoon asked.

Stiles quickly took another drink of his pint and then shrugged. "I might 'ave been. It's hard to remember."

"We know you were there," Barnes interjected. "We also know that you're banned from that pub, so why did you go inside?"

"That Callahan witch can ban all she wants, but I go where I want. She thinks she's better than the rest of us, tellin' this one and that one and anyone she thinks is beneath her they can't go into that ruddy pub. Well, Bert asked me to do him a favor, and I did it."

"What kind of favor?" Barnes suspected he knew what kind it was. But he couldn't be sure until he heard Dickie admit it.

"He wanted me to get a note to that police inspector." He grabbed his glass and drained it.

"Would you like another?" Witherspoon waved at the barman, who had been staring at them the entire time.

"You buyin'?" Dickie laughed. "That's a ruddy first." But he didn't say no when the barman slid another pint in front of him.

"Let me make certain I understand," the inspector said. "Bert Santorini gave you a note to give to Inspector Nigel Nivens. Is that correct?"

"I didn't give it to 'im. I put it where he'd find it. Bert told me to slip it to him and make sure no one saw me do it, and that's what I did. The copper was tossin' back whisky and had his coat slung over the back of a chair. It was dead easy to stick it in his pocket."

"But someone did see you do it," the constable said. "You must be losing your touch. The lads at the Leman Street Station said you were a good pickpocket."

"Who cares what they say?" Dickie snapped. "And I ain't admittin' to nuffink. You're just guessin' 'ere—no one saw me slip that note into his coat pocket. No one."

"It's too bad you can't read," Barnes said. "Because if you could, you could tell us what the note said."

"I can read," Stiles snapped. "I weren't raised on the ruddy streets. Me mam sent all of us to St. Giles church school until we was ten, and my sister Dolly was there until she was fourteen."

"Then what did the note say?"

"Why should I tell you?" He sneered. "You'll only think I'm makin' it up to get that ruddy copper in trouble."

"In other words"—Barnes smirked—"you can't read."

"I bloody well can," he yelled. "I don't remember the exact words, but it said for the copper to meet Bert at the Felix Mews on Monday evening just after full dark and to have his cash ready. There, that good enough for ya?"

"'Ere comes the Good Samaritan," the red-haired man said as Wiggins stepped back inside the Crying Crows. "Did ya catch 'im?"

Wiggins would have loved to ignore the man, but as he was still on the hunt for information, he said, "Yeah, I caught 'im. Nice old gent. Seems to think the owner 'ere isn't who she says she is. Kept callin' her Millie Slavik."

"Watch it." The barman looked nervously over his shoulder at the closed door behind the bar. "She goes mad when she hears that name. That's why the old feller isn't welcome here."

"What? Just because some poor senile old gent calls her by another name, she's turfed him out for good? Get me another pint. There's time for last orders." He was determined to find out something before he had to head back to Upper Edmonton Gardens.

"Be careful what ya say, then," the barman warned. "She's been in a miserable mood for days now, and if she hears ya use that name, she'll have a fit."

"Oh, don't be such a ninny, Alex." The red-haired man chuckled. "Get the lad a pint—he's earned it—and Mrs. Callahan has been in a bad mood for years, not days. I just about fell off my stool Saturday night when she gave Wilkie Bramwell and his mate them pints on the 'ouse."

"Shocked me, too." Alex put the beer in front of Wiggins. "Especially as Wilkie had been in on Friday night, and she'd ignored him. But who can understand women?"

"What 'appened?" Wiggins took a sip.

Alex glanced at the door again before he spoke. "Thursday night one of our customers got into a scuffle with another fellow, and Wilkie gave her a hand sorting him out."

Wiggins hid his disappointment by taking another drink. He'd been hoping to hear something directly related to the murder. "So she bought him a pint on Saturday—that don't sound so surprising."

"That's the first time I've ever seen her buy anyone a drink," Alex muttered. "What's more, it was right after Dickie Stiles had gone. I'd been holdin' my breath when I spotted him in 'ere, but she didn't seem bothered. But like I said, who can understand females?"

Red-hair snickered. "From what I 'ear, the late Bert Santorini understood 'er as well as a couple of others."

Alex ignored that comment. "It was right odd, too. I mean the fracas on Thursday night. Inspector Nivens and that other policeman were 'ere when Goddard started up with his shenanigans, but they was slow off the mark, and Bramwell was the one who showed Goddard the door."

"The policemen were off duty," red-hair pointed out. "You can't blame 'em for not wantin' to arrest Goddard and haul him back to Leman Street. And to their credit, they did get off their arses and make sure Goddard was well and truly gone."

Alex snorted. "Come on, they waited till it was over and then stepped outside for a minute or two. I don't know why Mrs. Callahan likes havin' the police in here all the time. Seems to me it drives people away. The locals don't much like coppers."

Witherspoon was uncharacteristically morose as the hansom pulled up in front of Frida Sorensen's lodging house. Barnes glanced at him before he swung out of the cab and held the door open for the inspector. "I can tell Dickie's statement is upsettin' you," he said as Witherspoon stepped onto the pavement. "But just because Dickie said it, doesn't mean it's true."

"It's not that I think Inspector Nivens is as pure as driven snow, but I don't believe he's a murderer. If Stiles is telling the truth about that note, we'll have no choice but to arrest Inspector Nivens."

"We don't know that Stiles was telling the truth."

"But why would he lie?" Witherspoon sighed heavily. "I know that he has no love for the police, but allegedly Stiles was Santorini's 'toady,' so why would he make up a story about Santorini giving him a note to slip to Inspector Nivens?"

"Think about it, sir. Stiles does have a reason to lie. If he really believes that Nivens is guilty and that the police are going to cover it up," Barnes suggested, "he might lie about the note to push you into arresting Nivens right away. He and Santorini might have been genuine friends." He stepped to the front of the cab, paid the driver, and rejoined Witherspoon, who was looking a bit less glum.

They went to the door, and Barnes banged the knocker against the wood. It was opened immediately, this time by Frida Sorensen herself.

She stared at them coldly. "What do you want? I've already told you everything I know."

"Please, Mrs. Sorensen, we know that you and Humberto Santorini were more than just landlady and tenant," Witherspoon said. "You had a close and intimate relationship with the victim, enough of a relationship that you confronted him at the Thistle and Thorn about his supposed feelings for the barmaid who works in that establishment."

Frida's mouth dropped open, and she hastily stepped back, opening the door wider. "Alright, then, come in and be quick about it before all the neighbors see you."

They stepped inside and followed her into the drawing room. Frida stalked to the fireplace, turned, and glared at them. "Ask your questions and then get out."

"You admit that you were at the Thistle and Thorn the night before Santorini was murdered and that you threatened him?" Barnes whipped out his notebook and propped it on top of a half-empty bookcase and then yanked his pencil out of his coat pocket.

"You already know the answer to that, so why bother asking me?" She smiled cynically. "Yes, I told him that if he tried playing me about, I'd make him sorry. No one, and I mean no one, makes a fool of me."

"Did Mr. Santorini come home that night?" Witherspoon asked.

"Yes, and he promised me that the gossip I'd heard, the talk that he was sweet on that barmaid, was just that, talk." She sucked in a deep breath and licked her lips.

"He promised you it was just gossip and you believed him?" The constable looked at her, his expression clearly skeptical.

"Bert wasn't a liar." She tapped her fingers on the top of the mantel. "I believed him, and we made up. Now, if that's all, I'd like you to go."

"I'm afraid we can't do that," the inspector said. "We've a number of other questions. To begin with, why didn't you tell us about the true nature of your relationship with the victim?"

"Because it wasn't any of your business," she snapped.

"Someone murdered him," Barnes retorted. "And if you and he had really made up, and you had feelings for him, you should want us to catch his killer. But instead, you deliberately gave us the impression he was just a tenant. How do you explain that?"

"I don't have to explain anything to you." Frida's eyes filled with tears. "You think I don't want whoever did this to get caught—course I do! But you're lookin' at me like I've something to do with it, and I didn't. If you want to find his killer, maybe you should look at the Thistle and Thorn. Bet *she* wasn't happy when he come home to me."

"Where were you on Monday evening between five forty-five and six fifteen?"

She shrugged. "Right here."

"Can anyone confirm that?" Witherspoon glanced at Barnes. The constable had already told him he'd heard from an informant that she'd been seen on the Commercial Road only moments before the body was discovered.

"No. Marianne—she's the housemaid—sets the dining room up before she leaves at five."

"What time do you serve supper?"

"Half past six. Some of the tenants don't get in until then. I don't offer a full evening meal—it's usually just a hot soup and a plate of cheese and bread. Some of my lodgers take their dinner meal out."

"What about one of them? Perhaps one of your lodgers can confirm you were here," Witherspoon suggested.

"How would they know?" She crossed her arms over her chest. "They don't come into the kitchen, and I don't open the dining room until right before I serve."

"At half past six you opened the dining room, and your lodgers can verify that?"

"Go and ask. Mr. Pruitt is upstairs. He can tell you I was here."

"Bert Santorini was killed in the Felix Mews just after dark. That's less than a twenty-minute walk from here. You could have done it and then got back here in time to serve your lodgers their supper." Barnes stared at her as he spoke.

"That's ridiculous." She uncrossed her arms and put them at her sides, her hands bunching into fists. "I told you—we'd made up, so why should I want to kill him? Besides, I've told you, I was here all afternoon."

"If that's true, ma'am," Witherspoon said, "then can you explain something for me? We have a witness that saw you on the Commercial Road within thirty yards of the entrance to Felix Mews only seconds before Santorini's body was found."

Betsy put the teapot on the table. She and the housekeeper were setting up the table for their afternoon meeting. The sun had come out, and she'd let Mrs. Goodge take Amanda out for a walk. She glanced at Mrs. Jeffries and noticed that the housekeeper's expression was serious, as though she was worried. "Are you alright?"

"Oh yes, I'm fine." She gave Betsy a quick smile. "It's just this case. It's a bit more complicated than I initially thought it would be."

Guilt flooded Betsy. "I'm sorry I haven't contributed very much."

Mrs. Jeffries turned and looked at her. "You've done your fair share."

"No, I haven't." Betsy plopped into a chair. "I've not even gone out except for that one time. The truth is, Mrs. Jeffries, I couldn't face it, not after that first time I went back to the East End. I didn't think it would bother me so much. I've been through the area a time or two in the last few years, but this was the first time I'd actually gone back to places I used to know."

"That must have been very hard," Mrs. Jeffries said. "But you've no need to apologize, Betsy. Over the years you've more than done your part and, to be perfectly frank, no matter how many of us were working on this case, I'd still be in a dreadful muddle."

Betsy drew back and studied the housekeeper. She realized that Mrs. Jeffries wasn't just trying to make *her* feel better—she actually meant what she said. "But that's nonsense. You'll figure it out. You always do. Give yourself a bit more time—it's only been a few days."

Mrs. Jeffries gave her a grateful smile. "I hope you're right. It's a very puzzling case. The only person who appears to have a motive that fits all the circumstances of the crime is Fiona O'Dwyer. She's the only person who could possibly have a motive to want Santorini dead and Inspector Nivens arrested. She did blame him for sending her sons to prison."

"Plus, she sent her daughter off to Ireland on the pretense that Santorini threatened the girl," Betsy added. "She might have done it so she could move about freely, you know, follow Nivens and find out where he lives. Besides, as you pointed out before, Mrs. O'Dwyer has a lot of connections because of her sons. She could easily have found someone to break into Nivens' house and steal one of those guns—" She broke off as they heard the back door open and footsteps moving quickly up the corridor. A moment later, Phyllis hurried inside.

"The others are right behind me." She took off her coat as she raced toward the coat tree. She spotted the teapot on the table. "Oh, good—it's ready. I'll get the milk from the wet larder."

Within minutes, everyone had taken their places at the table. "Who would like to go first?"

"Mine will only take a minute," Luty offered glumly. "The only thing my source knew was that Bryson's Brewery is havin' a tough time financially." She glanced at Ruth. "Seems like that Mr. Bryson, who bored your whole table at that charity luncheon, wasn't just talkin' to hear the sound of his own voice. My source claims that he's actively trying to find investors."

"Oh, perhaps that explains his behavior," Ruth murmured. "Helen Cavendish was at our table, and her husband is always looking for a good investment opportunity."

"Anything else, Luty?" Mrs. Jeffries asked.

"Afraid not."

"Don't be so miserable, Luty," Smythe volunteered. "The only thing I found out was that some of the locals have said Susan Callahan's barman was being paid to pass along any information he happened to overhear from the police to his boss. But my source couldn't confirm it, so it might just be gossip because there's so much resentment against that pub as well as the people who work there." He'd been disappointed that this was all Blimpey had for him today, but, as Blimpey had explained, on this particular case, he had his people workin' to help Fiona O'Dwyer. She'd hired him first. Blimpey was scrupulously fair in his business dealings.

Mrs. Jeffries forced a smile and glanced around the table. "Phyllis, did you have any luck today?"

"None," she admitted. "I'm sorry."

"Don't be sorry," Mrs. Jeffries said briskly. "Rome wasn't built in a day."

"I found out a little bit," Wiggins said quickly. From the expression on the faces around the table, he could tell none of them had anything more to add. What was worse, he sensed that despite Mrs. Jeffries' smiles and careful comments, she was worried, really worried they'd never solve this case. "It was a bit odd, and I'm not sure it's got anything to do with the case, but I'll pass it along." He told them about his trip to the Crying Crows, skipping over the bit where no one would talk to him and going directly into his chasing after the elderly Enoch Dinsworth. He made certain to tell them every single detail, focusing on what he'd heard from Rosemary Dinsworth. "But when we got back to the Crying Crows, I decided to give it one more go to see if I could find out anything else." He continued speaking, repeating the bits and pieces he'd heard from the other patrons and the barman. "It's not much," he concluded. "I wish I coulda learned more, but they're a suspicious lot in that part of London."

"Regardless of whether the information is useful or not"—Mrs. Jeffries gave him a genuine smile—"you did the right thing. That poor Mr. Dinsworth might have been badly hurt if you'd not been there."

Everyone at the table echoed her words to such an extent that the footman was embarrassed. "It were nothin' special," he muttered as a blush crept up his cheeks. "Any of you woulda done the same."

"Anyone else have anything to add?" Mrs. Jeffries asked.

No one did.

* * *

When the inspector arrived home that evening, his mood was almost as melancholy as Mrs. Jeffries'. They had their sherry together, and she listened carefully as he described his day. But she could tell he was upset, especially as the pressure from Scotland Yard was mounting.

"I don't know what to do, Mrs. Jeffries." He put his empty glass on the side table. "If Dickie Stiles is telling the truth, and we've no reason to believe he isn't, then the evidence pointing to Inspector Nivens' guilt is overwhelming. Not only that, but the only reason that Santorini would have instructed Nivens to bring cash is because he must have been blackmailing the inspector."

"And you think that he was being blackmailed because he paid Santorini to lie on the witness stand?" Mrs. Jeffries sipped her drink.

Witherspoon pursed his lips and shook his head. "I don't see that it could be anything else, Mrs. Jeffries. I know that Nivens is capable of behaving badly, but I simply cannot believe he is a killer. Unfortunately, I don't know how much longer I can delay his arrest."

"What about some of your other suspects?" Mrs. Jeffries suggested. This morning, she had told Constable Barnes her theory that Fiona O'Dwyer had the resources to commit the crime, and she knew that Barnes would have found a way to pass that idea along to the inspector.

"We're taking a second look at Fiona O'Dwyer," he said. "And Frida Sorensen. Neither woman has an alibi, and both may have had a motive to murder Santorini. But only Mrs. O'Dwyer had a reason to frame Inspector Nivens."

"You'll sort it out, sir." She hoped she sounded better than she felt. "You always do."

"I don't know about this one, Mrs. Jeffries." He exhaled sharply. "Nothing seems to be going right. We can't even keep the reports sorted properly. This sounds petty, but honestly, this is the third time the case reports haven't been in their proper place, so on top of being hard-pressed for time on most days, I've got to waste time searching the duty inspector's office for the file. Someone keeps moving the ruddy thing."

"Perhaps it's the cleaners, sir," she murmured. She was thinking hard about everything he'd told her.

"They don't have cleaners, Mrs. Jeffries. The constables keep the place tidy, and once or twice a week the prisoners scrub the floors. Ignore me, please. I'm just frustrated and rather depressed, if the truth be known."

"Of course you are, sir." She brought her attention back to the present. "Your 'inner voice' is telling you Inspector Nivens is innocent while your rational side insists you look at the evidence. But as I said"—she paused and forced a cheerful smile—"you'll sort it out. You always do."

Mrs. Jeffries tossed and turned as one thought after another skittered through her mind. She tried taking long, deep breaths in order to marshal her errant ideas into some sort of logical sequence. But it was difficult. She flopped onto her back and forced herself to start at the beginning and to go over each and every morsel of information or gossip they'd heard thus far; but the bits and pieces wouldn't behave, and she found herself drifting off as one thought after another poked into her brain.

She rolled onto her side as her own voice echoed in her head.

"You read the article in the *Sentinel*. Why else would our inspector be going to the East End?" A second later, she wondered why Santorini had eighty-five pounds in his possession, ten of which were gold sovereigns. But that wasn't all he'd kept in that box. Why keep bad whisky and inferior beer?

But try as she might, she simply couldn't come up with an answer. She went over the suspects one by one. Philip Graves hated Santorini, but he'd never had anything to do with Nigel Nivens, so why would Graves go to so much trouble to make it appear as if Nivens was the killer? Surely if it was just general hatred of the police, Graves could have found an easier way to publicly humiliate them.

Harvey Macklin hated Santorini as well. But both the inspector and Constable Barnes had thought Macklin hadn't the character to plan such a sophisticated crime. As she trusted both their judgment, she was inclined to agree with them.

Frida Sorensen and Alberta Miller were both involved with Santorini, and jealousy was a classic reason for murder. Hell hath no fury like a woman scorned, she thought as the idea took hold. Neither of them had alibis, and both of them may have had friends or relatives that could have helped them. She couldn't leave Susan Callahan off the "woman scorned" list, either. They only had the widow Callahan's word that she was the one that tossed Santorini out of her life. It could well have been him that left her.

She yawned as drowsiness overcame her. Just as she was falling asleep, she heard Constable Barnes' voice. *I just remembered something. Inspector Nivens asked me the same thing.*

CHAPTER 10

The next morning, Constable Barnes was almost as glum as Inspector Witherspoon had been the night before. He added a few details to the information Mrs. Jeffries had heard from Witherspoon but was even less optimistic that they'd find any evidence exonerating Nigel Nivens. "Much as it pains me to say it, from the evidence, it looks like Nivens is guilty."

"But Inspector Witherspoon seems sure he isn't," the cook pointed out. "And I can't help feeling he's right. But as I see it, that's not the problem here. We all know that rather than arrest someone he doesn't think is guilty, our inspector will quit the force."

"It won't come to that, Mrs. Goodge." Mrs. Jeffries tapped the side of her tea mug with her finger. "He's still got a few days before he has to take any action. The murder only happened on Monday evening, and surely Chief Superintendent Barrows will see reason about the matter."

"Don't be too sure of that, Mrs. Jeffries," Barnes said. "Dickie Stiles' statement is now part of the official report, and that'll be on Barrows' desk by tomorrow morning. The only reason it's not already there is because we got back to Leman Street too late for it to be included in yesterday's district report."

"Isn't there some way of delaying it?" Mrs. Jeffries needed time to think. The idea that had come to her in the wee hours of the morning needed to be examined against the witness statements, the bits and pieces of information they'd picked up from their collective sources, and local gossip they'd learned thus far. "Last night Inspector Witherspoon complained that the files on this case had been mislaid several times and that was just in the Leman Street duty inspector's office. Surely there's a way to 'mislay' yesterday's report from getting to Barrows' office for a bit longer."

"I doubt it, Mrs. Jeffries." Barnes shook his head, his expression gloomy. "You know our inspector—he'd not do something like that."

"But that would give you both time to have another go at Fiona O'Dwyer," Mrs. Goodge added. "The woman doesn't have a real alibi, and she's the only one who might have had it in for both Santorini and Nigel Nivens."

"As far as we know," Mrs. Jeffries murmured. She made her decision. She'd planned on bringing up her idea at the morning meeting so the others could weigh in with their thoughts, add to what she had come up with. But they no longer had that luxury. She'd hoped the others could help put the pieces together in such a way that she'd have no doubt her theory was right. In truth, she could well be wrong, but that was just a chance she'd have to take. They were out of time.

Barnes put his mug on the table and started to get up.

"Constable Barnes, have you ever heard of someone called Millie Slavik?" Mrs. Jeffries blurted.

Barnes stopped moving in midair. His eyes widened, and his mouth formed a surprised O as he sank back into the chair. "Ye gods, I've not heard that name in years," he murmured. He cocked his head to one side, his expression thoughtful. "Good gracious, no wonder she looked so familiar. It's her. It's really her, and Inspector Nivens must have recognized her, too."

"Who?" Mrs. Goodge demanded. "Who are you talking about?"

"Susan Callahan." Barnes exhaled softly. "This might change everything."

"We've much to do this morning," Mrs. Jeffries warned the cook as they hurried into the kitchen to get everything set up for the morning meeting.

"I understand." Mrs. Goodge grabbed her matches and lit the gas fire under the kettle. "I'm not sure what's going on here, but I know you're close to figuring it out."

"Thanks for the vote of confidence, but as of now, my theory is just that, a theory." Mrs. Jeffries grabbed the mugs out of the pine sideboard and put them on the table.

"Is that why you asked Constable Barnes to confirm those two bits of information?"

"Yes. If I'm right, then there will have been some contact between them." She broke off as she heard footsteps coming down the back staircase. "Good. Here comes Phyllis. I'm going to send her off before I do anything else."

"Send me off where?" Phyllis asked as she came into the kitchen carrying a tray with the inspector's empty breakfast dishes. She glanced at the housekeeper curiously as she crossed to the sink.

"To the East End," Mrs. Jeffries explained. "I want you to have a word with Janice Everly. I want you to waylay her before morning opening and ask her a few questions. You'll need to play your role of being a private inquiry agent."

Phyllis put the dishes in the sink and started to run the water.

"Leave the dishes," the cook ordered. "I'll take care of them. You get your apron off and get ready to go."

"What should I ask her?" Phyllis struggled with her apron strings as she hurried toward the coat tree. She finally got the garment off.

"The questions won't make a lot of sense at the moment, and I've no time to explain," Mrs. Jeffries said. "But you need to find out two things . . ." She trailed off as they heard the back door open and footsteps stomping up the hallway.

It was Luty and Hatchet. Mrs. Goodge ushered them in while the housekeeper finished giving Phyllis her instructions.

"Be as quick as you can and hurry back," she told her as Phyllis buttoned her coat.

"What if Janice isn't working today?" She put on her hat.

Mrs. Jeffries drew some coins from her pocket and held them out to the maid. "Then bribe someone for her address and go to her house. We need this information."

"Will do, Mrs. Jeffries." Phyllis grinned broadly and raced for the back door. "I'll be back as soon as I can," she said as she flew past Wiggins, who'd just come downstairs.

"Oy, where you off to in such a 'urry?" he called after her.

"Where's she goin'?" Luty demanded.

"You've figured it out, haven't you?" Hatchet added. "Well done, Mrs. Jeffries, well done."

"I'm not sure. That's why I've sent Phyllis off to the East End." The housekeeper frowned worriedly. "Frankly, this time, I'm not certain I'm right, but I might be. I do hope Betsy and Smythe get here soon. We've much to discuss."

"And we'll need Smythe and Wiggins to get out and keep an eye on things," Mrs. Goodge said. The kettle boiled, and she grabbed a pot holder and hurried to the cooker. "I've had one of my feelings again, and I know all of you make light of them, but I was right on that other case we had last year." She poured the water into the teapot and then put the kettle back on the cooker.

"Keep an eye on what?" Wiggins pulled out his chair.

"Let's wait until everyone arrives . . ." Mrs. Jeffries' voice trailed off as they heard the back door open and footsteps pounding up the back.

"Slow down, Amanda." Betsy's voice warned her daughter. "You're going to fall."

A moment later Amanda came racing into the room. She skidded to a halt beneath the archway and looked around the room, then she ran flat-out toward Mrs. Goodge, who quickly put the teapot on the table before scooping up her goddaughter into her arms. "Hello, my lovey," she cooed as the little one snuggled close.

Wiggins yanked out the cook's chair and steadied her by putting his hand under her elbow as she eased into her seat, arranging Amanda comfortably on her lap.

"Ruth is right behind us," Smythe announced as he and Betsy appeared.

Within a very few minutes, everyone was seated around the table.

Wiggins spoke first. "What's goin' on? Why'd you send Phyllis to the East End? Where do ya want me and Smythe to go?"

"You'll understand in just a moment," Mrs. Jeffries said. "First of all, I need to tell you what we found out from the inspector and Constable Barnes." She told them everything, speaking quickly but clearly so they'd follow her reasoning. "So I've sent Phyllis to speak to Janice Everly, to see if she can confirm something which must have happened if my theory is correct. But I also need someone to verify something else, but I've no idea which of you has a source that would know the answer to this question." She paused, took a deep breath, and then told them what she needed to know. For a moment, no one said a word. Then Smythe said, "One of my sources *might* know. But 'onestly, it's doubtful. I think 'e'd already 'ave told me if 'e did."

Betsy suddenly stood up. "If Amanda can stay here, I've got a source that will know."

"Betsy, no." Smythe grabbed her hand. "You don't need to do it . . ."

"I do." She smiled at her husband. "She'll know, and I need to do this, if for no other reason than to break the hold the past has on me."

"We'll take care of the little one," Luty offered. "Unlessin', of course"—she looked at the housekeeper—"you need me and Hatchet to get out and about."

"Only Hatchet," Mrs. Jeffries said. "I've a task for him, if he's willing."

"Of course I am."

"What about what you want me and Smythe to do?" Wiggins asked.

"Are we close to a resolution on the case?" Ruth reached for the cream pitcher and added a bit more to her tea.

Mrs. Jeffries hesitated. "It will depend on if we can find out a few more bits and pieces that might or might not have occurred between Saturday night and Monday evening. The truth is, I'm simply not sure."

"I am," the cook announced. "You always get this way at the end of a case, but I know you've figured it out." She looked at Wiggins. "And we want you and Smythe to keep an eye on the Crying Crows."

Mrs. Jeffries smiled as she looked at Hatchet. "If Luty doesn't mind, we'd like you to keep an eye on Nigel Nivens' house."

"Course I don't mind. I'm goin' to be here with the little one and the two of you." Luty gestured at Mrs. Goodge and Mrs. Jeffries.

"Is there anything specific I'm to watch for?" Hatchet asked.

"I'm not certain," Mrs. Jeffries admitted, "but you'll know it when you see it. If, indeed, anything happens at all."

"Something's goin' to happen alright," the cook muttered.

Hatchet got to his feet. "I take it you'd like me back for our afternoon meeting?"

"Yes, and let me apologize in advance. You might end up spending most of the day waiting for absolutely nothing to happen. My reason for wanting you to keep Nivens in sight is hazy at best. I might be acting precipitously here once again." Mrs. Jeffries frowned.

"You're not," the cook announced. "Something is going to happen. I've told you, I've got one of my feelings and, sneer at them all ya like, but I know I'm right."

"Are you alright, Constable?" Inspector Witherspoon asked as the cab turned onto Leman Street.

"Yes, sir. Why do you ask?"

"You've been very quiet."

Barnes smiled self-consciously. "I've been thinking, sir." He stepped out as the hansom pulled in front of the police station. "I've figured out why Susan Callahan looked so familiar to me," he said. He took care of the driver and then they headed for the front door.

"How very interesting," Witherspoon said as they went inside. "Why was it?"

"I think she's someone else, someone I knew quite well when I worked around these parts," Barnes said as they crossed the room. "I'm going to ask Constable Rhodes what he thinks. He might be able to help a bit."

"Morning, sir." Rhodes nodded respectfully at Witherspoon. "Help with what?" he asked Barnes.

"With my memory," the constable replied. This was the tricky bit. He'd thought about the situation on the ride over, and the only way it might make sense is if he could get confirmation of her identity and, more important, find out a few other essential facts. Facts that might only be available from old records, and Barnes wasn't even sure where such old records might be stored.

From behind them, they heard the front door open.

"Remember when I asked if Susan Callahan looked familiar to you?" Barnes asked.

Rhodes nodded. "I do. It was just a couple of days ago. Why?"

"Do you recall a pickpocket that lived around here, a woman named Millie Slavik? It was a long time ago."

Rhodes' brows drew together. "Millie Slavik . . . Oh yes, yes, now I remember her. She was a lovely little thing. Mean as a contrary goose and slippery as an eel, but she disappeared years ago . . ." His voice trailed off and his expression changed. "Good gracious, I can't believe I didn't see it before. Mind you, I've only seen her a time or two, and she looks so different now. She's gained a good two stone in weight, and her hair is red, but women can make their hair a different color. My wife claims a lady at the Women's Institute dyes her hair."

Barnes interrupted. "You think Susan Callahan could be Millie Slavik?"

"Now that you've pointed it out, I do." Rhodes' gaze moved over Barnes' shoulder. "What the devil is he doin' here?" he muttered. "Good day, Inspector Nivens. Can I help you with something?"

"I've just come to pick up my post and water Maude." Nivens shoved away from the far wall and headed for the duty inspector's office. "I'll just be a moment."

Rhodes scowled at Nivens' back. "He usually comes in the evening to water that wretched plant. I wonder how long he was standing there?"

"Standing where?" Witherspoon blurted the question before he could stop himself. He was a bit confused, but he had enough trust in Constable Barnes not to interrupt or ask too many questions until the two of them were alone.

"Just inside, against that back wall." Rhodes pointed to a spot beside the door. "He moved when I saw him."

"Was he eavesdropping?" Barnes asked.

"Probably."

"John, you've been here for years"—Barnes leaned on the counter—"and you've a decent memory."

"I wouldn't say that." He laughed. "I didn't remember Millie Slavik until you mentioned her."

"Nonetheless, was Inspector Nivens ever in this part of the East End? Could he have arrested Millie Slavik?"

"I doubt it. For starters, Millie did her best work in the West End. What's the use of pickin' pockets here? Most people are too poor to have much except a few ha'pennies. Also, when Inspector Nivens was first assigned here, it was obvious he'd never been in this part of London before."

"Where would Nivens' service records be kept?"

Rhodes shrugged. "The Yard, I guess. I don't know."

"I do." Witherspoon chuckled. "Really, Constable, have you forgotten where I used to work?"

Barnes thought for a minute and then he laughed. "Silly of me, sir. Of course, the records room at Scotland Yard." He broke off as Inspector Nivens stepped out of the duty inspector's office and into the short hallway.

"He's right here. Why don't you just ask him?" Rhodes said softly.

Barnes shook his head as Nivens came into the room proper. He nodded at Witherspoon and headed for the door.

"Why does he come every day to water a plant? My wife waters ours twice a week," Barnes said as soon as the door closed behind Nivens.

"Is it that aspidistra by the window?" Witherspoon asked. "If so, I do believe he's overwatering the poor thing. It's half dead."

"He comes in most evenings when things get a bit quiet," Rhodes said. "I told Inspector Havers about it, but he said that as long as Nivens didn't interfere with police business, to leave him be."

"Well, that's probably a wise course to follow." Witherspoon started toward the corridor. "I'll just nip into the office and get the file on this case. I'd like to look at Dickie Stiles' statement again before we interview Mrs. O'Dwyer."

Barnes chatted quietly with Rhodes as they waited for Witherspoon. But a good five minutes had passed when the inspector came rushing out, slamming the office door behind him.

Barnes shoved away from the counter as Rhodes straightened up.

"It's gone," Witherspoon cried. "It's gone. The entire Santorini file is gone."

"Blast a Spaniard," Barnes muttered, borrowing one of Smythe's sayings, "I'll wager I know who took it."

Betsy stepped out of the hansom and paid the driver. Smythe had wanted to come with her, but she'd told him that she needed to do this herself and reminded him he was needed elsewhere.

She turned and faced Mattie Mitchell's shop. Betsy had dressed in the same outfit she'd worn before. The only difference now was that she had half a dozen sovereigns in her purse rather than banknotes. Mattie was always partial to fancy coins.

Taking a deep breath, Betsy crossed the cracked pavement and stepped inside. Mattie stood behind the counter, watching her. Neither woman said anything for a long moment, then Mattie cackled. "I knew you'd be back."

"How very clever of you," Betsy said. "Since you knew I'd be back, care to have a guess as to why I'm here?"

Mattie reached into the open box of tobacco tins she'd been unpacking, pulled one out, and placed it next to the others on the counter. "Same reason you were 'ere the first time. You're wantin' to stick yer nose in somethin' that's none of yer business."

"That didn't stop you from taking my money." Betsy crossed the small shop. If anything, the place looked even worse than the last time. The layer of dust on the display case was thicker, more dirt was caked on the floor, and the windows were so streaked with grime, it was hard to see the street. The place was falling apart and that meant one thing: Mattie was in dire straits.

"That's true." Mattie carefully placed a tin on the bottom shelf of the small glass display case on the counter, angling the colorful tobacco case to hide the beginning of a long crack. "What do you want to know now?"

"I want to know everything you know about Susan Callahan."

Mattie stopped, her hand resting in midair before she picked up another tin. "Susan Callahan? Why do ya think I'd know about 'er? She's not goin' to be friendly to the likes of me, not that one. Walks around with 'er nose in the air like she's too good to breathe the same air as the rest of us." She put the tin in the display case. "Nah, I don't know anythin' about that one. You've wasted yer time comin' 'ere."

Betsy pulled the smart gray suede purse out of her pocket, opened it, and pulled out a sovereign. "That's too bad, Mattie. I brought several of these with me. But seein' as you've just said you can't help me, I might as well try elsewhere."

"Just a second," Mattie cried. "Let's not be hasty 'ere. Maybe I do know a thing or two. I was just 'aving a go at ya because of the way ya stomped out of 'ere last time."

"I'm in no mood to play games, Mattie. If you know something, tell me."

"How many of them do you 'ave?" Mattie jerked her chin at the coin.

"Enough. Start talking, Mattie, and don't try lyin' to me. I've plenty where this came from, and if you lie, I can make your life right miserable."

"There's no need to threaten me—I'll not lie." She snorted.

"How long has Susan Callahan been here?" Betsy asked.

"Seven years, maybe seven and a half." Mattie put another tin in the case. "Old man Callahan went up north somewhere—Leeds, I think it was—and when he came back, he was married to her."

"Was she from Leeds?"

"Course not—tried to pretend she was, but you could tell by the way she talked that she'd not been born or bred up there, and her name ain't Susan. It's Millie Slavik, and she was born less than a quarter mile from that pub she owns now." Mattie stared at the coin in Betsy's hand. "I think I've earned that one."

"Not yet." Betsy clasped the coin tighter. "I already knew that bit. You'll get this when you tell me something I don't know."

Mattie snorted. "You didn't use to be such a 'ard one."

"You think you know who I am?"

"Course I do. You're Betsy Berry," she said, using Betsy's maiden name. She looked Betsy up and down, once again taking in the expensive clothes and shoes. "And you've done well for yerself. You think you were 'ard done by when you used to come in 'ere, but I was poor, too, and I needed every penny I could lay me 'ands on to keep this shop goin'."

"I'm sure you believe that's true." Betsy refused to feel anything other than contempt for this old hag. The memory of how her family had been treated, how her mother died flooded back in a rush. But she forced the memories away. "Let's get back to business here. What else do you know about her?"

"She killed old man Callahan, that's for sure," Mattie announced. "One day he had a touch of bronchitis, and the next day, he was dead. The day before he died, Susan was at the chemist's buying a big bottle of laudanum. But when the undertakers come to get his body, most of the bottle was gone."

Betsy handed over the coin. "You've earned this one. If you want another one, keep talking."

Hatchet pulled back the blue velvet curtain covering the carriage window and stared at Nigel Nivens' home on the other side of the street. He'd had the coachman pull the carriage up to a spot farther along the road, rather than directly in front of the house. He had a good view from here, but the trouble was thus far, there was nothing to see.

He yawned and shifted on the seat. The only thing that had happened since he'd arrived was the housekeeper had gone out with her shopping basket. He wasn't concerned with any of the neighbors getting curious about him; Luty's expensive carriage fit in perfectly in this neighborhood.

He was bored, but he wasn't going to desert his post. He'd no idea why Mrs. Jeffries had sent him here, and apparently she hadn't a clue herself. Nonetheless, he would do his duty, no matter how dull it was. Just then, a cab stopped at the corner, and a man stepped out and hurried along the pavement. The hansom stayed where it was.

The man wasn't quite running, but he was moving fast. His bowler was slightly askew, and he had some sort of small box clutched to his chest.

Hatchet squinted at him and wished he'd brought his spectacles. But they were on the table next to his bed. The man reached the short, paved walkway leading to Nivens' home, turned in, and raced for the door. Hatchet realized it was Nivens.

He had no idea why he was suddenly sure that he needed to find out what Nivens was up to—he'd only been told to keep an eye on the place. Perhaps it was because Mrs. Goodge had insisted that something was going to happen today or perhaps it was because Nivens was acting so odd, but nonetheless Hatchet decided to take a look for himself.

He waited a moment until Nivens went inside and then got out of the carriage. Glancing up, he nodded at Cecil, the coachman, and crossed the road. He didn't need to look around to know the layout of the property; the first thing he'd done when arriving here had been to take a walk past the place.

He plunged down the side of the house, moving fast and trying to be as quiet as possible as he approached the window. He stopped, peered inside, and saw nothing but a nicely furnished drawing room. He moved to the next window, and, as Luty would say, he hit pay dirt. Nivens was there. He was at his desk, still wearing his coat and reading the papers on his desk.

Hatchet eased to one side, far enough from Nivens' line of sight so that he wouldn't be spotted if Nivens looked up. But he didn't. Hatchet stood quietly for a good twenty minutes while Nivens sat at the desk, his attention focused on whatever was in the pages in front of him.

All of a sudden, he looked at the window, and Hatchet hastily stepped back. He held his breath, expecting at any moment that Nivens would throw open the casement and demand to know who he was. But nothing happened. After a few moments, Hatchet peeked inside again.

Nivens was at his bookcase. He pulled a flat, wooden box off the shelf, took it to his desk, opened it, and reached inside.

Hatchet's eyes widened as he saw it was a gun. Specifically, a dueling pistol.

Nivens held the gun in his hand and stared at it for a good two minutes. Then he opened his coat and put the weapon into the inner pocket. He moved fast now, stopping only long enough to grab the bowler he'd tossed on the chair before disappearing out the door.

Hatchet raced back the way he'd come, getting to the carriage and inside it just as Nivens exited his front door. He watched Nivens stride to the hansom that was still on the corner and step inside. A moment later, the cab pulled away from the curb.

"Oy." Hatchet thumbed the ceiling of the carriage, stuck his head out the window, and yelled at Cecil, who awoke with a start. "Follow the hansom." Hatchet pointed at the cab, which was now turning the corner. "Don't lose it."

Cecil didn't hesitate. He cracked his whip in the air and took off after the cab. They followed closely, moving across the busy streets of the West End to the smaller, more congested streets of the City of London and then on to the East End.

Hatchet held on to the handhold as Cecil weaved the vehicle in and out of the heavy traffic while keeping the right hansom in sight. Hatchet was thinking furiously. He wanted to get word to Mrs. Jeffries about this startling turn of events, but his instincts, which he'd learned to trust years ago, were screaming at him that he didn't have time to get back to Upper Edmonton Gardens. He had to do something now. But what?

The hansom pulled onto the Commercial Road, blending in with dozens of other cabs. Hatchet watched from the small window, trying his best to keep the right cab in sight. At one point, he was sure that Cecil had lost it, but he was only changing lanes, jockeying and moving fast. Finally, after what seemed like hours but was in truth far shorter, Cecil swung the big carriage past the hansom as it pulled up at the curb. Cecil slowed down, and Hatchet, hoping his bad ankle wouldn't pick this moment to fail him, leapt out. He nodded at Cecil, who pointed at a side street farther up the road.

Hatchet ran to where the hansom had stopped and got there in time to see Nigel Nivens hurrying along the pavement just ahead of him. Nivens turned a corner, and Hatchet dashed after him. He rounded the corner and watched Nivens easing back into a darkened walkway between two buildings. Hatchet quickly crossed the street so he'd not be spotted and continued walking. What on earth was Nivens doing? Hatchet slowed his steps as he walked, and he was almost past the place before he realized exactly where he was. He was in front of the Crying Crows Pub, and Nigel Nivens was hiding across the street with a gun.

No matter how one looked at the situation, it wasn't good. Hatchet moved a bit faster now, trying to put the pieces together. Betsy volunteering to see what she could find out about Susan Callahan's past. Mrs. Jeffries sending Phyllis to speak to Janice Everly, the barmaid from the Crying Crows, and sending Wiggins and Smythe to keep an eye on the pub. They should be close by, and right now, he could use all the help he could get.

Hatchet stopped and surveyed the area, his gaze raking both sides of the road. But he couldn't see either of them. Where the devil were they? He knew something horrible was going to happen if he didn't take action. He could feel it in his bones.

Hatchet didn't know how much attention Nivens had paid to him when he burst into their meeting the other day, but he didn't want to risk Nivens' recognizing him. Hatchet went to the end of the street, far enough away so that if Nivens stuck his head out of his hiding place, he couldn't see him.

As he walked, he yanked his pocket watch out of his waistcoat and looked at the time. It was already twenty past twelve, and the pub would close at one p.m. When he reached the busy corner, he surveyed the area quickly and spotted what he was looking for across the road. Hatchet dashed across the busy thoroughfare to where a young brown-haired lad, no more than twelve, ambled down the road, his attention fixed on a pretty lass much older than himself walking ahead of him.

Hatchet stepped in front of him. "How would you like to earn a shilling?"

"Huh?" The lad blinked and stepped back. He was slender, blue eyed, and wearing a black jacket that was a bit too big for his thin frame. "Did I hear you right? You're offerin' me a shilling? To do what?"

"Get to the Leman Street Police Station and find Inspector Witherspoon or Constable Barnes. Tell them there's big trouble at the Crying Crows Pub and to get there quick. Go fast and then get back here. If you're there and back in fifteen minutes, I'll give you two more of these."

"They'll not believe someone like me." He bit his lip.

"They will if you tell them you saw that police inspector everyone knows killed Bert Santorini going into the pub and that he was carrying a gun."

"I know where she went when she disappeared." Mattie cackled. "She pulled a good one back then, she did. Up and vanished like a puff of smoke. Mind you, she'd been arrested a time or two before, but when she got out of prison that last time, she vowed she'd never go back. She meant it, too."

"Is that when she went to Leeds?" Betsy asked.

Mattie shook her head. "Nah, she took up with a troupe of actors, not one of them respectable ones like you see in the West End. It was one of them kind you don't see much of anymore. Small groups that put on plays and such wherever they can find a village hall or pub that'll pay a bit to see 'em perform. That's where she learned them tricks."

"What kind of tricks?" Betsy stared at her skeptically.

"The ones she used to fool everyone 'round these parts." Mattie laughed again. "She dyed her hair that ugly red, put on a good two stone in weight, got them spectacles, and changed her voice."

"You mean she got rid of her accent?"

"I didn't say that, did I? She changed the sound—her voice sounded different when she come back as old Mr. Callahan's bride. She didn't sound at all like Millie Slavik. But despite her best efforts, she couldn't fool everybody. She didn't fool me, and she didn't fool that Inspector Nivens. He was always askin' her questions about where she was and what she was doin' twenty-five years ago."

"How do you know that?" Betsy demanded.

"Alex Parker, her barman, he's been braggin' to some of his mates, one of which is my grandson, that Susan Callahan paid him extra to keep his ears open whenever that Inspector Nivens was in the pub. Seems that fellow likes the sound of his own voice and wasn't shy about givin' his opinion or tellin' that stupid police constable that was always lickin' his boots lots of details about himself."

Betsy dug another coin out of her purse. "What kind of details?"

Mattie held out her hand, and Betsy handed over the money.

"Seein' as you've asked so nicely, I'll tell ya. He complained about 'avin' to stay at his mother's house on Sunday and Monday night. Mickey—he's my grandson—said that Alex was whining that Susan started in on him on Saturday night, when Nivens showed up at the pub. She claimed Alex said that Nivens was leavin' town, so what in blazes was 'e doin' in the pub? Alex corrected her and said he'd told her that it was Nivens' *mother* that was leavin' town. He was right scared she was goin' to sack 'im, but all of a sudden she got sweet as pie, grabbin' a couple of beers and givin' 'em out to a couple of fellas for free. Alex was stunned when she did that. Susan never gives anythin' away for free."

"We've wasted half the morning looking for that wretched file box. Sometimes following proper police procedure is very inefficient." Witherspoon shook his head in disbelief as he and Barnes came out of the lockup and headed for the front foyer. "You don't suppose that someone took it upon themselves to send the file to the Yard?"

Barnes knew exactly where the file was. "I don't think it's likely, sir. Who would do such a thing? Inspector Nivens isn't well liked, but most officers would think twice before doing something so outside the normal channels. I suspect it was Nivens himself who took the file."

"I agree, but we can't accuse him of that unless we've searched everywhere. We'd look like fools if we accused him and the file had accidentally been mislaid somewhere here in the station. I hope you're right that no one has sent it along to the Yard. If Chief Superintendent Barrows gets wind of Dickie Stiles' statement, he'll insist we arrest Inspector Nivens."

They went to the reception counter, and Witherspoon drummed his fingers on the wood, wondering what to do next.

"Has Inspector Havers been in the office?" Barnes asked Constable Rhodes.

Rhodes shook his head. "No. He's used the chief inspector's office since you've been here. Other than yourselves, the only people who have been in that office are Constable Donner—he takes the evening post in—and Inspector Nivens, who, as you both know, was here this morning. None of us like to think it, but I've a feeling that the inspector wanted to have a good look at the evidence against him . . ." He broke off as a young lad burst through the front door, dashed across the floor, and skidded to a halt.

"You'd best hurry up and send some constables to the Crying Crows Pub," he shouted. "That copper that killed Santorini is there, and he's got a gun." The boy turned and raced out the way he'd come.

Barnes was the first to react. "We'd better go see what's wrong, sir." He was already heading for the front door. "This sounds very bad."

Inspector Witherspoon hurried after him. "Send along some constables," he called to Rhodes as they raced out of the station.

"Janice told me that Susan Callahan walked right behind Inspector Nivens when she was taking two pints to a couple of men that helped her with a nasty customer. She gave them free beer, and when I pressed Janice, she remembered that after Susan put the pints down, she dropped her handkerchief and bent down to pick it up," Phyllis reported as she tore off her outer garments and hung them on the coat tree. She hurried to the table and took her seat. "As for the other thing you asked about, Janice was sure that when Alex was outside Susan's flat on Saturday night, he was shouting loud enough for her to have heard that they were out of gin."

"Yet she didn't buy any," Mrs. Jeffries mused. "Thank you, Phyllis. You've done well. I hope it wasn't too difficult getting Janice to speak with you."

"She's got the day off, so I went to her house." Phyllis grinned. "But she spoke to me readily enough. Seems she's decided to look for work someplace else."

Luty shifted a sleepy Amanda to a more comfortable position. Ruth, who realized the toddler was just a bit too heavy for the elderly American, quickly moved to pick up the little one. "I'll put her in her cot if it's alright with you." She looked at Mrs. Goodge as she spoke. The cook had a sleeping cot for her godchild in her quarters.

"Thank you, Ruth," Mrs. Goodge said. In truth, the little one was a bit too heavy for her as well, though she'd die before admitting such a thing to anyone else. She glanced at Mrs. Jeffries. "I've got a feeling this case is comin' to a head very soon."

"It may well be," the housekeeper agreed. "If I'm right, by tomorrow."

Hatchet gave the lad another three shillings and, as soon as the boy had scarpered off, took note of his surroundings. He still couldn't see hide nor hair of Smythe or Wiggins, but he dared not search for them. Nivens was still in his hiding spot, but he might stick his head out any second and see him.

He leaned against a lamppost and frowned as he watched people empty out of the front door of the pub. Time had run out; the pub was closing for the afternoon. He glanced toward Nivens' hiding place just as the man himself emerged and ran across the road and down the small narrow opening between the pub and the building next to it.

It took Hatchet a moment to realize that Nivens was heading for either a back or a side door to the place. Suddenly, from the other side of the pub, Wiggins and Smythe stepped from between the buildings onto the pavement. Hatchet raced toward them.

"Cor blimey, what are you doin' 'ere?" Wiggins exclaimed as he drew closer.

"Following Inspector Nivens." Hatchet pointed to the front door. "He's inside, and he's got a gun."

"Blast a Spaniard." Smythe was staring at the corner. "When did 'e get 'ere? We've been takin' turns watchin' the place from the side so we wouldn't get spotted by Inspector Witherspoon. Oh Lord, look." He pointed. "Speakin' of the devil, there he is along with Constable Barnes. We've got to move. Now!" He ran back to the slender opening between the buildings they'd just left. Wiggins and Hatchet charged after him. The three men crammed themselves into the cluttered space, moving as fast as they dared while dodging splintered wood pallets, broken kegs, and the rusted metal strips from the cooper's barrels.

All of them were panting hard as they reached the end of the space and flattened themselves against the cold brick of the pub. "Is there a window anywhere?" Hatchet whispered.

"Yeah, but it's at the back of the pub." Smythe pointed as he spoke. "That's why we come in here. We were hopin' to find a window to see inside, but the only one we found is in the back, and the opening between the pub and old flour mill behind it is too narrow for any of us to use. We're stuck 'ere until this is over."

Hatchet gave them a quick summary of his morning. "When I saw Nivens had a gun, I had to follow him. I sent a lad to Leman Street Station with a message, so if we're lucky, Inspector Witherspoon and the police will be able to stop any further bloodshed."

Wiggins looked grim. "I don't like this. Sounds to me like Nivens has gone off 'is 'ead. There's no tellin' what 'e'll do. Cor blimey, I wish we knew what was goin' on inside."

"Sh . . . sh . . . sh." Smythe shushed them as they heard banging on the front door and a second later, Constable Barnes calling out, "Open up in the name of the law. Unlock this door, I tell you." They waited for a few moments, then Barnes said, "We'll have to go around to the side door."

"What's going on out there?" Startled, Susan Callahan looked up from the stack of bills and coins she'd been counting and frowned at the front door. She started to get up from the stool and then stopped as she caught a movement out of the corner of her eye. "Good Lord, what the hell are you doing here?"

Inspector Nivens ignored the commotion going on outside. He'd planned his entrance well, waiting until he'd seen Alex step outside before rushing out of his hiding place and getting to the side door before Alex was able to lock it. He'd grabbed the door key, pushed the stunned barman to the ground, shoved his way inside, and locked the door. Then he'd calmly taken the dueling pistol out of his coat pocket and entered the pub proper. As expected, Susan was sitting behind the till, counting money.

"Hello, Millie." Nivens raised the gun. "You and I have some catching up to do."

CHAPTER 11

"That fellow's gone mad," Alex shouted as Witherspoon, Barnes, and four uniformed policemen came racing around the corner to the side door. "And he's locked the ruddy door." He scrambled to his feet.

Constable Poole tried the handle.

"I just told ya he locked it," Alex called as he turned and raced toward the corner. "I live close by. I'll get the key."

"Hurry," Witherspoon ordered. He knew that Susan Callahan was inside and, if the young lad who raised the alarm was telling the truth, apparently so was Inspector Nivens. He looked at Barnes. "What do you think? Should we break the door down? *If* that boy was telling the truth, then Nivens came here with a gun. If that's the case, we have to assume he's prepared to use it."

But it was Constable Poole, rather than Barnes, who spoke up. "I don't think he was larking about or lying, sir. He's Charlie Hickam's boy. They're a decent family, and young Nevil is to be apprenticed soon to learn carpentry at Fitzgerald's Workshop. He'd not risk losing his place by lying to the police."

Barnes looked back at Witherspoon. "Trouble with breaking it down, sir, is that if Nivens has lost his mind and he hears us, he might do something rash."

"Why would Nivens bring a gun here?" Witherspoon muttered. He was frantically thinking of what they could do. "It doesn't make any sense whatsoever."

"It does if he thinks Susan Callahan murdered Santorini and then maneuvered the bits and pieces for him to take the blame," Barnes pointed out. Some of the comments and questions from his meeting this morning with Mrs. Jeffries and Mrs. Goodge were finally beginning to make sense.

"We've got to get into this pub." Witherspoon looked at the constables. "Is there another entrance, a window on the other side or the back?"

Poole shook his head. "There's just the front door and this side one. There's a narrow window at the very back, but the space between the pub and old building behind it is too small for anyone to climb inside."

"Right, then. Let's try banging on the door again; perhaps we'll be able to get through to Inspector Nivens. After all, he is an officer of the law." Witherspoon clenched his fist and began pounding on the wood.

"My name isn't Millie. It's Susan Callahan, and what the hell is goin' on 'ere? Police poundin' on the door and now one of them standing in my pub without so much as a by-your-leave."

"Interesting how your accent changes from one word to the next. Why, now you sound just like little Millie Slavik." Nivens smiled at her. "You were a pretty little guttersnipe twenty-five years ago. Even when I was arresting you, I couldn't help noticing."

He studied her carefully. He could see who she really was now. Beneath the flesh on her cheeks there was still a hint of the lovely bone structure; behind the thick lens of the spectacles, her eyes were still a vivid blue; and even the shape of her jawline was almost the same, barely distorted by the sagging skin of age and fat.

"You're out of yer 'ead." Susan's bosom heaved as she dragged in one long breath after another. "I don't know what's got into you. You've no call to come here wavin' that stupid pistol around."

"This stupid pistol is what's going to make you tell the truth. Now, we can spend the next few minutes debating who you really are, but, as the police are already here, you're going to walk outside with me and tell them yourself."

"What truth?" Susan slipped off the stool and stumbled slightly before steadying herself.

Nivens sighed impatiently. "Alright, if you insist. We'll do this the hard way." With his free hand, he reached into his coat and pulled out a sheaf of folded papers. He tossed them onto the floor. "I know exactly what happened. I know that on Saturday night, Dickie Stiles came in and slipped a note into my coat pocket. Moments later, you, on the pretext of giving the customers at the table behind me a couple of pints, pretended to drop your handkerchief and retrieved that note from my jacket."

"You're mad! I did no such thing."

"You've never given out a free drink in your life." Nivens nodded at the folded sheaf of papers on the floor. "After I read the case file, it didn't take long to realize what must have happened. I knew that there was no note in my coat pocket, so if Dickie was telling the truth, someone must have taken it out. Dickie came in that night even though he knew you'd banned him from the premises, and he did it because Santorini paid him to do it. He put the note in my pocket, but you took it out. Good to know that you're still a decent pickpocket. It means that old skills never die." He stepped closer and aimed the gun. "Now come out from behind that counter."

"I don't know what you're talking about." She glanced toward the side door. "They're here now, but it's you that'll be arrested. They're going to hang you for killing Bert. You mark my words, you'll be hanging soon."

"You know good and well I didn't kill Santorini. You did—and if it's the last thing I do, I'm going to get you to admit it. This is your last chance. Come out of there before I put a bullet in that black heart of yours."

"You'll not shoot me." She sneered. "I know your sort. You're a coward. Just another little rich boy that plays at being a copper so you can feel like a man."

"Shut up!"

She cackled with glee. "I don't take orders from little men like you. You should 'ear what the other coppers say about you, what they call you behind your back. They call you that dumb toff. No one has any respect for you. If it weren't for your family's influence, you'd have been tossed out of the police years ago . . ."

Nivens tightened his grip and then stumbled backwards as the gun went off.

"Dear God, that's a gunshot. We can't wait any longer—we'll have to break it down," Witherspoon cried as they heard the shot. He started to step back, intending to get the constables to put their shoulders to the wood.

"Let me through! I tell you, I've got a bloody key." A disheveled

Alex Parker pushed his way through the group of constables crowding around the door.

"Good Lord. Get over here, man," Witherspoon yelled as all of them stepped back and made room for the barman.

Alex, his shirt collar askew and his jacket dusty, shoved the key in the lock. "When her nibs had the place fixed up, she was too cheap to change the locks. Old man Callahan gave me this one when I first come to work here after he'd locked himself out and had to break in through the front door."

Witherspoon shushed him and everyone else as he stepped in front of the barman. He pushed Alex's hand away and slowly turned the key. But before he eased the door open, he glanced at Constable Poole. "Have any of your constables ever played cricket?"

Poole looked surprised by the question. "No, sir. We like football, not cricket."

"That'll have to do, I suppose."

Inside Nivens stared in dismay at the gun in his hand. The slightest pressure on the handle, and the newly repaired finger spur had sent a bullet flying. "Bloody hell, I paid a pretty penny to have this wretched thing fixed."

"You stupid fool. Only a toff would be dumb enough to bring a one-shot dueling pistol to do your dirty work." Susan Callahan stepped out from behind the counter. "You don't have any more bullets in that gun. But I've got plenty of bullets in this one." She lifted her arm and in her hand was a revolver. "Good God, you really are an idiot. Any minute now the police are going to break down that door, and when they get inside, you'll be dead."

"You're going to shoot me?" Nivens stared at her in horror.

"You tried to shoot me."

"I did not." He edged backwards. "It was an accident. You're no good to me dead. The only way they're not going to hang me for Santorini's murder is if you're alive to tell the truth."

She cocked her head in the direction of the side door. "Listen, it's gone quiet now—that means they've sent off to the station for more men so they can break the door down. That should give us a few minutes."

"You're the one that's gone mad." Nivens eased farther back, hoping to get out of range of her revolver.

"Stand still, or I'll put a bullet in you right now," she threatened. He stopped.

"Good man." She smiled. "This actually is working out better than my original plan."

Nivens swallowed heavily. If he got out of this mess alive, he was going to have a word with that wretched gunsmith. "What plan?"

"I thought you had it all figured out," she mocked. "But you're not so smart, are you? When they break in here, they'll find me weeping and distraught because you attacked me, and I had to defend myself by shooting you."

Nivens' heart was pounding so loud it sounded as if it was vibrating off the wall. "They won't believe you."

"They will." She laughed. "You're the only one who knows who I really am. To the police, I'm a hardworking woman named Susan Callahan who took this hovel of a pub and made it something special. I wasn't going to let Bert Santorini ruin that. So I shut him up for good, and I fixed it so that you're going to get the blame for it."

"Santorini figured out who you were as well?" Nivens was desperately trying to keep her talking. It was his only chance to make it out of this room alive.

She snorted derisively. "Don't be daft—Santorini wasn't that smart. Besides, he never knew Millie Slavik. No, he found out something else and, stupid fool that he was, instead of keeping his mouth shut about it, he started blackmailing me."

"Blackmail?" He slowly and quietly tried to force air into his lungs. He had to stop panicking. Otherwise, he'd end up dead. "If he didn't find out who you really are, what else is there?"

"Unfortunately, the brewery loan on this place costs a bit more to service each month than I'd thought, so let's just say I found a nice way to increase profits, and Bert, sneaky bastard that he was, found out about it. Despite his words of love and devotion, he was always lookin' out for number one."

It took a moment before Nivens realized what she'd just said. "You mean you watered the beer and the spirits."

"Not all of the spirits, just the whisky and the beer." She shrugged. "But that's enough to ruin me. Bryson's won't care that I never filtered the gin. I paid Bert for six months, two gold sovereigns a month. Can you believe that? Gold sovereigns instead of banknotes. It was a ruddy pain in the arse getting hold of the damned things, but he insisted."

"But the police only found ten gold sovereigns when they searched his rooms." Nivens felt calmer.

"I didn't pay this month. I kept the sovereigns as a bit of a souvenir after I killed him." She shrugged.

"Why did you decide to frame me?"

She stared at him as if he were a half-wit. "Good Lord, don't you understand? You were askin' too many questions about my past. You recognized me. You couldn't pinpoint exactly who I was. After all, I look and sound very different than I did twenty-five years ago. But it was only a matter of time before you recognized me as Millie Slavik." She shrugged. "I couldn't risk that. Bryson's would call in the loan if they found out I was watering their liquor or who I'd been in the past. So Santorini had to die, and frankly I was hoping you'd hang."

"You served six months in prison," Nivens muttered. "That's right. I was the arresting officer. Good Lord, I can't believe I didn't recognize you right away. I arrested you several times."

"Yeah, but it was only that last arrest that got me sent up." She shrugged. "It was a horrible place, but it taught me a few things. For starters, how to pick locks."

"Is that how you managed to get my gun and that pillow from my study?"

"It was dead easy. I followed you home on Saturday night so I could find out where you lived. I already knew you weren't going to be home on Sunday and Monday nights—you'd complained to everyone about havin' to do your old mum a favor. Sunday night, after the pub closed, I took a trip to your place. Gettin' inside was child's play. For a copper, you've got miserable locks on your back door. It took me less than five minutes to get inside. I got the gun and the pillow and put them back early on Tuesday morning."

"How did you know my housekeeper wouldn't be there?" Nivens wondered what the devil was taking Witherspoon so long. Surely, they hadn't just gone away?

"I followed her to the train station on Sunday morning, and I heard her ask the clerk for a return ticket from Leicester, then I heard her ask him if there was an express back to London on Tuesday morning. I'd been keeping watch on your house, waiting to see what time you'd been leaving for your mum's and making sure I could get in and out easily. It pays to be thorough." Susan raised her gun. "I don't know why you're pestering me with all these questions. It won't matter to you when you're dead." She steadied the revolver and started toward him.

"Drop the gun, Mrs. Callahan," Witherspoon shouted. "You are surrounded by the Metropolitan Police Force, and we've heard everything you just admitted."

Susan whirled around just as Witherspoon, Barnes, and three police constables burst inside, flipped up the bar barrier, and raced into the room. Susan pointed the gun at the mass of police just as a loud crash banged hard against the front door.

She jerked her head toward the sound as Witherspoon, Barnes, and Constable Poole rushed her, slamming into her with such force she dropped the gun. Barnes kicked it to one side as she began to scream.

"You bloody bastards! You can't do this to me," she cried as she struggled to fight them off. She banged her fist into Poole's cheek before he managed to snag her arm and kicked out at Witherspoon, connecting with his shin bone. Throwing her head back, she smashed against Constable Poole's chin and stuck her elbow into Constable Farrow's ribs. Another two constables raced through the door and into the fray.

Finally, they got her subdued.

Witherspoon took a deep breath, stepped back, and stared at the woman being held by the constables. "Susan Callahan, you're under arrest for the murder of Humberto Santorini."

Unrepentant, she glared at them. "I'll beat this. You broke into my place and unjustly accused me so that you could protect one of your own. That's goin' to be my story, and not you or that idiot Nivens will be able to prove otherwise."

"Don't be absurd, Mrs. Callahan. No one will believe you," Witherspoon warned.

"Won't they?" She laughed. "You're all coppers, and everyone knows they protect their own. I'm a respectable businesswoman, someone who is known and admired by her friends and neighbors. The press and locals will all believe me and so will the court. I'm just a poor woman who is being used to make sure the police don't have another black mark against them."

"Stand back, Witherspoon," Nivens ordered.

Witherspoon turned and couldn't believe what he saw. Nivens had her gun, and he was pointing it at her heart. "Ye gods, Inspector Nivens, have you gone insane? What on earth are you doing?"

"I'm making sure the police are protected," he said softly. "Now stand back. I don't want to shoot you."

"You really have lost your mind," Witherspoon warned. "Put that weapon down."

"I won't." He kept his gaze fixed on her. "She's right. They'll believe her—and all of us, all of our careers will be over. She's got to be stopped. Someone as evil as she is must be stopped."

"Don't be ridiculous, Inspector." Witherspoon couldn't believe it himself. "No one in their right mind will take her charges seriously. We can prove she isn't who she claims to be."

"Oh, but I am." Susan chuckled. "My real name is Millie Susan Slavik, and I married Callahan, which makes me legally Susan Callahan. There's no law against using your middle name."

By this time Witherspoon was beginning to think that she was as crazy as he now thought Nivens might be. He opened his mouth, but before he could speak, a voice said, "I'm not a copper, Mrs. Callahan. I'm just someone who 'as worked 'ere for years, and I know what kind of person you are. The copper's right: You are evil, and, what's more, everyone will believe me, and I 'eard every word. You're a bloomin' murderer, and you deserve to meet the hangman." Alex Parker stood behind the bar glaring at his employer.

"And if that copper"—he nodded at Nivens—"has a brain in his 'ead, he'll put that gun down and let the law handle this."

No one said a word as Nivens stared at the barman. After a few tense moments, he lowered the weapon and put it on a nearby table. "Believe it or not," he murmured, "I do believe in the law. It's the only thing that keeps us civilized."

"You're not going to believe what's happened," Betsy cried as she raced into the kitchen. "Susan Callahan's been arrested. Oh, my gracious, I couldn't believe it myself." She glanced at the faces around the table. Mrs. Jeffries, Mrs. Goodge, Luty, Phyllis, and even Ruth stared at her in confusion. The only female missing was her daughter. "Where's Amanda?"

"She's taking a nap," the cook said. "Come on, then, sit down and tell us what happened."

"I'll pour the tea." Phyllis jumped up and grabbed the kettle, which had just boiled, from the top of the cooker.

"You didn't expect this, did you?" Ruth asked Mrs. Jeffries.

"Not this fast," the housekeeper admitted. "But let's hear what Betsy has to say."

"Go on, then, talk," Phyllis directed. "I can listen while I'm making the tea."

"I was on my way back here after seeing my source." Betsy sat down. She quickly related everything she'd heard from Mattie and then told them the rest of the information she'd learned. "I knew you'd sent Smythe and Wiggins to watch the Crying Crows. I had the cab stop so I could have a quick word. But I couldn't get near the pub—there were police everywhere, and I was afraid I'd be spotted by our inspector."

"So how did you find out that Susan Callahan had been arrested?" the cook demanded.

Betsy smiled. "I batted my eyelashes at one of the policemen, a sweet young constable named Farrow, and he said they'd arrested the owner of the pub for murder. I asked if anyone had been hurt, because I was a bit worried about our men being there, but Constable Farrow assured me that she'd been taken into custody without anyone being harmed, though a shot had been fired. I tried to have a quick look around to see if I could find Smythe or Wiggins, but I couldn't see them."

"So we'll just have to wait until they get back to find out what's what," Luty muttered. "Dang, I knew I shoulda gone with 'em. Now I've missed out on all the excitement."

"Indeed you have, madam," Hatchet exclaimed. He, Smythe, and Wiggins stood in the archway.

"We didn't hear you come in." Betsy jumped up and ran to her husband. She looked him up and down, her expression anxious. "Are you alright? It's true, right, no one was hurt?"

"I'm fine, love—you don't need to fuss," he said, but the big smile on his face proved he loved her fussing over him.

"It was ever so excitin'," Wiggins exclaimed. "Smythe and I 'ad been there for ages, crammed into a narrow strip beside the pub so we'd not be spotted by the locals or, even worse, the police while we was watchin' the place. When we finally stuck our heads out, there was Hatchet as big as you please. Two seconds later, our inspector and Constable Barnes come barrelin' around the corner like the 'ounds of 'ell was after 'em." He paused to take a breath.

"Tea is ready." Phyllis brought the big brown teapot to the table and then went to the cupboard to grab the mugs.

Mrs. Jeffries stood up. "Everyone sit down, please. We're dying to hear what happened but, please, do it so we can understand."

Smythe, his arm around his wife, gave her a squeeze as they headed for their seats. "We're just excited, Mrs. Jeffries. Hatchet needs to go first— 'e's the one who started it all."

"Just my danged luck." Luty shot a quick glance at her butler. "You always git to have the fun. You okay?"

"I'm fine, madam." He grinned broadly as he took the chair next to her. He waited until everyone settled into their chairs and had a steaming mug of tea in front of them. "First of all, Mrs. Jeffries, credit to you for having the foresight to send me to keep watch on the Nivens house. That's the only reason this case came to a head without a great deal of blood being shed."

"I'm glad no one was hurt," she murmured.

"So am I," he replied. "I'll admit, after I'd been in Belgravia for what seemed hours, I was beginning to think you were wrong, but then Nivens showed up and that's when things got interesting." He told them what happened. He took his time, making certain to include each and every detail so the sequence of events would make sense. "Luckily, even though I hadn't expected Inspector Witherspoon to still be at the Leman Street Station, he and the constable were."

"But they were supposed to see Mrs. O'Dwyer this morning," Mrs. Goodge said.

"They were delayed because the Santorini file had gone missing," Hatchet explained. "Constable Barnes spotted me hovering at the edge of the crowd gathered in front of the pub. Apparently, police activity attracts people very quickly in that part of London."

"Don't be a snob, Hatchet. It attracts people in every part of London," Luty interrupted. "But go on."

"As I was saying, Constable Barnes saw me, and when the inspector and the other constables were occupied putting Mrs. Callahan in the police wagon, he was able to spend a few minutes telling me what had transpired." He told them the details Barnes had shared with him, including the fact that Nivens had been at the station.

"Nivens was there?" Phyllis exclaimed when he finished. "But wasn't he on some sort of leave?"

"He was, but he came into the station this morning with the excuse that he needed to water his plant. Apparently, he's been coming in most days and has been reading the Santorini file all along. It was the file that sent Nivens to the East End and his confrontation with Mrs. Callahan."

"He realized she was the killer from reading the file?" Mrs. Jeffries mused. "Right?"

Hatchet nodded. "It appears that way, but again, I don't know all the details, only that she admitted to murdering Santorini and to creating the circumstances so Inspector Nivens would get the blame for it."

"But why did she kill him?" Ruth asked. "Was it because she was jealous of Alberta Miller, the barmaid at that other pub?"

Hatchet sat back and folded his arms over his chest. "I believe I'll let Mrs. Jeffries answer that question."

Mrs. Jeffries hesitated. She didn't want to steal his thunder, but he simply smiled at her and nodded. "Go on, Mrs. Jeffries—tell us why you sent everyone to the Crying Crows and me to watching Nivens."

"Two things. One, Dickie Stiles' statement that he put a note in Nivens' pocket; and two, the alcohol Santorini kept locked up in his box. Up until last night, I was certain that Fiona O'Dwyer was the killer." Mrs. Jeffries took a quick sip of her tea. "It appeared she was the only person to have a reason for both hating Inspector Nivens and wanting Santorini dead. Then last night I realized I was looking at the facts incorrectly. Susan Callahan could also have had a reason. She was afraid of losing her pub."

"How'd you come to that conclusion?" Phyllis exclaimed.

"I almost didn't until it was too late. But when Wiggins reported that Susan Callahan had banned Mr. Dinsworth from her pub merely because he kept insisting she was Millie Slavik, I realized that her reaction was extreme. Mr. Dinsworth was known to be senile, so why go to such lengths?"

"Because she really was Millie Slavik." Phyllis nodded her head in understanding. "I should have realized that as well."

"What about the alcohol?" Luty asked.

"I suspect we're going to find out it was those beer and whisky samples that signed Santorini's death warrant," Mrs. Jeffries replied. "Remember, he dated both of the vials, and those dates were from when he was actually in residence at the Crying Crows. My theory was that he witnessed Susan watering Bryson's beer and whisky. Perhaps by then things weren't going well between them as a couple, and he wanted a bit of insurance to have the upper hand."

"Oh, my goodness," Ruth said. "Of course. Mr. Bryson himself went on and on about how they called in loans from people who watered the liquor."

"And she had a loan from Bryson's," Mrs. Jeffries said. "What's more, years earlier, she was a known pickpocket, and I suspect that she didn't want that coming out as well." She glanced at Phyllis. "Another reason that I thought she might be the killer was because of what Janice Everly told you. After the pub closed on Saturday night, she supposedly went upstairs to lie down, leaving Alex

Parker and Janice to close up. Before they left, Alex shouted that the pub was almost out of gin and for her to order more; but come Monday, the gin wasn't with the order, and Susan got furious. But Alex insisted that he'd shouted loud enough for her to hear him."

"She didn't hear him because she'd left to go to Belgravia," Phyllis cried. "Goodness gracious, it's so obvious now. She must have followed Inspector Nivens home to find out where he lived."

"That's what I suspect must have happened. Then on Sunday night, after her pub was closed, she went back to Belgravia and broke into Niven's house," Mrs. Jeffries explained.

"That's when she stole the gun and the pillow." Phyllis nodded.

"And Tuesday morning after she'd murdered Mr. Santorini, she put them back," Mrs. Jeffries said. "At least, that's what I think happened. We'll have to confirm the details with Inspector Witherspoon."

"I thought she was just a pickpocket," the cook muttered. "But if you're right, she can pick locks as well."

"I think so, but, once again, we'll have to hear what the inspector says about the situation," Mrs. Jeffries said. "And it was her skill as a pickpocket that set her plan in motion. She used the excuse of giving two customers, who were sitting at the table behind Inspector Nivens, beer on the house, something she'd never done before. That was when she picked Nivens' pocket—I think we can assume she spotted Dickie Stiles that night and saw him slip the note in Nivens' coat. Once she read the note, she came up with a plan for getting rid of Santorini and Inspector Nivens."

"She thinks fast, I'll give 'er that," Smythe muttered.

Mrs. Jeffries looked at the coachman. "She does, and that's one of the reasons she was always able to stay one step ahead. I think that the hansom cabdriver that told you he'd picked up the same woman twice on Saturday night was right. It was her. She used the time in Belgravia to get a look at the lay of the land, so to speak, and probably had a good snoop around Nivens' property. Nivens was getting close to recognizing her as Millie Slavik, and, according to what Betsy learned today, she had even paid her barman to pass along everything he overheard either about Nivens or from Nivens when he was at the pub."

"That's why the note was so important," Ruth said. "Once she knew that Santorini was to meet Inspector Nivens, she knew she could arrange the situation to make it look as if Nivens was the killer."

"Thus killing two birds with one stone," Mrs. Jeffries concluded. "But we'll have to find out the rest of the details when the inspector gets home."

"My source thinks she killed her husband," Betsy murmured. "With him out of the way, she had free rein to do what she liked with the pub."

Mrs. Jeffries nodded. "That's certainly possible." She looked at the carriage clock on the sideboard. "The inspector might be late tonight. Murder always involves a lot of paperwork."

But for once, he wasn't particularly late. Betsy and Smythe had taken Amanda and left, but Luty, Hatchet, and Ruth, along with the others, were still there discussing the case when the inspector arrived home.

The visitors started to leave when his hansom pulled up outside, but Mrs. Jeffries waved them back to their chairs. "Stay. I know you want to hear what he has to say. Ruth, can you feed the inspector dinner tonight?"

"Of course, I'd love to. Cook won't mind—she loves it when we have a guest, even one at short notice."

"Excellent." She dashed upstairs and met him as he came through the front door. "Goodness, sir, you're home a bit early."

"We've had a very exciting day, Mrs. Jeffries, and even better, we've solved this case." He grinned broadly as he handed her his hat and slipped off his coat. "You'll never guess who we've arrested."

"Oh, don't tell me, sir." She hung up the hat and coat. "Lady Cannonberry is here. She came to invite you to supper tonight, and then Luty stopped in with Hatchet because they wanted to borrow one of Mrs. Goodge's cake recipes for a birthday celebration. You know how much all of us love hearing about your cases, especially as you've just solved this one. They'll be thrilled to hear it directly from you."

"Ruth is here?" If possible, his smile got wider. "And I've not seen Luty nor Hatchet in ages. Gracious, how lovely."

They went downstairs, and, after the greetings were exchanged, Witherspoon took a seat at the head of the table while Phyllis made another pot of tea for all of them.

"Well, where to begin?" Witherspoon beamed proudly. "It was quite startling—this young lad came running into the Leman Street Station and shouted that we'd best get some police to the Crying Crows Pub." He told them much of what they already knew, but all of them played their parts well and reacted appropriately as he explained the sequence of events.

But everyone leaned just that bit closer when he got to the point in his narrative where he and the other police constables were inside the Crying Crows. "So, being as quiet as possible, we crept up to the side door, which leads into the pub proper, and we could hear Susan Callahan, who is really Millie Slavik, practically bragging that she'd murdered Santorini and had manipulated the evidence to ensure the police thought Inspector Nivens had done the crime."

"How did she do that, sir?" Phyllis asked.

"She was very clever." He took a sip of tea. "She'd kept her widow's weeds, including the veil, from when her husband died. That's a very pertinent point, as it allowed her to use hansom cabs from the East End to Belgravia without being identified."

"Hansom cabs, sir?" Mrs. Goodge gave the housekeeper a quick, congratulatory smile.

"Indeed, she used one to follow Inspector Nivens home on Saturday night—this, of course, is after she'd taken the note that Dickie Stiles had slipped into Nivens' pocket out and read it. She then came back to the Nivens home on Sunday night, picked the lock, and stole Inspector Nivens' dueling pistol and the pillow from his study. She used them on Monday evening when she murdered Santorini. She didn't want to lose her pub or keep paying Santorini. She saw this as an opportunity to rid herself of Inspector Nivens." He continued with his narrative, making certain he explained all the pertinent details of the case.

"Let me make sure I understand," Luty said. "She was worried that he was gettin' too close to recognizin' her as Millie Slavik, right?"

"Correct." He smiled at the elderly American. "Unfortunately, Inspector Nivens' behavior wasn't very good, though I must say, he does have a bit of an excuse, as she tried to shoot him. But luckily, I'd instructed Constable Mayhew to heave a rock at the door just to buy us a bit of a distraction, as we didn't know what we were going to face once we got inside. Because of that, we were able to stop her from shooting the inspector."

"It was your 'inner voice,' Inspector," Mrs. Jeffries assured him.

For once, she wasn't saying it to bolster his confidence. This time, she was absolutely certain she was right.

"Thank you, Mrs. Jeffries." He told them the rest of it—how Susan Callahan had boasted she'd use the press and the local community to make the case that the police arrested her to save one of their own, and that, if it hadn't been for the barman, Nivens might have committed murder himself. "But the inspector came to his senses once he realized Alex Parker was going to tell the truth."

"Why was it only Inspector Nivens who recognized her?" Mrs. Goodge asked, though in truth, Enoch Dinsworth and Mattie Mitchell had both seen through the woman's disguise.

"That's an interesting observation," Witherspoon acknowledged. "But she left the East End twenty-five years ago, and when she came back, she spoke differently, was married to a respected member of the community, and disguised herself to some extent. Also, I suspect some people are just better at recognition than others."

"I'm amazed that she was so forthcoming when she was being questioned," Hatchet said.

"As was I, but once we had her at the station, she was quite candid as to what she'd done, how she'd done it, and why she'd done it."

"Doesn't she know she'll face the 'angman?" Wiggins exclaimed. "Cor blimey, she killed Bert Santorini and tried to kill Inspector Nivens."

Witherspoon thought for a moment. "I don't think she does." He frowned slightly. "As I was leaving, she looked at me and gave me the oddest smile. Then she said, 'I'm not done yet, Inspector. You think you've won, but there's something you don't know.' When I asked her what it was, she said, 'Don't worry, you'll find out soon enough. But know this, I've got friends in very high places.'"

"Was she threatening you?" Ruth asked, her expression worried.

Witherspoon patted her hand. "Don't worry, Ruth dear. I'm not in the least concerned. As a police officer, I've heard that, or words very much like it, many times. Once arrested, a lot of criminals are full of nonsense and bravado. But it's all empty talk. No matter how many important friends she thinks she has, she'll not escape justice."

"What about Inspector Nivens, sir?" Mrs. Jeffries asked. "What's going to happen to him?"

Witherspoon sighed. "I'm not sure. When we went back to the station, as we were busy questioning Mrs. Callahan, Inspector Havers took his statement and then he left. One of the constables said they saw him getting into a hansom cab."

"Surely he'll be taken off the force permanently, won't he?" Ruth said. "He tried to take the law into his own hands. That's not right."

"True, it's not the sort of behavior that can be overlooked," Witherspoon replied. "Especially in light of some of the other charges levied against him. But I suspect that Chief Superintendent Barrows will give him an opportunity to resign rather than sacking him outright."

"I think they should arrest him," Mrs. Goodge declared. "He's tried to harm you and interfere in your investigations more than once, and he's as bad as the criminals he's supposed to be catching."

"Now, now, Mrs. Goodge. We'll let justice take its proper course. Being sacked will be punishment enough. But I appreciate your sentiments, and I am always delighted with the way my household looks after me."

"There's one thing I don't understand, sir," Phyllis said. "If Susan Callahan took the note out of Nivens' coat pocket, that means he never saw it, so he never knew he was to meet Santorini Monday night at the mews. Right?"

"That's right."

"Then why did Inspector Nivens lie about the time he had dinner on Monday night? You said he told the staff he needed to eat because he had 'an important appointment.'"

Witherspoon smiled faintly. "According to what he told Inspector Havers, Nivens said it because he was hungry and wanted to eat what he called, 'a decent meal.' He was afraid they wouldn't let him into the restaurant because it hadn't opened yet, so he made up that story about having an important appointment. When he arrived at the Leman Street Station on Tuesday morning, as soon as Chief Inspector Boney and Inspector Havers began to question him, he realized he needed an alibi for Santorini's murder, so he lied about the time he was actually at the restaurant."

"Didn't he know you'd confirm his story?" Ruth asked.

Witherspoon shrugged. "I don't think he realized Mr. Caladini, the maître d', was so observant and so eager to cooperate with the police."

"So what did he do after leaving the restaurant?" Hatchet asked.

"He went to his mother's house and availed himself of her very good whisky. It was only when he got to the station on Tuesday morning that he realized he was a murder suspect."

The letter was delivered by messenger at nine o'clock the following morning. Mrs. Vickers carried it into the dining room on a silver tray. "This just came for you, sir. Shall I put it in your study or would you like it now?"

"I'll take it now." Nivens took the envelope and stared at it for a moment before sliding his finger under the flap and tearing it open. He knew who it was from and what it would say.

> *Dear Inspector Nigel Nivens,*
> *Please report to my office at one o'clock today. I*
> *shall expect your letter of resignation as well as any*
> *property in your possession that belongs to the*
> *Metropolitan Police Force.*
> *T. E. Barrows, chief superintendent of the*
> *Metropolitan Police Force*

Nivens read it again, rose to his feet, and went to his study.

He stood there for a long moment, staring at the cheerful fire he'd had Mrs. Vickers light this morning.

He shook himself out of his stupor and went to his desk. Sitting down, he opened the top drawer, pulled out a sheet of stationery, and picked up his pen. It took less than two minutes to write the resignation letter.

Nivens folded the page properly, reached for an envelope, and then stopped, his fingers just brushing the wood of the cubbyhole. He looked at the folded paper and got up. He walked to the fireplace, where he stared at the flames for what seemed hours but was, in truth, only a few minutes. Then he crumpled the paper into a ball and tossed it into the flames.

Resign, humph, he thought—that's not going to happen. I can weather this storm. I've weathered plenty of others.

ABOUT THE AUTHOR

Emily Brightwell is the *New York Times* bestselling author of the Victorian Mysteries featuring Inspector Witherspoon and Mrs. Jeffries.

Ready to find
your next great read?

Let us help.

Visit prh.com/nextread

Penguin
Random
House